Peg reached for her. "No." Paris stepped back, undressed quickly, lay Peg down once more, lay on top of her, kissed her face, her neck, her shoulders, those breasts again, kissed down to her belt line.

"Paris," Peg said, trying to rise, that tender amused look in her eyes, a slight smiling curve to her lips, her hands reaching.

"Hey," she said, pushing her down, pushing her again, a third time, unbuckling her belt as she did, unzipping her slacks, pulling them off with her underwear. "Umm," she crooned at the glorious sight of her and parted her legs like the two ends of her tie.

"This doesn't work for me," Peg said, her voice tight, but her telltale breathing a pant. One hand kneaded Paris's shoulder, the other had a fistful of her hair. "I need to make love to you first."

That lisp was a turn-on. "You're gorgeous," she told Peg and plunged to the knot in the tie of her legs with her mouth. "Butch," was the last thing she said before she took a faintly cinnamon mouthful of her. The word was a challenge.

MORTON RIVER VALLEY

BY LEE LYNCH

MORTON RIVER VALLEY

BY LEE LYNCH

The Naiad Press, Inc.
1992

Printed in the United States of America on acid-free paper
First Edition

Edited by Christine Cassidy
Cover design by Pat Tong and Bonnie Liss
    (Phoenix Graphics)
Typeset by Sandi Stancil

Library of Congress Cataloging-in-Publication Data

Lynch, Lee, 1945–
    Morton River Valley / by Lee Lynch.
        p.   cm.
    ISBN 1-56280-016-7
    I. Title.
PS3562.Y426M67   1992
813′.54--dc20
                                                        92-18552
                                                        CIP

For Carol Seajay
and all the booksellers

Acknowledgments:

Thank you, Akia Woods, for your generous help and gentle understanding.

I'll always be grateful to the late writer and teacher, Con Sellers, for sharing his wealth of knowledge.

Heartfelt thanks to:

Akia, Jo Pierce, Christine Cassidy, and Moonyean, for helping me to approximately depict femme behavior and point of view; Ben Eakin and Tom Hayes of Austin; Carol Feiden for a harrowing drive into Morton River Valley; Deb Lovely, Morton River Valley born and bred; Ray for his assistance with the Italian language; the members of the Listen and Be Kind Writers' group and the Ansonia, Connecticut Public Library.

Morton River Valley and the characters who live there are entirely fictional.

MORTON RIVER VALLEY

BY LEE LYNCH

CHAPTER 1

A freight train shouted a husky, boisterous greeting to the hills gathered along the Morton River, to the houses that jostled for space on the hillsides, to the woman just arrived in town.

Paris Collins climbed the steepest street buoyant with excitement, hot even in the cool morning air of early autumn. The houses she passed were practical yet fanciful and emphatically individual. A dog barked in the yard of a dull brown clapboard which boasted stained glass windows to either side of its front door. A score of wary cats watched the dog from the sloping porch rail, steps and windows of a peeling wooden one-story. Next, sideways, was a bright pink ranch-style duplex of 1950s vintage. Across the street a brick Cape Cod was having its elaborately detailed trim repainted. Other than the whistling white-capped painter she saw no people. The hillside felt like a ghost town. She looked over her shoulder, back toward the river below, and felt her gut contract: she was terrified of heights.

"Nice day!" called an old woman at a corner mailbox.

Paris inhaled with shock. The ghost town had produced a genuine ghost. Paris realized she was sweaty and her shins ached from the climb. In the shade of a healthy old oak the woman craned her neck to see beyond the leaves and Paris looked too. Honking geese were flying south. "I can taste your New England fall in the air," Paris said, giving a big smile.

The woman was heavy but sharp-featured. She narrowed her eyes. "You're not from around here," she told Paris.

"That's a fact." How did she look to a local? Paris Collins, an almost middle-aged woman in trendy stone-washed Levi's and jacket, bright cotton tropical shirt, tinted glasses and long hair turning dusky gray. Her style of dress was left over from two years in Florida, which she'd left just yesterday, and was aimed at females other than heterosexual grandmas.

"You moving onto the Hillside?"

She'd never owned a home in her life, but with a laugh she imagined moving into one of these

Connecticut originals, planning a total restoration with enlarged thermopane windows and a lavender hot tub just for the sake of decadence. Perhaps she'd spent too much time on the west coast, where she'd lived before Florida. "I'm not sure where they're putting me up. I just got in yesterday."

"I suppose the new factories brought you to the Valley. All these newcomers taking the jobs out from under our men."

Her first reaction was annoyance, but she'd been around enough not to take native hostility personally. She laughed again and opened her arms. "Please! I'm here to help folks, not steal their jobs! I'll be teaching at Rafferty Center."

"The teacher! You were in the *Valley Sentinel*. You're here for those Vietnamese and Spanish pouring in. And the people in the projects. Tsk."

Would any of her students live in these houses? The nearest home was faced with split red asbestos shingles which faded, lighter and lighter, to the chalky pink of the original salt box building. One section seemed to lean against another, all at different heights, windows obviously sized to available materials. The magnificence of the garden made up for the distress of patchwork architecture. Wild growth began at either side of the walk and surrounded the house completely. Somewhere in the dense vegetation hidden tomatoes gave off their warm ripe scent. Blue jays scolded as she passed, grackles clucked at a weathered feeder, sparrows chittered, flitting from tree to tree. She touched a leaning splintery post that pulled down instead of propping up the wire fencing. Within, green acorn and yellow patty pan squash, roses from yellow to deep purple, apples little more than nubs, jostled for life. She'd never had a garden.

She swallowed a sad, tired sigh. People like this woman could make a newcomer squirm for a long time. "I reckon you always lived in the Valley," she replied, nurturing, no, exaggerating, the soft old Texas accent which was all she'd kept of home.

With a possessive sweep of her arm that took in the town, the river and the hills, the old woman answered, "A thousand years! My father built Rafferty Brass, the factory down there. My husband retired from Rafferty's as a mechanic. Our boys followed in their footsteps and retired before it shut down, all but my baby. Everything's plastic these days. They laid him off without a cent — two years he's been out of work. Now that's wrong."

As Paris took leave of the woman and went on up the hill she wondered which home fit the woman, but she didn't look back: a stranger's curiosity is always nosiness. She wandered slowly past grey cinder block fencing and perfectly symmetrical terracing, past turreted three-story relics which cast their shadows onto tiny bay-windowed cottages.

The climb had become work; she was heavy with the old woman's anger, with the worries she always brought to a new home. She was used to having to prove herself to communities, but this woman had gotten to her. *I'm only 41*, she thought, *it's too soon to be sad and tired.*

The touch of fall had melted by noon; summer's heat had returned with a vengeance. After picking up her luggage and dragging it through the small downtown peppered with grimy but ornate granite banks and columned civic buildings, she collapsed into an air-conditioned diner booth. She swirled a long-handled spoon in a tall glass of crushed ice and lemony tea. If she hadn't known it was Friday she could have guessed by the smell of fish chowder steaming in the kitchen. Earlier she'd passed two Catholic churches within blocks of each other. At the counter a toothless man crinkled open a cellophane packet of saltines and broke them into his soup. A girl with spiked hair joked with the waitress. Someone banged pots onto counters in the kitchen.

Miss Valerie had suggested meeting at Dusty's Queen of Hearts Diner because it was close to the apartment the Center director had chosen for her, but Miss Valerie was ten minutes late already. Paris idly studied the decor. The floor tiles were red with bold black patterns. Silver cylinders reached up from the floor to support red vinyl stools. The counter was red too, the tiles beneath it cream-colored all the way down to a red-tiled footrest that ran the length of the counter. She supposed this funny old diner in this funny old factory town touched a memory in her heart that led directly back to her childhood memories of the forties and fifties, a past life of nickelodeons and a victorious America full of plans. This diner gave her excited flutters in a way cities like London and Rio de Janeiro never had.

"More iced tea?" asked the waitress, a thin woman with frosted hair and a nice touch of makeup.

"No, Elly, thanks," she replied, reading her name tag. "I'm waiting for someone."

"Oh! Are you the teacher Venita Valerie's meeting? She was in for breakfast this morning."

"I hope I haven't slipped her mind."

"Is the old character late?" asked Elly with a laugh and a Southern drawl. Not Texas, but it sounded good to Paris: a stranger who looked happy here. No wedding ring. Maybe she took it off at work, but there was something about Elly that brought up Paris's lavender antennae. "Typical. She's probably explaining algebra to somebody like me with about as many brains for math as it takes to run that cash register." She sank into the booth with a weary relieved sigh. "Did you find a place to stay, honey?"

"I spent last night in an enormous musty, nineteenth-century guest house. I can't believe Morton River doesn't have a motel, not even a Y."

"You'd have to stay in Upton for those kinds of frills," Elly said.

"I don't have a vehicle. I sold Honkey."

"Honkey?"

"My spunky old Comet. I taught in Florida last. To liven up grammar classes I threw in slang. The students were all Island people and started calling me Honkey. I passed it on to my car. She had the strangest sneezy horn."

"How in the world did you get here without wheels?"

"Let's see. From LaGuardia I took a limo to Upton and waited three hours for a half-pint MetroNorth train."

"Our rolling litter box. I hate taking that filthy thing. Do you move around much?"

"Every two years."

"You must have been born with a heck of a restless soul!"

"A stint in Vista hooked me fourteen years ago. I liked moving on so much I gave myself an ultimatum to keep going, to meet new people, see new sights before I got too comfortable. Before I settled for something — or someone — not quite right."

Was it still comfortable, she wondered, this uprooting, resettling, goodbye syndrome? No town, no woman, had even tempted her to stay once her clit stopped throbbing at the sight of them. Nothing got her up and going anymore but the kick-start of a move. All she wanted was some romance, some glamour, a strong woman extravagant in flowers, caresses, compliments — *Oh, Lady Be Good!* she chided herself in silent song, and smiled into her coffee.

The waitress shook her head. "I got too old for traveling about the time I started." Like a conductor, she sang, "Last stop, Morton River! I don't know how you do it."

"It may be in my blood. My folks were teachers too. They could only travel summers, and then on a shoestring, but they never missed a year."

Elly got up with a groan. "It's time I started traveling the length of this diner again. Look! Here comes Venita Valerie now," she said. "You can see her galloping down the hill."

There was a figure hurrying along Railroad Avenue toward the diner, passing a fenced lot filled with heavy equipment, an old wooden warehouse with one charred wall and a tavern too down on its luck for a neon sign, its door propped open for air conditioning.

The woman, who looked at least seventy, was

squinting toward the diner. Elly waved and pointed to Paris. Miss Valerie raised both arms in the air, then hit the heels of her hands against the sides of her hat, waving and smiling. She was so tall and had such straight, thin, stiff-looking legs she could have been on stilts. Paris hadn't expected her to be black. Under a floppy blue jacket with huge pockets she wore a silky white dress and a jaunty wide-brimmed straw hat with a red band.

"Miss Collins?" She came with the smell of talcum powder like a cloud around her. Her voice was quick, whispery.

Paris popped up.

"My, you're slender," said Miss Valerie.

"Small bones, big muscles," she joked.

"Are you one of those lady weightlifters?" Miss Valerie asked, dropping into the booth. She lifted her hat off and fanned herself.

Did she look like one? This really was old-fashioned Yankee territory. She worried for a moment that she wouldn't fit in here in New England. "I've worked out, but mostly to keep in shape."

"You won't need to here, you know. Between the hills, the budget cuts and the literacy rate we'll run you ragged."

"Thanks for the warning, but I'm used to skimpy staffs and ragtag texts. It's a pleasure to meet you, Miss Valerie. Your letters were a treasure-trove of Morton River lore."

"Venita, my dear, Venita," she said, offering long fingers in a ladylike handshake. They felt papery dry and warm. Venita wore no wedding ring either, just a huge amber stone in an antique gold setting. Her quiet speech never slowed, as if breathing were a waste of time. "Mr. Piccari asked me to greet you when he realized his wife's people would be descending just before the start of school and his life wouldn't be his own. He couldn't even predict if he'd be in town today at all, much less if he could be on time, though look at me late anyway. So there, that's my apology and now let's get you to your new home. Mr. Piccari sent his youngest up to give me the key and I hope you don't mind what an awful mess I am today. I'm so disorganized and I don't want you to think ill of me so soon. Or ever!"

Paris finished her iced tea slowly, a little worried about Venita Valerie's breathiness and waited in vain for it to disappear.

They walked along the river past the muffled clanging of a long red brick factory, a small wooden church with a sign in Spanish on its rough patch of grass, an American flag prominent over the door of a liquor store, an insurance office with glass brick windows, and houses half stone, half wood or covered with stained and dented aluminum siding. The slow early autumn river gave off a minty scent as if ground cover thrived in the mud.

"You young people like swank addresses: two-two-two Railroad Aven-oo. Sounds like an old song, doesn't it?" said Venita. "It'll be handy for you starting out, close enough to the diner and the pizza parlor that you won't have to cook. But here I go talking a blue streak when I don't know a thing about you." Miss Valerie stopped short and stared at her. "Except that you're cute as a button. You could pass for under thirty, even graying so early, even behind such great big round glasses. And I don't think I've seen lashes that long in my life. They are real? Yes, of course. Come." She started again, but stopped almost immediately, chanting. "Here. Two-two-two."

The building was three-storied, and newly painted a pale yellow with white trim. On the bottom floor, the Valley Pizza House had put in an arched entryway. A green neon beer sign blinked in one window. The top floors were entered from the side over a small parking lot.

"This is the bad part of your little home," Miss Valerie said as they turned off Railroad Avenue to a long iron stairway that led to a landing outside the top floor. "But, you see, we've always had male teachers."

Her heart felt like a bass drum. "Which floor?"

"That's what I meant," said Miss Valerie, starting slowly up. "Third."

Just the sight of those pitched stairs made her feel weak, shaky and slightly nauseous. Silently she calculated how many times each day she'd have to face this ordeal, move up or down this virtual fire escape. She supposed she could say no, that she'd find another apartment, but Venita had already written about the lack of affordable housing in Morton River. She could stay in the guest house until she bought a new Honkey, but hadn't she signed on for new experiences, people — challenges? She reminded herself of her isolation in North Dakota, fighting rattlesnakes in Montana with nothing but a hoe, the tons of impassable snow in Buffalo. She lifted her suitcases, their weight anchoring her.

"Don't these sound like dungeon steps!" called

back Miss Valerie, holding her dress close to her legs and laughing. "You'll wear pants a great deal this winter, I'd guess."

She said nothing, just shook, fear chilling her as if this were February already, while Venita searched in her bottomless purse for the key. Paris squeezed her eyes shut, heard the lock and stepped through the door on the strength of her sense of Venita's back.

"What's wrong, Miss Collins?" asked the older woman, even more whispery, removing her hat again. "You're pale as snow!"

"Paris," she answered. "Please call me Paris. I'm just worn out."

"Of course you are. Now sit down. I'll fix us something."

Paris slumped on a short dark couch. It smelled like mildew at war with some cleaning chemical. She hoped the mildew would win. Her legs were rubbery, and she felt sweat trickle down the small of her back. "Great," she said.

"Shall I go out for something stronger than tea?"

"That's all right. I don't drink." The cartons in which her life was stored had been delivered and stacked neatly along the walls. There were her stereo boxes, her Gershwin and Broadway tapes. She slowly stood and made her way to her new kitchen.

The kitchen was huge, with an old green table against the window. Tie-back yellow curtains framed a vacant lot and a row of boarded-up buildings, haunted-looking warehouses and feed and garden stores lining Water Street down to the river. The white refrigerator was very old, but clean, with a silver *Frigidaire* across the door. She'd grown up with appliances like that. Morton River was evidently where all the recycled furniture came to live.

Venita led her through the apartment, keeping up her sibilant chatter. "You'll find a use for this second bedroom, knowing how teachers carry their work home with them. I've heard," she whispered, "that the last teacher used it to grow marijuana. See? It's lighted from both sides. I was frankly sorry to see him go. He was quite a character." Venita stopped short and smiled a great loose delighted smile. "But I'm so glad to have another woman to talk shop with. It's never the same with a man."

Paris looked her in the eye, but Venita turned away.

The other bedroom boasted a four-poster colonial-style maple bed, scratched but matching dresser and night tables. A large braided rug, once red and blue, now very faded, was the centerpiece of the room. Clunky old venetian blinds hung at the windows. "Perfect!" she said, forcing strength into her voice.

"You like it? Really?"

"It's fine. Clean and spacious and close to everything." No need to confess to her earlier fantasy. Lavender hot tub indeed. And it looked, if today was any indication, as if her life would be populated with everything but mysterious dykes who slouched, all too attractive, hands in pockets, whistling old show tunes. At least the whistling kettle would keep her company. She moved back into the sunlit kitchen to pour tea. Dust motes swarmed in the warm rays.

Venita passed her a mug painted with boldly bright flowers. Was that how she looked to the world? She was pleased. "That reefer-teacher," said Venita, "must have left these supplies. We can have some of his Oreo cookies too." Again the delighted smile. "Double creme."

Venita was a dunker. Paris watched, swallowing a smile, as the teacher dipped exactly one half of the cookie in her steaming tea.

"You must be dying of curiosity," said Venita, laying the other half on her saucer. "The school is back over the river, across Route Eighty-Three. It's a fifteen minute walk from here. Mrs. Rafferty willed the Center to Morton River. She never had an education as a girl because she went to work in the factories so early. She married widower Mr. Rafferty and it was quite the scandal." She dunked the other half and put it in her mouth. "Plant owner falls for floor girl. She brought up his boys and then he started failing. Instead of staying home to nurse him she went off to school herself. Morton River was shocked — this thirty-year-old woman in class with the town children. But she graduated and was ready to take over when he died — his boys would have squandered everything in a year."

Venita took a breath, looked under her eyebrows at Paris, and then they both grabbed more Oreos. And laughed. "I'm afraid chocolate is my downfall," whispered Venita.

"It's the frosting that lays me flat," Paris confided, with a twinkle of a memory: Jilly back in Montana, red-cheeked, under a snow-covered watchcap, dropping one last brawny armload of wood and leaping into bed for an orgy of Oreos. And more. Then afterwards, going back to their push-pull relationship, Jilly wanting more, Paris suffocating.

"Mrs. Rafferty wanted the Center to teach the whole person. She loved music and would go to New Haven for concerts and museums and theater. She knew she couldn't give enough money to teach classes in the arts, but she built in money for chamber concerts, readings, and for art exhibits in the halls. Mr. P., for all his faults, encourages us to take extracurricular trips, just like the grammar schools do, to acquaint the students with the fine arts. This is a special institution, Paris. It's a school with a spirit."

"I've dreamed of a school like that. I would have been here years ago."

"You'll meet Mr. P. Monday morning. His wife's not Italian, you know. Mixed marriage of any kind is frowned on around here so you won't find too many of the older Italians at the center though we have a lot in the Valley. But there I go again. I'll talk about Morton River for hours. Tell me about Paris — what an unusual name. How did you ever —"

"I was conceived in Paris: Maudie Paris Collins. Maudie is my least favorite aunt, so straight-laced she'd wear underwear on her mind if she could." She twisted the ring on her finger. "She objected to Dad giving me Grandmom's ring —" She held out the translucent opal in a fragile-looking gold setting on her pinky — "because I wasn't much like them, and wouldn't stay in Austin."

"It suits you though. And goes well with that fine gold necklace. I've been admiring the design."

"It's a lambda." She hated the suspense and

14

waited for Venita to ask what it meant. There was no way she'd swallow her feelings around this issue.

"The Greek letter? Of course." Venita looked at it again, as if about to ask a question, then dunked another cookie. "What brought you to adult ed? Where are you from originally? Most people want to teach children."

"I've never been much drawn to small sticky terrorists," she said, again watching Venita's eyes for recognition. Did it mean anything to her that Paris was in Levis, wore a lambda slung around her neck, that she, like Venita, had no man, no kids . . . Was there an outside chance that Venita might be a lesbian too? "Every September my parents and I would return to the same old routines in Hyde Park, an Austin suburb. It's the most boring home town in the universe."

"No cowboys?"

Paris laughed. "Our neighbors weren't brazen legendary Texans. They were full of unbearable anxieties about a blade of grass too long or a blond hair out of kilter. That's where I developed my passion for kids," she said with sarcasm. "If I was just back from Germany they'd call me a Nazi-lover, if we'd been to France I was a Frog. They threw ethnic slurs at me no matter where I'd been. I wanted to stomp the little bigots, but the first time I tried I was in trouble up to my ears. After a while I treated them like something the dog left in the gutter."

"I love children! I've taught half the business owners, lawyers — the teachers themselves! in this Valley. But I was at retirement age and they didn't want such an old fogey in the elementary schools. I can't imagine living like you, leaving all my work behind me."

"I know I've helped a few people. Letters follow me."

"Now tell me how Morton River got on your list."

"It wasn't premeditated." She pushed the cookies across the table. Venita took another. Paris split hers in two and scooped up half the frosting with her tongue. "I get newsletters, government bulletins. I applied for openings in the states where I haven't taught yet. Morton River offered what I wanted: teaching people who know English but are still wrapping their tongues around it like it's a golf ball they're trying not to swallow."

"No English as a Second Language?"

"When I was a kid we'd go to countries where I could just about get by with the words I had. I wanted to fit in like a snake wants its new skin before winter, and I never could because I didn't know the passwords that stamp you as native, the idioms. Without the jargon you're always a stranger. I like my students to have the basics before I get at them."

"So you're the stranger who teaches others to fit in."

"I see language as a survival skill."

"And I'm a numbers runner," said Venita with a dare in her eyes. "The odds of success, no matter how smoothly you speak, go down until you can count your change."

It was feeling like a friendly duel. "I teach them poetry for the cultural references, not art for art's sake."

"And I teach them how to use three-ninety-nine

calculators — the new math is useless." Venita clapped her hands together. "We're going to get along just fine, my dear."

"I believe you're right," Paris answered, pushing the cookies toward Venita, glad clear to her toes to have found a friend so soon.

CHAPTER 2

Mr. Piccari was much shorter than Paris, with a bald spot as big as a saucer and brown eyes that seemed to beg forgiveness for every word out of pursed, badly chapped lips. He didn't seem to know what to do with her once she declined coffee. She didn't know what to make of him either.

"Let me explain your time sheet to you," he said, enthusiasm in his reedy voice. He stretched his chin up from his tightly starched collar, dark bristles scratching.

She tuned out, rolling a number two pencil

between her palms, smelling a lifetime of classrooms, pencil lead and wood shavings. At the little downtown mall on Saturday she'd prescribed a new Gershwin tape to cure the dispiritedness which had returned after Venita's visit. All last night, as she finished setting up her household, she played the tape over and over, whirling in her floor-length bathrobe with a dust rag, dancing chairs into their proper positions, sweeping her kitchen floor as if waltzing in some great old ballroom. Gershwin was her magic music and her heart ached from all the dreams that had danced in it last night. There was a seventeen-year-old lurking inside her.

Mr. Piccari finished. The unpleasant task was at hand. She'd insisted on doing it from day one, her first teaching job out of college. It was another of her numerous reasons she would teach only adults, this insistence on honesty. And she made a point of telling employers in person even though it was more risky. The rewards of confrontation were much greater than hiding behind a long distance phone connection. It hadn't backfired yet, but the spark of anxiety, and her retreat into fantasy, were sure signs that she was still scared.

"I'm gay, Mr. Piccari," she said. She felt as if a flock of hummingbirds were locked inside her chest.

He stretched his chin up again like a restless turtle, the window light on his wire-rimmed glasses hiding his eyes. "Let me show you the building now, and your classroom," he replied.

She hesitated before rising, wanting to say, *Knock, knock, is anyone home in there?* He was out the door, though, hands fluttering. It was always a letdown after she broke the sexuality barrier. Most people either couldn't care less or were reluctant to show any other reaction.

The worn bannister was smooth and cool, the steps uneven under her feet from years of erosion. Her classroom was pleasantly enormous, with original woodwork as well as floor-to-ceiling windows. It smelled as if someone had devotedly oiled the wood recently. Mr. Piccari?

"I love it!" she said. "But I want to hold dances, parties, salons in it, not grammar classes." And live in it, she thought, with a Rhett Butler of a woman, all tailored clothes and ruffled shirts, charming her guests in a parlor just like this.

"Now," he said, returning to his natural bustle, lifting his chin, "a staff meeting and you'll want to acquaint yourself with your texts and equipment."

Paris used to get nervous meeting co-workers, but like most adult ed staffs, this one was a benign cast of characters. Hattie Echols, the ESL language teacher, immediately tried to build an alliance with Paris by warning her about the other teachers' peccadillos.

"That fool!" Hattie hissed in her ear about the history teacher. "Someday he'll get caught with his hands on the innocent girls —"

"Whoa," Paris told her, spitting mad. "First off, I do *not* want to hear all this. Second, he acts like he wouldn't know what to do with *any* girl, much less an innocent one, and third, I'm gay, so I try not to cast stones."

Hattie listened to that. "Gay? Well, there's nothing wrong with gay. I have gay friends."

Hattie sped away from her almost as soon as was polite. *Thank goodness for gossips,* she thought.

They saved her from having to declare herself to every last soul in the universe. She should have told Venita on Friday.

For all the good it does me to be gay, she thought, her depression rushing back in like dark, roiling storm clouds.

Why bother coming out to the world when she hadn't done anything in an age except flirt like a twenty-year-old and pose in bars? Social life was the major drawback to her two-year plans. She could find the gay people in a small town without any problem, but no one wanted to get involved with a Kelly-gay, as one ex called her. "I'm not into temps," Lynn had said, her tears soaking Paris's bare shoulder. "But I told you I'd only be here till summer," Paris had reminded her. "I know, but I thought you'd stay. For me." They all thought that. Even she sometimes thought that. She hadn't bothered to fall in love at all in Florida.

She came out to Venita after the meeting.

Venita chuckled. "Oh well," she said in a breathy undertone, offering her a wintergreen LifeSaver. "As long as you don't grow little lesbians in your back bedroom windows and then smoke them. Let's have dinner at the diner tonight and I'll introduce you to some of your folks."

"Then you're —" Paris concluded, her curiosity raging.

"No," Venita said. She seemed excited. "Not me, but that's where to go if you want to meet them."

At dinnertime she stayed in a skirt, but grabbed her jean jacket as a compromise. The usual terrifying descent toward the street was always embarrassing once it was over. Her heart beat as if

21

she were going into combat. It took all of the five minutes between the apartment and the diner to calm down. On the way she saw herself reflected in the window of the beflagged liquor store, hunched, scurrying. How could such a competent woman of the world have such fear of a few steps?

This time, Venita was there ahead of her. Monday must be spaghetti day. Spicy-smelling sausages popped and spit as they grilled. Her stomach growled. She could tell, though, from the way no one on the diner staff looked at her, as opposed to the professionally cheery welcome she'd been getting since her arrival, that everyone "knew."

She sat across from Venita. Their booth by the door was in everyone's path and noisy with the bustle of the restaurant. "Thank you," she said. "You've done your job well."

Venita's skin flushed darker. "I confess," she said in a stage whisper. "I tried to smooth your way, but they already knew."

"They didn't know last night, I can guarantee you that. I'll never have to take out a personal ad around here — Hattie Echols works faster. Normally, I'd have to crop off my hair or walk around on the arm of Martina the tennis player before they'd give me a second glance. I've never looked like a dyke even when I've tried," she said, tossing her jacket into the booth and displaying her lambda.

"That's good, isn't it?" Venita asked.

She tried not to be impatient. The most liberal of straight liberals had no inkling of how obtuse they could be. "How would it feel to know you were black by heritage — and by some accident of birth and environment had white skin?"

"Isolating. No, stifling. I'll take being who I am over every social and economic advantage in the book."

"Well, me too."

Venita pursed her lips. "Must be this new generation. This gay revolution generation."

"Liberation."

"Whatever. My big brother killed himself over it forty-five years ago."

"God, I'm sorry."

"Right here in Morton River." Venita's eyes clouded, her words barely audible, but more staccato than ever. "He'd come to me crying and praying for the man of his dreams and wishing he'd never been homosexual, or never been born. Then he'd flee to Harlem, but he didn't like the big city. He wanted to meet some nice boy and bring him home. No one would leave the wild nights, the rent parties, to come hide in the Valley." Venita's fingers tapped one another as if she were playing scales on them. "So he got involved at home, with a sixteen-year-old. Bubba was only eighteen, but the young man's parents had him arrested. Father was the first black officer of Morton River Savings, of any Connecticut bank; it had taken generations to get there. He threw Bubba to the wolves." Venita shook her head, eyes far away. "But these are happier times for you," she ended, leaning against the seat back with a smile. "I like to think of Bubba in the diner laughing with you all."

"Don't tell me this Valley is the Garden of Eden for gays. Blue collar, working class — that's hardly likely in my book." She played with a split end in her hair, waiting for Venita's testimonial.

23

Venita tapped her fingertips together again. "Perhaps these are extraordinary gays. I don't mean that they're marching down Main Street. But a few years back the town was ready to give up, to let the failing industries wash it down river. The young people were all leaving. The whites hated the blacks, the blacks hated the Spanish and everyone hated the Asians. Yet with civil rights the only ones left to pick on were the homosexuals."

The waitress came by; Venita waved her away. It was that Southerner named Elly who had a wiggle in her walk a mile wide. Was she one of the dykes? If so, would Paris fit in?

"A few years back, Dusty and Elly and their friends were the backbone of the fight against a flood. They fed the sandbaggers, sent everyone who came in to work on the line regardless of color or accent, collected blankets and food and clothing for the people who were evacuated and generally kept up everyone's spirits. After the waters receded the Red Cross and the diner remained the center of activity for flood relief. When the federal government didn't want to cough up funds, some of Dusty and Elly's gay pride friends raised the money to send protesters to Washington. They knew how to do these things from raising their own money. People suddenly were reading about Morton River Valley in their papers and seeing it on TV and we got what we needed to fortify the dam and the riverbanks and to rebuild what we lost."

Venita paused, drank some water and went on. "That was the work of the gays, no one else. And," she gestured toward the white-uniformed woman on the other side of the kitchen window with a deferential look, "of that plucky Dusty Reilly. She's got the stuff heroes are made of. I'd fall for her myself if I were gay."

The waitress returned. "Venita, you old character, you're talking this girl's head off and I know you're telling tales on us. Why don't you just introduce her?"

"Because I know you're too modest to tell your exploits yourself. The Valley is still losing businesses and people, but you two helped make it livable in its failing years."

"Failing? Heck, it's just changing. Something will come along to make this Valley as grand as it once was, not some bedroom community for Upton and New Haven."

"Elly," said Venita, "is a transplant. We used to get a lot of Southerners here when Rafferty's was going."

"She means rednecks — I don't even know your name."

"Paris. Paris Collins." The woman had deepening friendly-looking laugh lines at her eyes.

"We've been hearing a whole lot more about you, honey. Let me drag Dusty out. It's just about time to get on home anyway and that woman wouldn't stop work to sleep if I didn't lure her home nights." Elly turned back immediately. "By the way, what all do you want for your supper?"

They ordered and Paris asked Venita about Morton River Valley's situation now.

"We're not under water, dear, and that's about it for the good news," Venita said in a sad tone. She sighed as quietly as she spoke. "When the Rafferty plant closed its doors two years ago there wasn't much more we could do. They'd had state and federal help and new management and layoffs and retooling and employee purchases till even their strongest booster, the *Valley Sentinel,* started to agree that they were jinxed. Now the old plant is like a ghost we tiptoe around, pretending it's not right there in the middle of town. Oh, there are a few of these light industries coming in, moving into failed garages, but they hire fifteen, twenty people at most and then at minimum wage. The unemployment rate is twenty-three percent!" Venita's hands came up, appealing.

"You know," said Paris, puzzled, "I've been in towns that have died because a mine played out, or the timber industry went kaput, but this is my first one where everything looks ready to go: cheap power, industrial properties for a song, a big labor pool. Why isn't anyone taking advantage of it?"

"One developer converted a small factory to a mall with a restaurant right on the river, but he was crooked, the work was shoddy and no one in Morton River has the money to buy expensive clothing or support a teddy bear shop. He thought he'd rejuvenate the river tourist trade, but with no motels all we have are people who've owned summer cabins for generations."

It was some time before Elly returned. When she emerged from the kitchen it was with a parade of staff. Dusty, one of those bashful, bright-eyed dykey grins on her face, bore dinner. They were singing "The Yellow Rose of Texas."

She felt her eyes well up. "This is a first!"

"We want you to know you're welcome," said Elly.

She was introduced. Dusty was handsome, with an air of unruffled authority about her, but it was the tall waitress with broad shoulders and a languorous yet purposeful stride, and dark hair gathered at the nape of her gorgeously long neck, who'd caught Paris's fancy at meals over the weekend. She'd pictured the woman in a tuxedo, poised at open French doors, champagne in hand, watching as Paris danced with another partner, then striding over, classy, appraising, taking her elbow with a gentle, unquestioning pressure. The waitress stood apart from the rest, eyes smoldering as if her dignity were being assaulted by being there.

"You need to come out and meet our ducks sometime," said Dusty, genial, offering her hand. Even in bifocals and a soiled white uniform she looked dapper. She wasn't Paris's type, but Elly had her arm through Dusty's anyway, claiming her at the same time that she smiled a real welcome at Paris. "We're ten miles from town."

"I don't have a car yet."

"No *problem*," said a willowy young man with arrestingly blue eyes. "I'm John." He shook her hand briskly.

Elly laughed. "He's our relief cook now, just back from the Navy. Dusty didn't trust him to whip up your dinner."

"Might stick hardtack in your spaghetti sauce," Dusty warned, but patted him on the back with a fond look.

John elbowed her. "Come off it, old timer! They haven't served hardtack since you were mustered out." He turned back to Paris. "I have a friend at the Jeep dealership in Upton. Louie. Tell him you're from Dusty's Queen of Hearts Diner. He'll treat you good."

"*Friend,*" teased Dusty. "I'll bet these ladies want to eat before it gets cold. On the house."

Paris was embarrassed to hear her voice tremble when she said, "I really, really appreciate this. You've won yourself a customer for the next two years."

"What happens in two years?" Dusty asked, peering into her eyes with a look that made Paris feel like she'd just been adopted into a big, welcoming family.

"This Cinderella turns into a pumpkin every twenty-four months, not hours," said Venita.

"I like to move on. I get to see the country that way and nothing gets stale, including me."

For the first time the tall woman looked interested. *God, she's beautiful,* thought Paris. Her back was straighter even than Venita's, her eyes huge, deep brown, her nose a little heavy for that delicate neck, but it gave her face strength. She couldn't stop staring.

Dusty's look was admiring now, even cruisy. "You don't look like a candidate for stale to me," she said. "Elly, let's see what we can do to turn this one around and plant her here for good."

"Twenty-four months? It took me a lot longer to land you, Dusty Reilly, but I can do just about anything else in the world in twenty-four months. Consider that a challenge, Tex."

"You're on, Elly," said Paris, a sense of excitement that she might really have lighted at last from her restless chariot. "But don't hold your breath."

CHAPTER 3

"The first day of school is always a madhouse, wherever you teach!" cried Venita in a strangely loud, harried voice, books and file folders in both arms. "One of my math geniuses is giving me a ride home. He can drop you if you'd like."

"I'll need the walk after today, but thanks for asking."

Venita sped off.

Paris dropped to her chair, feeling stunned. The room still smelled of lemon wood polish, but now it was crowded with the dozens of personalities that had swarmed into it all day. She'd taught through the afternoon, rushed to the diner for dinner with Venita, then taught two more classes. She had a stack of introductory compositions to take home, her way of getting to know the students and their skill levels. She didn't expect a whole lot. The classes seemed to attract recent high school dropouts who wanted to pass military entrance exams, displaced workers back to school after a dozen or more years, and well-drilled graduates from ESL. There were two displaced homemakers and a few refugees from Southeast Asia who might be college material.

Someone knocked softly at her open door. *Not Mr. Piccari,* she thought, too exhausted to deal again with his fussy concern. But it wasn't him at all. The stunning, broad-shouldered woman from the diner watched her from the doorway.

The woman had been so aloof at work Paris never had been able to get beyond please, thank you and bring on the eggplant parmigiana. Now the waitress was presenting herself on a platter? This is too easy, she thought, a second wind, all nervous energy, infusing her.

"I'm Giulia Scala, from the diner." Giulia casually leaned against the door jamb, diffident, but chin upthrust. Her eyes were stern, her proud manner disdainful, her voice resonant with self-assurance, yet Paris realized she was barely out of her teens. The smell of pink soap from the diner's restroom softened Giulia's guarded air. She wore the white uniform dress that always looked incongruous on her. She looked too handsome, too regal for Morton River

Valley. As if to point this out a freight train hooted one very long blast which faded as it left the town behind.

"I know."

"May I come in?" There was an old-world air about Giulia. Her demeanor unleashed a potent memory stuffed way back in Paris's head of Mademoiselle, the woman her parents rented a flat from in Paris — haughty, obviously struggling to keep her little building from shabbiness, too proud to act like a landlady. Just the sight of Giulia brought on the scent of her apartment: European cigarettes spiced with oregano. She felt the old butterflies of allure Mademoiselle had always held for her, echoes of the massive crush that had engulfed her at ages nine and fourteen, two of the summers they'd spent in France.

Giulia triggered the challenge she'd felt to romance Mademoiselle, to wring love from her dignified rejection. Giulia was so young though, she told herself, thinking of Bubba Valerie and the temper of the Valley. *Lady be good.*

"I live with my mother and younger sister up there," continued Giulia, vaguely gesturing toward the hills behind the Center. Paris saw the hills of a small Italian town she'd visited on another trip — or had it been in Greece — felt cobblestones under her feet. Giulia lowered her gaze for the first time, hands deep in the pockets of her black blazer. Paris fleetingly stood her at a dark bar, cruising. "My mother doesn't speak English and she is very, very heavy." She thrust up her chin again and a hot anger was in her voice. "My father left us three years ago. She won't learn English even to get off

32

welfare. My sister is still a child, but in a few years there won't be any money."

Giulia's face was a battle of arrogance and pleading. How could she know that Paris was frantically searching her bag of tricks just to tease a smile from this woman?

From the pocket of her blazer Giulia pulled a referral to Rafferty Center. "The welfare is pushing her to prepare. She can't work without English, but she can't get here either. Cabs are too expensive. The buses don't come close enough to our house. We live at the top of the hill, behind everyone else. We don't have a car. Because of her weight she can't climb the hill. And she's ashamed."

"Of what?" Paris asked, although she remembered perfectly well how she'd wanted to scream, traveling with her parents, locked into her own language and a smattering of others. She'd wanted to talk, to joke with the people they met, and felt ignorant for not knowing how, felt gagged and despised when she couldn't say what she felt, especially to the women who looked at her so kindly, wanting to understand. "Of what?" was really beside the point.

"That he left her," spat Giulia. "That she's fat, that she can't speak English, that my sister runs wild."

"How does your mom get to welfare?" She felt the lasso tightening around her and rapidly rolled her pencil between her palms.

"My fiance drives her."

Oh, well, Paris thought, abandoning Giulia's tuxedo.

"But he can't take her to school. He works."

"Does she read and write?"

With an indignant tone, Giulia answered, "She was educated by the nuns. My grandparents wanted her to catch a rich man. She isn't stupid."

Fiance or not, Paris felt the first teasing words leap to her lips. She couldn't help treating the woman like a dyke. "I'll just bet pride runs deeper than bone in your family."

Giulia's chin rose a fraction higher. "I earn good money at the diner. I'll pay a teacher to come to the house. Once my mother has decent English she won't be as afraid to go out. Once she goes out she'll want to lose weight." The anger never left her eyes. "Or else she'll always live with me."

"Not good," Paris sympathized, thinking of another out. "But she needs to learn the whole ball of wax. I don't teach beginning English. You'd better ask the ESL teacher."

"She said no last year." Giulia tossed her chin toward her shoulder in a clear gesture of dismissal.

"Yes, well," Paris said, hoping she'd never be on the wrong side of this lady. "How about you, your little sister?"

"We're only her daughters. What do we know? She won't learn from us. The little one is just there enough to sleep anyway, when would she teach?" The chin toss wrote off the sister too.

She pictured a smaller, dissipated, prepubescent version of Giulia, heavily made up, smacking gum and smoking clove cigarettes, watching some punk-haired boy play Nintendo. "So I'm it," she said, mostly to herself. She moved to the window and studied the trestle across the river. There was no way she could think while she looked at that should-be lesbian beauty.

What else did she have to do with her time? She couldn't exactly live at the diner. And for what other reason was she in teaching? Whatever it was that drew her to a poorly paid profession working with even more poorly paid workers and the unemployed also drew her to Giulia's dilemma. She reminded herself that she could say no, but apparently her heart wasn't buying that one. Not with the added attraction of getting to know Giulia. When she turned back to the room she asked, "And if someone were to volunteer?"

"No," Giulia said with force. She was so self-assured, so authoritative, Paris couldn't imagine not doing her bidding. "I didn't come for more welfare. I'm prepared to pay for a service. If I can't give you what you want then I'll think of something else."

"Looks to me," she said, trying to find something besides a seductive smile, probing for the woman's sense of humor, "like I have you over a barrel. I can make you pay through the nose or you can snap me up for free. Take your pick." She chuckled.

Giulia drew herself up even straighter. Blood flushed her face a smooth pink. "You're making fun of me," she accused. She stood and folded her arms, a level look willing Paris to agree with her terms. Every one of them.

"Whoa. Sorry. What if someone wanted to exchange services? I picked up a little Italian in Venice, but I haven't had a soul to talk to since I was nine."

"You speak Italian?" Giulia looked disconcerted.

Point, she thought, feeling guilty at her sense of victory. She watched the lovely face in thought.

"If she took some money for her time," said Giulia firmly, "and didn't reduce her charge out of kindness."

"Nothing wrong with kindness in my book," Paris said, wondering if the woman's iron determination was charm or flaw. Damn, if she wasn't going to do it, if she wasn't going to get involved with some sick family that needed a stranger to bounce off. She felt seduced. Which of those crazy hillside houses was Giulia's? "Where do you live?"

"Straight up the hill in back of the school. Just below the top there's an unpaved road. We're at the end."

"Nine tomorrow morning?"

"I'll be there. I don't have classes until afternoon."

"You're in college?"

"Of course."

"Of course."

She spent the night searching for Giulia's house in her dreams: castles, gingerbread cottages, glass-walled feats of balance, all tumbled together. Every dream ended with Giulia stroking her in some outrageously erotic way.

The next morning she dropped her book bag at the Center and trudged up the hill, legs straining, eyes heavy and squinting in the daylight from late night reading. Someone was burning leaves already. The hillside was a festival of fat red tomatoes, outsized zucchini squash and chrysanthemums. The cracked and pitted sidewalks became occasional, then rare. At the turnoff she heard a rooster crow. Who said the east coast was all cement?

Giulia's house was like a good-size squared stucco hut. The dirty white walls had not recently been painted, but the crumbling corners and cracks had been patched with a darker cement. The structure perched at the edge of the cliff. There was no garden here unless this land grew junk along with crabgrass and weeds. Wild pink asters fought for space with tangles of purslane, tiny clusters of yellow open to the sun. A rusted car, a bicycle without wheels, lumber scraps, a cement mixer —

"Yo!"

A burly teenager strutted from behind the mixer.

"Hello," she answered with a start. *Curiouser and curiouser,* she thought. Stained red football jersey, faded black jeans strategically torn, dirty turquoise hightops and a gray fedora — surely not the sister?

The girl strode though a maze of loose flagstones and abandoned tools toward Paris, wiping her hands on her jeans. Paris saw a hint of large breasts then, hidden in the oversized jersey. She had Giulia's impressive brown eyes, her even dark brows, and the same mouth, only this one smiled. It was a closed-mouth smile, but so big it made lines in that perhaps fifteen-year-old face. When the girl took off her hat wild curls tumbled over her forehead and ears. Paris couldn't help herself, that face brought out her own best smile and she reached down to shake the dirty hand the kid offered. Here was Giulia's warm side.

"I'm Maddy," said the girl. "Short for Maddalena, not Mad As a Hatter like a lot of the kids say. So you're the teacher — Miss Collins?"

She hesitated only a fraction of a second —

warning herself that this was one powerhouse little dyke budding out — before responding. "Paris," she offered.

"Really? What a cool name."

The ornately carved front door opened. Giulia, in a plain light dress that made her look smaller, softer, called, "Miss Collins!" Even if the sight of Giulia didn't draw her like a bear to a bee's nest, it wasn't a summons to ignore.

"That's my little sister. Don't let her bother you."

"Bother me?"

"All she wants is attention."

She looked at Maddy who shrugged and twirled a finger at her head. "*Essa e pazzo*. That's okay. I'm trying to get this thing going. If I can make it work I'll put a sidewalk in front of our house. What do you think?"

"Why?" she asked.

The kid shrugged again, a surprised look on her face. "Everyone else has one. Just because we live up here in the boonies doesn't mean we don't have class."

"Miss Collins?"

" 'Bye, Paris. Good luck."

"You too, Maddy."

She followed Giulia into a small hot room dominated by an empty fireplace. A short woman in black sat in the middle of a couch. The room looked like her parents' den when she was growing up, all blond wood with turquoise and gold upholstery. Speckled lamps made to look like Chinese lanterns hung from the ceiling on tarnished gold chains. Paris felt both comfortable and appalled all at once.

"Mama," Giulia said in Italian, "this is Miss Collins."

Sophia gravely nodded and gestured for her to sit.

"Please call me Paris," she said, in her most professional, reassuring tone.

Giulia explained in Italian.

Her mother's eyebrows raised. "Paris?"

"Like the city."

Again Giulia translated.

"This will never work," Paris said, tossing professionalism out.

Giulia's eyebrows shot up. Paris could see that the eyebrows grew naturally together over her nose like Sophia's and Maddy's and that they'd been pulled out. *Ouch,* she thought. "This *has* to work," Giulia instructed, her speech almost threatening.

"Not the English. You," she said. "I'll never get through to your mother with you between us. Go help Maddy fix the cement mixer or something."

"Do you have enough Italian?"

"I don't need a thing but words and a student."

Giulia glided into another room, skeptical and huffy. Some people thought their penny's worth brought dominance.

"I like your house," she said to Sophia more conversationally.

The woman looked puzzled.

"I like your house," she repeated with gestures.

Eyes narrowing, the woman leaned forward as if she could catch the meaning better.

"House." She rose and pointed to the walls, the ceiling, the floor, the doorways. Giulia's beauty was

in her mother's face along with the plucky orneriness
of her younger daughter. She could sense reluctance
— to learning, to anything new, to her? She
crouched at the end table next to her and sketched
a house. "House," she said, pointing to it. "House,"
she repeated, pointing to the one they were in.

"*Casa,*" Sophia said, her hands, absolutely still
until now, lifting a bit, like baby birds struggling to
fly.

"Your house." She pointed first to Sophia, then to
the drawing.

"*Mia casa.*"

"*Mia casa,* my house."

"*Mia casa.*"

"My house."

"*Mia casa.*"

She sat in front of Sophia, legs crossed. "My
house," she said stubbornly.

The woman was silent.

She sighed, frustrated. She wasn't going to waste
her time. Some people wanted to stay locked in their
closets. "My," she said.

Sophia scowled, but her hands fell open, palms
up, on the black skirt. "My."

"My *house,*" she insisted.

The hands began to lift, well-fed white birds,
then fell back. "My," Sophia said, teeth gritted. The
hands began their ascent again. "House."

She smiled. "Good!" Fifty percent of teaching was
winning the student's cooperation. That moment of
triumph always gave her a tingle along her sternum.

Sophia jabbed a finger at her. "*Vostre.*"

"*Vostre casa,*" she answered, glad at the quick challenge. She pointed to the woman and her house. "*Vostre casa.*"

Sophia nodded, then looked toward a door, eyes flaring like Giulia's. Giulia had been watching them. Sophia banished her.

Satisfied, the mother turned back. "Your. House. *Dovè?*"

Paris guessed. "*Mia casa* — down the hill, over the *rivera,*" she gestured. They played with that until Sophia had the new words *where, river* and maybe *down.* Then Giulia appeared again, this time balancing a tray.

Sophia took over immediately, not leaving her seat. She pointed here and there, giving orders. With ease, Giulia moved the coffee table so that her mother could serve. Paris would not accept anything until Sophia named it in English. Coffee she already knew. The pastries, when Paris let herself accept one, were flaky, just sweet, better than bakery.

"Is she learning?" asked Giulia.

"She's *teaching!* This is more intense than a whole day at school." Sophia's head came up. She looked wary. "Whoops. Wrong move. I don't want to exclude her."

Giulia began to translate.

"No!" Paris directed.

"It'll take forever in English," Giulia complained.

Giulia's obtuseness was wrecking Paris's fantasy of her. "Do you want your mother to learn or what? I'm only going to be around two years." Giulia strode out, as if swirling a royal robe around herself and

41

planning retribution against this rebellious peasant. Paris slowly explained what had been said. It felt like a battle. Sophia would intone a word, she would translate, Sophia would repeat it in English, she in Italian, until they could exchange a whole thought. No, even if Sophia had been physically capable of getting there she wouldn't have lasted a day at the Center. She was too truculent, challenging everything, as if Paris should teach Americans to speak Italian for her student's convenience.

Paris kneaded her aching calves. Their last lesson of the day was in the language of walking, hills, of aches and pains. Sophia summoned Giulia.

"*Per voi.*"

Giulia brought a jelly jar of salve. Was this an apology? "Mama makes it herself. Alcohol, red pepper and myrrh. It's wonderful for sore muscles."

"Thank you," she said, rubbing it immediately in. Sophia folded her arms and watched. "Yow!" She could feel it in her nostrils.

"*Calda?*" asked Sophia. "*Calda?*" she repeated, fanning herself and blowing.

"*Molto calda!* Hot!" she managed to choke out, tears stinging her eyes. "Wow!"

"Wow?"

Oh shit. "Wow —" she looked to Giulia for help. "Wow, Mama, is like —"

Maddy burst into the room. She went directly to the pastries. "Wow is right! *Pasticcera* on a weekday!" Crumbs fell to her shirt. Sophia reached to brush them away, but Maddy jumped back. "You trying to teach her to say wow? How about *grody to the max*? Think she'd learn that one?" She rushed to her mother, gave her a hard hug and a loud kiss, nuzzled her cheek, then grabbed for another pastry.

"*Basta!*" cried the mother, struggling to rise, but the front door slammed shut before she could.

"Wow," Paris said. A tornado had just come and gone. She didn't know whether to be amused or saddened by Maddy.

"*Cattiva,*" said Sophia, shaking her head and scraping her index fingers together.

"Bad?" Paris asked.

"Rotten to the core," answered Giulia.

"*Voletta mangiare?*"

She looked at Giulia. "Eat?"

"She wants to know if she can feed you lunch. You'd better say yes or she'll be insulted."

"After all that dessert?"

They worked a while longer, then Giulia called out the back door for Maddy. They were halfway through the meal before the kid bounded in, sailing her fedora across the room onto a counter. Sophia rolled her eyes.

"*Paisan!*" cried Maddy, lightly punching Paris in the arm. The girl ate fast. "Ma's the best cook in the world," she said, her mouth neatly full, "but I hate sitting at the table. Ma always tells the same stories. And you," she accused, pointing her fork at Giulia, "you always act like you have heartburn, with that sour look on your face."

Giulia never paused as she cut a long loaf of bread. She was obviously the queen of this roost. She kept the family together and coerced it to function as if she'd taken on her father's role and brought to it the strength of a mother. She was a magnet for Paris. Imagine, she thought, a lover who knew how to make a home, who could be counted on, leaned on, who knew how to do life.

"I don't understand you, Giulia," mimicked Maddy, in a perversely accurate imitation of her mother. She pulled at her bra, grimacing in her own discomfort.

"Don't make fun of her, brat!" Giulia looked at her with an exasperated scowl. She said to Paris, "Ma does all the cooking and cleaning and this ingrate doesn't appreciate any of it."

Maddy dipped bread in her sauce and continued with a straight face, obviously reciting one of her mother's favorite speeches, "A girl, a young girl like you, Giulia. Why do you work all the time? You should have fun, dance, let Peter take care of you. You're as beautiful as I was, with your hair so black, your skin so white. And so modest! Not like me. I knew it. Too much, I knew it."

Maddy told Sophia's story with histrionic sighs and gestures. It was, with her interpretation, a comically sad tale of an arrogant young Sophia who thought herself too good for any of the boys in her village. She'd waited too long to marry and her beauty began to fade. By twenty-five she'd resigned herself to being the daughter who stayed home and cared for her parents. Then Maddy's Dad had come to the town, a tall, curly-haired, dreamy-eyed traveling junkman, intoxicated with the promise of life. He was looking for the right bride to take to America. He smiled and sang and laughed Sophia across the ocean.

"Nothing true," Maddy spat. Paris laughed at the impassioned acting, though she was embarrassed for the mother, whose puzzled eyes followed Maddy. "Junkman in Italy, junkman in America. From poor to more poor and no family to turn to. I'm glad he left. I didn't want to look at him every day and think about the mistake I made. I don't want you to make mistakes, Giulia."

Maddy pointed a finger at herself. "You! Born to make mistakes! A shadow of your father with his face and ways."

Even Giulia cracked a smile, but she became grim again as she said, "It's true. She's like his son, followed him everywhere, the two of them rolling along like bowlegged sailors, from one unfinished project in the yard to the next. My mother tried to teach her to sew, to cook, but the brat cried until she choked. She wanted to do what her father did: bricklaying when he made the barbecue outside, welding when he put up the half-fence out front, engine repair on all those lawnmowers and his crazy half-dead Plymouth. My father could do anything except earn a decent living."

Grabbing one of Maddy's grimy hands, Sophia herself spoke then, adding to the rancor at the table. Maddy translated, echoing the scolding tone. "You didn't wash your hands again! What kind of wife will you make? Wash!"

When Sophia didn't stop, Maddy swaggered to the sink.

"Just like him. She walks just like him. Don't you know you're a girl, Maddalena?" Giulia asked. Paris almost laughed. What did Giulia see when she looked in the mirror, a powder-puff?

Maddy swung around, her face red. "Don't call me that!"

"What's wrong with it?" asked Giulia, baiting her.

"It's some girl on a stained-glass window, not me. It's who I'm supposed to be." Paris felt Maddy's humiliation: she couldn't be the kind of kid her mother had wanted when she chose the name Maddalena. Sophia took spumoni from the freezer. Maddy ran her fingers through her short curls, hesitated and dug at her bra again, grimacing as if it cut into her. But she sat down; where else could she find spumoni?

Giulia said in slow English, "We have to go to the welfare tomorrow, Mama."

Maddy, obviously restored by dessert, returned to her imitation, "When Peter marries you, we won't have to go to the welfare. You're my hope, my jewel. Who wants this other one?"

But the storm had passed. Sophia reached to play with Maddy's curls.

Maddy grabbed her mother's hand. "I don't want to get married. I'm going to get a job and take care of you. You don't need a man."

Giulia interrupted. "You stay in school. You need an education. Maybe nursing."

"I don't want to take care of sick people."

"Babies. Take care of new babies."

"I don't like babies. They cry and stink."

"You were a baby."

"I outgrew it as soon as I could."

"Peter will be here at seven-thirty tomorrow morning," Giulia said, dishing out the last of lunch.

"I wish he'd teach me more about heavy equipment. I can rip up trees as good as anybody."

Paris had kept her silence long enough. "Whoa. Why would you want to?"

"They're building that industrial park. I'm for Earth Day and all that, but, you know, it'll make lots of jobs. And jobs mean more people want houses and offices and that's what I want to do, build them!"

"Ripping down trees," Paris said with sarcasm.

Maddy looked stricken. Hadn't anyone ever challenged this way of thinking before? "All right, *teacher*," she defied Paris, "I suppose you think I ought to be a nurse too."

"Not on my life. I wouldn't want you taking care of me with that attitude."

The girl was constantly fiddling with her bra, pushing up the straps, pulling down on the elastic. "Then what?"

"You want to build?" She thought for a moment. "How about a solar technician?"

"What, repair the sun?"

"Jerk," said Giulia. "You've heard of solar energy."

"Who's going to pay me to do that?"

"You'd have to be an independent contractor. Do some selling. Aluminum siding had to start somewhere."

Maddy looked thoughtful. "How do you get to be a solar technician? We don't have a shop for it at school."

"I suppose you'd have to study electricity first."

Meanly, Giulia added, "And algebra and trig and physics."

Maddy leapt up. "I get it, this is all a conspiracy," she yelled. "You just want me to go to school too," she said, banging out the back door. Loud hammering started almost immediately. Paris noticed that Maddy had finished her spumoni before storming out.

Sophia rose with difficulty and slammed a window down. *"Basta,"* she cursed.

"This industrial park is Peter's big opportunity," explained Giulia. "His older brother's a contractor and Peter will be promoted if they get the job."

Paris had heard all the arguments. Did it always have to be a choice between the earth and making a living? "It's just a shame to mess up the land when Morton River already has all these old factories moldering away."

But Giulia was clearing the table, arms full as only a waitress could fill them.

The cuckoo clock sounded, Sophia's bird hands waved, and the first day of battle was over. She felt drained. *But I wouldn't have missed them for the world.* Problematic though it might be, the family's dynamism was as magnetic as Giulia herself. *I might just fall in love with all of them,* she threatened. *It'd surely be safer than what I've been chasing.*

Walking downhill the liniment still warmed her legs. A breeze shifted the just-turning leaves. It felt good after the stuffy house. A group of teenagers leaned against two classic Chevrolets and she heard the whispered word *teacher.* She felt like a celebrity. A dog walked with her. She stopped to send him home and caught a quick movement at the top of the block. Had someone ducked behind a hedge?

She thought of Giulia again, so reserved, as if she'd checked her emotions with the hat check girl and wouldn't take them back until she was ready. The strange little house felt warm despite the conflicts it housed, was clean and organized. Had

Giulia pulled the craziness of life together into a whole? Could she with her will keep lives from unraveling no matter how hard they tried to mess up? Paris couldn't even do that for herself. *That's what I've been needing,* she thought. *A Giulia all my own.*

Outside the Center she looked across Route 34 to draw strength from the powerful sound and sight of the river. Again she saw the furtive fast movement at the periphery of her vision. This time she was sure it wore a gray fedora. Maddy might be blood sister to Giulia, but she had that natural fascination for her sisters in kind. She hugged herself, warm with the joys life had in store for Maddy. Had the baby dyke come out yet?

CHAPTER 4

By the end of the third week of school she felt settled enough in her schedule to relax. Friday night she ate leftovers at the apartment and spent some time reading a Marion Zimmer Bradley novel while she listened to the public radio station. She was anxiously avoiding sleep. If she didn't sleep she wouldn't have those ever-worsening stair dreams.

Her roost was warm and comfortable, but too much of a good thing could drive a woman stir crazy. About ten o'clock, bored, she checked herself in the mirror, ran a brush through her hair and walked in the cool night to the diner for dessert. The trees spoke incessantly, rustling as they dried. Behind the still factory there was more silence in the railroad yards, but the river tumbled over itself in its usual rush, sending up to the street a muted scent of damp banks.

Elly and Dusty were long gone, though their personalities seemed to inhabit the old diner, Elly's through those bright heart-studded curtains, Dusty's through the calm order of the old streamliner despite the crowd. John cooked. Giulia waitressed, serving sodas and desserts to the gang from the 8:00 show at the Mine Cinema with her air of ruined royalty, her frosty beauty like a dare. Her sharp tongue and defusing laugh kept rowdiness to a minimum.

Paris hadn't had a chance to go in that late before and was pleased to recognize regulars. A fried-batter smell lingered from dinner, warring with the sting of ammonia. The floor was still wet. The booths were full, the counters nearly so. There were at least three lesbian couples and an assortment of singles, most of them very young or acting like they'd just come from a bar. She sat a few stools away from a tall woman in precisely pressed slacks, tweed jacket and buttoned vest. The woman was bantering familiarly with John across the kitchen counter.

"Hi, Tex!" John called when he spotted her. "Haven't seen you since I started here."

"My schedule puts me to bed practically before you get up."

The woman, near Paris's age, was looking at her, eyebrows raised. "Now that's a real accent. You *are* from Texas."

"Born and bred, but I don't answer questions about my daddy's billion-dollar ranch and I have personally never so much as had a pony under my rump in my life."

"No bronco-busting?"

"Disgusting sport."

"No oil wells in the family?"

"I wish."

"Your daddy ran a savings and loan then."

Paris laughed loud and long. The woman knew how to play just the way she liked. "What's your name? I have a feeling you're an original."

"Just a damn Yankee who reads the paper. Texas is no longer known for a fort called the Alamo, but for Alamo Savings and Loan, also known as First Texas Waterloo. I'm Peg Jacob."

"Paris Collins." They shook hands. Peg's hand was cool, but lingered like her eyes.

"Your real name?"

"Oh, yes. My parents were entering their second childhood and got absolutely silly. I have a fifty-eight-year-old brother, Donald Junior, and my sister Mary is fifty-six. I was the little afterthought. That's spelled m-i-s-t-a-k-e."

"Have you ever been to gay Paree?"

"Every five years until I left home. Mom and Dad are the most in-love couple in the universe. They spend all their second honeymoons in Paris."

"Romantics."

"Don and Mary think it's disgusting. I'm afraid I inherited all the romantic blood."

"That could be an asset," said Peg in an undertone.

They'd been watching John chop vegetables as

they talked, but now she looked at Peg. How many times had she heard a come-on like that? How many more times would she follow the lure of romance down a winding twilight road to disappointment? How many times, to the crescendoing strains of "Rhapsody In Blue," would she hover over the abyss of love?

Peg's hands were decorated only by a pinky ring. There was a strength to them despite their manicured care, nails buffed and prudently short. The jacket and slacks were not off any rack, women's or men's, she'd ever seen. Peg's hair was the masterpiece, though. Short but thick, maple syrup brown, it was molded around her head in waves and dips that looked perfectly natural, but were far too neat. It was as if when she had the cleaners press her pants, they ironed each hair into its location.

"How do you do that?" she asked, despite the alarm sounding in her heart. This alarm sounded like the song "I've Got A Crush On You."

"What?" Peg turned toward her and Paris saw a face with lines set perfectly: sharply cut jaw, crowded laugh lines, cleft chin. If ad agencies ever wanted the perfect dyke face, she wanted to be this woman's agent. Managing Peg would be about the only thing to keep Paris out of trouble.

"Your hair." She lifted the ends of her own. "This stuff's about as well-behaved as dandelion fluff in a breeze. How do you keep it so neat? Do you spray it?"

"Don't you know better than to ask the butch's secrets, darlin'?" Peg answered, smiling through lidded eyes. Paris noticed that she had the slightest lisp, almost an affectation. "On the other hand, you look like a woman I might want to share a secret with. I just comb it. It's coarse — feel it. I'd like just once in my life to experience hair blowing in my face."

"Poor baby. Maybe I'll buy a convertible just to try and mess up your hair." She couldn't believe she was flirting like this, within the first five minutes, but she couldn't stop. It was second nature. Maybe even first.

"Am I being asked out?" Peg inquired.

"Not till I get the car."

"And I suppose that'll happen when you win the lottery."

"No. I think it may be about time. John?" she called.

"Yo."

"What did you say your friend's name was who sells cars?"

"Louie. At the Jeep dealership on the Post Road."

"Is there a bus going down there or do I have to make another train trek?"

"Sure —"

"Hold on," Peg interrupted. She had a habit of patting her hair down as if expecting it to go into some sort of wild paroxysm. That was fine with Paris, who watched Peg's hands and their delicate touch. "If I'm going to be getting a friend with a convertible out of this allow me to have the honor of driving you to Upton."

"That would be heaven." Had she been hinting for this? She could say no. *Try it Paris: no. No. No! NO!*

For the first time she swiveled on her squealing

stool to look into Peg's eyes. They jarred her, holding a sadness so deep she wondered how Peg was able to laugh and joke. "I'm going down there tomorrow anyway," Peg said. "Are you free?"

She'd looked away, but those hurting, longing, shaded eyes called to her. Paris surfaced again, forcing humor. "You'll find me at two-two-two Railroad Avenoo-oo-oo —" she sang.

Am I free, she thought the next day, sitting on her cold narrow bottom step waiting for Peg, trying to forget the stair dream she'd had the night before. It'd been the worst one yet, with iron steps and rails that disassembled and reassembled as she was halfway down. Wherever she put her foot was not a sturdy black step, but nothing. Now, that wasn't fair. She could take dreams of rotted-out wooden steps; they just scraped her ankles. She could take the glass stairways to the sky; at least her destination was worth the terror of risk. And she could take the endless circular stairs that ran deep into the earth and got hotter and hotter to the touch; all she had to do was wake up and kick off some covers or turn down the heat to escape. But these constantly moving pieces of iron below her, like black Tinker Toys which collapsed on sight — there seemed no way out.

She hadn't wanted Peg to see her tortuous descent. As a matter of fact she worried that the whole outing was a tortuous descent for her. She'd sworn and she'd sworn that she would not fall for one more of those darned women who promise the world with their bedroom eyes and in the end just want a mama to comfort them when real life plays rough, or a drinking partner, or worst of all someone at home to make it more exciting when they ran around.

Dykes my ass, she muttered. *Infantile narcissists is more like it.* She'd be safer pursuing impossible Giulia. She got into Peg's 280Z and slammed the door so hard the car shook. Peg looked at her, one arm down behind the seat. Paris managed a smile.

"I have someone I'd like you to meet."

"A pup!"

"This is The Reverend Minister."

"I can see why." The dog was all black except for a white bib, white paws and a white monocle. Peg held it, her hands controlling but light on the animal.

"If I put her in your lap she'll probably let you call her Reverend for short."

Peg laughed as forty pounds of dog came over the seat, clean-smelling as Peg's dog would be, and soft to touch, with odd feathers of fur curling over her fingers.

"Do you mind?"

"Mind? It's the biggest drawback to the traveling life. I won't drag an animal from home to home, not knowing what landlord I'll have two years from now. So I depend on friends to bring furry things around for me to love. Reverend, I already took my shower this morning. I'm pretty sure you don't have to clean my neck again." The Reverend's tongue was rough and her doggie breath moistly hot.

"Rev," chided Peg, putting on sunglasses which made her even more attractive.

The Z picked up speed along Railroad Avenue. Of

course it was a gorgeous warm day, a bright autumn sun saved from being too hot by a cool soft wind. Of course the woman drove like a professional, whistling as she went. Of course Paris's heart was racing faster than the damned car. Lights flashed and bells went off each time they passed an intersection, signaling an oncoming train. They finally met it on the outskirts of town, the passenger train returning from Waterbury, rumbling almost empty on a Saturday on its way through Morton River to Upton. She remembered her arrival in the Valley, that lonely frustrating train ride, with no one to greet her at the old stone station.

She patted the Reverend. "It's all right. An extra bath is a small price to pay for instant love and affection."

"That must be another drawback to your traveling ways."

Paris looked at Peg, the alarm blaring this time. "Not really," she said, noticing that Peg's Levis were creased and the plaid sports shirt was starched. She was hesitant to use her standard line about not finding anyone to make her want to stay put, since folks around the Valley seemed to take that as a personal challenge. She didn't feel an iota of need to be a challenge for Peg Jacob. Well, maybe just one iota.

"Have you ever seen a New England fall before?" Peg asked.

"Not in person. Not like this," she said, suggestively lowering her voice.

"What a treat. I've been here all forty-five of my falls so I don't appreciate them enough."

"You're a native?"

"From Brockett Lake, just south of Morton River."

"And you came up just to get me?"

"Ten minutes. No big deal."

"Where do you work?"

"Brockett High."

"A teacher?"

"P.E. For the last twenty-three years to be exact."

At least freeloading wasn't this one's sin. "Like it?"

"It's my life. Except for my house and the Rev here."

"Then traveling isn't the only thing that gets in the way of love and affection."

"That's my choice," said Peg. "I found out long ago that love is more pain than pleasure."

"So you don't —"

"I enjoy having women friends. It's great to have a lady on my arm at a concert or a show. But sex leads to trouble and trouble usually gets misnamed love. I've had enough."

She expected relief to fill her, but instead her mind seemed to sit at attention. *Oh?* she thought, raring up for her own challenge. *Stop it!* she told herself. "Then we can be friends?" The question was as much for herself as for Peg.

"As long as our definitions of friendship don't clash."

She leaned over and kissed Peg on the cheek, not feeling safe, but as chaste as good intentions could make her.

"Hey!"

"Now, no objections. I could have cleaned your cheek like the Reverend would."

"Then maybe in your case it's affection we need to define," Peg complained. She was smiling at the road, though, and Paris cuddled hungrily with the dog, lulled by the smooth purr of the Z.

Twenty minutes later Louie was shambling ahead of them to the used cars. He wore tight black slacks and a shiny double-breasted, light blue jacket. He showed her several cars, newer-model sedans, mostly red, that Louie obviously thought would appeal to a fortyish dyke. "You want one with a history?"

"Like what, a safari through the Everglades?"

He took them to a pale green bare-bones Jeep that looked as if the body shop had given up before it started. "It belonged to a hermit."

Peg asked, "That guy who died a couple of years ago and the family's been fighting over the spoils ever since?"

"That's the one. The son brought this in."

"He lived on the outskirts of Morton River, next to Bromsberrow State Park," Peg explained, "and as long as he was left alone, and no one hurt it, he let people use his land as an extension of the park. The developers wanted to put in an industrial park, but he wouldn't budge. I've lost track, but he had a handwritten will leaving his ten acres or so to a land trust."

"Seventeen. Primo. The courts decided the old coot was cracked and gave everything to the relatives," Louie said.

"The judge probably had money in the industrial park," suggested Paris.

Louie nodded. "He did. There's a big scandal about it now. The day after he made his ruling the family sold the hermit's acres. They didn't have the capital to develop it."

"To a development company called CIFRV — City Fathers Renew the Valley," Peg continued. "They've bought up enormous amounts of undeveloped acreage around the Morton River."

"So that's the industrial park the Scalas were talking about. I understand it's pretty much a certainty."

Peg looked at her. "That hasn't been in the papers."

"One company already put a bid in."

"This is news to me. I'll have to ask my brothers. They usually let me in on their little investment schemes and I know they were interested in this one."

"You mean you'd invest in a project that would rape what little wooded land you've got left?" She realized that she was coming down on Peg a little roughly for a new acquaintance. She turned to Louie. "It's the same from one coast to the other," Paris said, "men have got to destroy Mother Earth."

Peg watched her, an amused smile on her face, and glanced down at the Save the Whales sweatshirt Paris was wearing. "So you're a Greenpeace type?"

"I'd like to think people are smart enough to take care of their home. I'm not an activist, though, unless you call sending a check once a year to the Sierra Club activism."

Peg looked as if she were holding her counsel and Paris knew they had their first bone of contention.

She turned back to Louie. "How do you know so much about this hermit?"

Louie tapped the Jeep. "We couldn't offer what his son wanted on this baby. He was spitting nickels at the lawyers' bills. Said between them and taxes he might as well give it all to the Land Trust. They're contesting the sale deal in court now. He's still the owner of land he can't legally touch."

"He's a contractor," said Peg. "I suppose he'll bid on the contract."

Paris wondered briefly if the hermit's son was the same contractor Giulia knew, but she didn't want to be distracted from the car deal. "So if you didn't pay the hermit's estate much, you can give me a good deal on this Jeep, is that what you're saying?"

Louie's grin looked as fake as his jacket. "No problem. The insides are perfect, like it never left the lot. The son replaced the canvas top. See? No cracks or scratches in the windows." He studied his muddy moccasins. "I'll talk to the sales manager on the price if you like the way it drives."

She looked at Peg to gauge Louie's various levels of honesty. Peg nodded, but raised one eyebrow. Paris circled the car. For all the dents there was no rust. "It certainly has personality." She leaned on the bumpers to test the shocks.

Peg checked the oil. Paris noticed that she limped.

"Are you okay?" she asked.

"Me? Why?"

"You're limping."

"I'm afraid that's a permanent defect, darlin'. Busted the old pelvis at a field hockey game. They pinned me up and ever since this left leg's been a little shorter."

"I'm sorry. I didn't —"

"Think nothing of it. Let's just make sure your car isn't gimpy."

While Louie went for the key Paris sat in the driver's seat. Peg leaned in the passenger window, hands hanging loosely. Paris noticed a thin gold watch which accented the womanly shape of the hand without modifying its strength. Why did it feel so natural to be buying a car with Peg? "What do you think?"

"I think it looks like a hunk of junk, Paris, but it's your decision."

She tried to curb a defensive feeling. "You should've seen my last car. I wonder if this heater can handle your winters."

"I doubt it."

With each negative Paris grew more attached to the Jeep. The shift fit snugly into her palm and she depressed the clutch to run through the gears. "On the other hand, four wheel drive would be just fine on the hills in the snow."

"Sure. So would a Subaru with a roof."

"You wanted a friend with a convertible." She twisted around. "Not much room for luggage if I did take it along in two years.

"None."

"But I wouldn't."

"Then it doesn't matter."

"You wouldn't buy it, would you, Peg?"

"You know what I drive. I bought her new and babied her all these years. I like a sporty car." She gave Paris an appraising look. "We're very different people, Paris. I wouldn't buy something because some dreamer like you took a stand."

"I'm no dreamer."

"Oh, right," said Peg with playful sarcasm.

Peg had been leaning against the 280Z, hands deep in her pockets, whistling, while Paris drove off the lot to test the car. Louie directed her to an off-road tour where she played with the four wheel drive. It wasn't exactly a Cadillac ride, but it wasn't any worse than Honkey's.

"Did you ever feel like you clicked with somebody just like that?" she snapped her fingers.

"You mean love at first sight? Only in my dreams. But I'll tell you, I'd grab him if it ever happened to me."

"I don't know if I do mean love at first sight." She did find that Peg was absolutely right. Though she dickered over the price, there was no way she'd let some hunter or off-road enthusiast buy the hermit's car. Was she that transparent or was Peg that astute?

She followed Peg and the Reverend to Brockett Lake in the noisy, energetic little Jeep, her hair blowing wildly with the windows open. The light was golden on the turning trees and there was a smell of sun-toasted leaves in the air, yet the grass was as green as spring. She wanted to drive forever, Peg's low fast car leading her where she belonged.

I should go home, let this rest. She wasn't in love, not after a twelve-hour acquaintance, but she could make major purchases with this woman for life. Had anyone invented shopping dates yet? In a moment, it seemed, it had become she and Peg allied against the rest of the world. In her standard operating procedure, she'd be pushing and tugging with a lover, looking outside for support.

They left the highway and curved into narrower country roads. The closest she could get to "Rhapsody In Blue" on the radio was opera. She blasted it, singing along to familiar snatches as the Jeep roared from patches of sunlight to tree-shaded pools of road. Would today have been as much fun with Giulia? The woman was stiff as a sunflower in its prime. Dealing with her was one big negotiating process. Shopping with her would be nothing but head-butting. Yet she wiggled her hind quarters against the ripped seat just thinking about outfitting Giulia in Amazonian elegance. Just thinking of grinding down all that propriety, preferably crotch to crotch. Straight she might be, but what was a little heterosexuality?

Peg's home was in a fairy glen. Paris was enchanted.

"How old is it?" she asked.

Peg bent to let the Reverend off her leash. "Ancient. Pre-Civil War."

"Don't tell me you're —"

"I'm afraid so. Blue blood all the way back through my mother's family. They were Tories and on the shit list, so they just kind of faded into the woods here. My father comes from a line of merchants that arrived not long after the Goodboddies and settled in Upton. They've had all kinds of specialty shops through the millennia, but now they're just Jacob's Department Store. It's a local chain."

"How did you end up with this wonderful relic?" The house was a peeling gray, with broken gutters along the roof, but a new wraparound wood porch. It was surrounded by fields of grass, fall wildflowers and wooded areas beyond. The raw porch rail still had a layer of sawdust which came off on her fingertips.

"I only have seven acres. And the shoddy old house. My two brothers each have bigger pieces of land — off that way and that way — with newer homes. Well, practically new: 1880 and the 1920 building we grew up in. That's because they run the business. I'm the black sheep."

"I'd volunteer for black sheep any old time for this." The seductress in her came to life, whispering *grab 'er*. She straightened her sweatshirt and pulled the hair from her eyes. "You ought to see my piece of ancestral land — in a subdivision."

"I'm not complaining." There was that haunted look in Peg's eyes again. "It's just gotten to be my life work trying to make my home livable. I decided to move in two years ago when I swore off relationships. My friends say I married the old homestead. Since then I've put in all new plumbing, the electric and the windows."

"They blend in well for — Thermopane?" she asked, remembering her first Morton River fantasy.

"I'm trying to keep the integrity of the original farmhouse. The foundation was the only thing in good shape. Come on in. Let's throw lunch together. I picked up some fresh cider at a roadside stand on my way home from school yesterday."

She was relieved to see no early American furniture, just wide comfortable chairs and a couch. Peg had also installed the universal stereo system, TV and VCR of their generation. A few compact discs lay face up: Manhattan Transfer, Betty Carter, Bobby McFerron. Throw rugs and afghans of varying colors and patterns harmonized. There was so much personality in the room she wondered if the house really had become Peg's love object.

Paris glanced at the books. No Marion Zimmer Bradley, no *Wanderground*, but off in a corner, in protective bindings with clear plastic revealing the covers, was a row of pristinely preserved paperbacks. Several Ann Aldriches, *The Grapevine* in hardcover, *Return to Lesbos* and *Stranger in Lesbos*.

"Are these what I think they are?"

"What — my old lesbian classics? We used to pass those around in college, the whole P.E. department. I have a couple from those days, but most of them I found at secondhand bookstores."

"I've read about them, but I've never seen one."

"Aren't those covers something?"

"Vixens in slips. I'm afraid they don't appeal to my prurient side."

"That's because they never put real butches on the covers. Nothing for you to drool over."

"You believe in that old stuff?"

Peg deftly poured cider from a glass gallon jug into a saucepan. "What old stuff?"

"Butches and femmes."

"Facts of life, darlin'."

"Really? Then what am I?"

"Don't be dense."

"I'm serious. How do you tell?"

Peg snapped a stick of cinnamon in two and dropped one into the heating cider. "Put it this way, I'm butch. What does that make you?"

"I don't have any rules."

"Then you're feeling your way in the dark."

"How about Giulia?"

"The waitress at the Queen of Hearts? Butch to her teeth, darlin', whether she knows it or not."

"Venita?"

"Not out, but she's got a femme soul. A safe friend for another femme."

At least Peg was consistent with her old ways, thought Paris. "That smells delicious," she said of the cider. There was no sense talking about role playing. She'd met women like Peg before and as attractive as they could be, they were so self-limiting. Why, there was a world of women out there! Who'd want to stick to one type? "Look at all these P.E. books. Anatomy and physiology, *The History of Recreation,* volleyball rule books, basketball, field hockey, *Geriatrics and Exercise* — you'd think you'd gone for your doctorate."

"I did."

"Well, I'll be. Pleased to make your acquaintance, Dr. Jacob." She reached out a hand.

Peg held hers for a moment. "The pleasure is all mine," she said, then released her. "After those students plowed into me during a field hockey game I thought teaching at the college level might be more sedentary. It can be, but academics have to follow the jobs. I like it right here in the Valley."

Would she ever figure this one out? The old-fashioned butch doctor. "A woodstove!"

"That's all I need for heat. Lunch is about ready. The john's that way if you want it."

The bathroom was cluttered and only adequately clean, though it smelled of Clorox. She sat on the cold toilet seat and looked out the window. She smiled. Thermopane. Peg put some classic Lionel Hampton on the stereo and whistled along. *So Peg liked the old music too.*

Outside a woodpecker thwocked against a pine trunk and shadows of feathery branches bounced in the sunlight. She could see her battered Jeep parked next to Peg's carefully polished Z. Even Peg's car looked ironed, its exact yellow pinstripe like a crease. From the sink she had a glimpse of a meadow, bright yellow grasses bending gracefully. What must it be like to belong to land like this? To be lovers with an enigma? Could she seduce Peg if she wanted to find out?

CHAPTER 5

For the next week it rained and Paris holed up all the time she wasn't working. Home alone she could frantically bite her nails, as if that would keep her from sinking them and herself into an unwanted relationship. She didn't even answer the phone for fear it would be Peg and her alluring hands. It didn't make her feel one bit safer that Peg was sour on love; she considered herself too damned good at getting her way where handsome women like Peg were concerned. As much as she wanted the perfect romance, she was going to be careful. She didn't want anything so perfect she'd be stuck in little Morton River. She only dared spend time with Sophia and Venita.

"Why *not* fall in love?" Venita asked, her tired teacher's voice like the last rustle of fall leaves. They'd stopped at the Queen of Hearts after school, soggy and chilled from the walk, for ice cream sodas. "It's a trick I've never been able to learn and always missed."

"I wish I could share my propensity for the stuff with you then. It's my greatest talent."

Venita battled a chunk of strawberry up through her straw. "What about your talent for languages, young woman? Don't sell yourself short."

Laughing she quoted, " 'Unlearned, he knew no schoolman's subtle art, No language, but the language of the heart.' "

Venita's hand flew to her lips and tapped. "Oh dear, it's on the tip of my tongue. Not Shakespeare —"

"Pope."

"You are a joy. I think the angels brought you here to keep me entertained."

Once more, she'd steered the conversation into safer waters. She didn't want to have to avoid Venita to stay away from the conflicts in her life. There'd be nothing left then but teaching Sophia Scala and that was like going into a boxing ring. The fact that learning was a matter of survival for Sophia and for her kids was the only thing that kept Paris stepping through those ropes. Sophia fought every step of the way as if knowledge might hurt her.

"She's ready for you," Giulia would say by way of

greeting her at her front door. Then she'd stride on those long legs into her room to study or dream of getting rich with her boyfriend. If she'd ever had the feelings for women that Paris sensed beneath those broad shoulders, she'd ditched them as counterproductive. Once when Paris stayed for another of the delicious but pitched-battle Scala lunches Giulia became practically expansive.

"Tell me about your school," Paris suggested, to put a momentary halt to their constant harassment of Maddy.

Ironically, it was Maddy who bragged, "Giulia graduated from the community college last year!"

"You say that like she won three gold medals in diving at the winter Olympics," Paris teased.

Maddy shrugged, backtracking. "So she got an A.S. That makes her an official a.s.s. in my book."

"What's your degree in?" Paris asked Giulia.

Scowling, Giulia used the family shrug too. She projected the same sort of strength, an ability to move decisively in the world, that Maddy did. "Accounting and data processing. An associate's around here, though, isn't worth the paper they print it on. I earn more waitressing part-time than I could cooped up in a tax office forty hours."

"So you're getting a bachelor's?"

Giulia's glorious eyes lost their dogged anger for a moment. She seemed to be contemplating a future as exquisite as a work of art. "In business administration. Peter will have his own company, I'll run the financial and marketing side of it while he's building."

"Or tearing down," Paris muttered. Maddy squinted at her over a heap of *pasta fagioli*.

71

Her sister was still describing greener grasses. "That's why this industrial park is so important to us. Peter will work with the other bosses. He won't just be carrying and hammering. Mike'll let him do some of the subcontracting and supervision. He'll make a name for himself."

"And then compete against his own brother?" Paris asked.

"Mike's all talk. If he gets the industrial park it'll be because of who he is, nothing else. He'll work for Peter and me someday. Whitcombe Enterprises," she said, that future look in her eyes again.

Maddy slammed down her milk glass, wiping a white moustache off with her sleeve. "Never happen," she grunted. "Mike's got the get-up-and-go. Pete's a wimp."

Giulia's glance might have taken her head off. "Mind your business. You don't know anything about him."

"Whoever heard of a guy waiting till he's married?" scoffed Maddy. "He thinks he's going out with the Virgin Mary here. And he's not even Italian." She looked straight at me. "Don't women do dumb things to get their mitts on a man?"

"Like wash, Maddy?" Giulia sneered. There was a shifting of gears. Maddy had loosed the vindictive kid in her sister.

Maddy jumped up from the table and took out a pack of cigarettes. She wore the same black jeans with the fashionably gaping hole below one knee.

"Maddalena!" Giulia said, glaring.

Maddy drew a cigarette out of the pack with her

lips like a TV tough. Sophia sniffed the air, threw up her hands and let out a stream of complaints at Maddy, then at Giulia.

"At least open the window, you little pig," Giulia said.

Maddy did. The autumn trees were splendidly costumed in reds, yellows, oranges and lingering greens. River scents came in and dissipated Maddy's cigarette smoke. "Look at that," she said. "I bet I know who lives in every house in town and what they're doing right now."

"If you'd spend more time in school instead of on the streets you'd learn something useful."

Maddy ignored Giulia and dragged deeply on the shrinking cigarette. Paris joined her at the window. Below them cascaded curving streets, houses that seemed to hold up the ledges of land by unseen roots which kept everything from tumbling into the river.

Out of nowhere, Giulia was behind Maddy, deftly grabbing the cigarette from her hand and tossing it far below. She slammed the window down.

"Sneak!" cried Maddy, wheeling to accuse Giulia. "You see what an evil Joker she is? No wonder Dad ran away."

"He should've taken his son Robin with him."

"I'm no son," Maddy hissed. "No way I want to be a man. I can work as hard as a man any day if somebody would only show me how to make things like Dad made!"

Paris just smiled. Maddy wasn't out yet, but she spouted dyke-talk like a music festival separatist.

"Walk me down the hill," she said to Maddy. She might have preferred an invitation to Giulia's bedroom, but she needed time to melt stone.

"Wish I could be in your class," Maddy said first thing.

"Was that you following me the first day I came up here?"

Maddy blushed a very feminine pink and pulled her fedora down over her eyes. "I was curious."

"About what?"

"About where you lived. How come you're in such a dive?"

"What dive? I love the smell of pizza."

"I never knew a teacher to live, you know, practically on the railroad tracks."

"So you follow all your teachers home?" Paris teased.

Maddy faced her with a defiant thrust of her chin. "I've *got* to know what makes people tick. They're like machines. If I can understand them then I know what to do with them. Otherwise I get in trouble."

"Seems to me trouble's just about your middle name at home."

"Those two — there's no acting right for them. Not if I got a degree in good behavior."

"What *do* you do with all this time you're not in school?"

"I build stuff."

"Sidewalks."

"Like that. I really can fix any lawnmower on earth. And clocks. And I was pretty good with woodworking shop till they kicked me out."

"Why did they do that?"

" 'Cause of my grades. Shop's a privilege," she said nasally, in imitation, Paris assumed, of some unyielding authority. "First you have to know algebra, then they'll let you hammer nails. I mean, it's *so* dumb."

"What else?"

"I play softball."

"You have teams around here?"

"You bet. Some of the best. Like the Raybestos Brakettes in Stratford. Man, I wish I could be that good. That's where Joanie Joyce got her start, you know."

Paris admitted she didn't.

"She's just the best softball player in the world. I saw her once, when I was little. I've got a poster of her hidden. I'll show you sometime. Giulia doesn't like girl athletes."

"Who do you play for?" Paris asked.

"Dusty's Diner. No one else would let me on their team 'cause of me being so young. Dusty's cool though. Said she remembers being fifteen in this town. She stood up to the whole team — and Elly — and put me in left field. I have a good throwing arm. Someday I'm going to pitch."

They were at the Center. She studied Maddy's face. What a waste it would be to see this one drugged or pregnant and desperate. "You want to sit in on a class, sugarplum?" A look of dread passed across Maddy's face. "Just to sit in. You don't have to participate."

Maddy licked her lips. "They say if I don't go to school they're going to send me to a girls school upstate where you can't get out at all. Do they let kids go to the Center?"

"No. But see how you like it and maybe we can work something out." She wanted to wrap her arms around this little one.

Maddy tried to hide her scared eyes. After a silence she pulled her hat down and warned, "Don't tell Giulia."

She didn't act out at all in Developmental English and Paris talked Venita into letting her sit in on math. Maddy came in every day that week.

Friday night rolled around again. Paris planned supper at the diner with Venita. Though the clocks hadn't been turned back yet, nips of her first northeastern winter had arrived. As usual, the diner smelled like a fish fry back home. It felt toasty warm. She took the chill off her fingers over a cup of coffee.

Elly came for their orders, laughing. "Miz Valerie, you manage to trick me every year with that darn pelt."

"Isn't that the most enormous fake fur you ever saw?" Paris agreed. Venita had set her coat in the booth beside her.

"I swear," Elly said, "it's so big I think you're a party of two all winter long."

Venita patted her coat all through dinner, laughing with infectious little ripples.

"How's the little kid I sent you doing?" Paris asked.

"They'll have our heads for letting her in when she should be at the high school."

"But she's not at the high school anyway. Are they that unbending?"

Venita laughed. "I forget you've only been in adult ed. It's like night and day. We big people are so scared of children we tend to make rules about our rules to keep them in line. They'll be afraid a move like this will start an avalanche of kids falling out of traditional classrooms. Mr. Piccari is apt to faint."

"Whoa. It's better than having them drop out. And what would be even better is if this town offered some vocational courses somewhere. *Privilege*," she sputtered, explaining what Maddy had been told. "If shop is what someone needs, is good at, can relate to, young or old, that's what should be provided. And it looks to me like it's the folks that run this town, never mind the factories, who need retooling."

"That's quite an indictment."

"I'm sorry, Venita, but there're things about Morton River Valley that haven't changed since the Dark Ages."

"You mean like race relations?"

"That's another one. But even if they won't deal with that, they know these old New England towns have been either dying off or changing. What's going to happen to the Maddies of tomorrow if they don't get training today?"

Venita laughed. "I've asked that same question. I'm still hearing the old tale about getting married and raising a family being a respectable occupation for a woman."

"Not that woman."

Venita's eyebrow arched. Although she wasn't

attracted to Venita, Paris found it hard to believe that no one had ever lured her into romance.

"You think she's —"

"Oh, please. Have you looked at her?"

"Come to think of it, she doesn't quite look like the marrying kind. She's got a head on her shoulders too. She won't say a word, but I've seen the kind of look on her face that the adults get when they come in convinced they're too old to learn — and then realize their brains are younger than their attitudes." She shook her head, a soft smile on her lips. "That look of absolute wonder."

"She keeps coming to class, but I haven't been sure why. I think she senses a kinship with me."

"She suspects she's — funny — like you?"

Elly delivered steaming blue plate specials. "Who's *funny*?" she asked, with a wink.

"Maddy Scala, the young woman on your softball team," supplied Paris.

"Oh, you bet, sugar. She's as funny as they come. I can't wait till she finds someone to show her the light of day. She's been drooling over every femme that comes her way for two years now without a clue about why."

Paris teased Elly. "Like yourself?"

"Among dozens of others. Enjoy your dinner."

"Elly — wait. Is there somewhere a kid like that can go around here? A hotline or something she could call?"

"You *are* a foreigner, aren't you? This is the Valley. They'd probably arrest anyone who answered the hotline and commit the caller. There's one in New Haven, but what kid can make a toll call like that without having a lot of explaining to do? Besides, I'm not sure she knows she needs to call anyplace." Elly left to refill a coffee cup.

"You're absolutely right, Paris," said Venita, her face suddenly tired-looking. "Things haven't changed much here since Bubba died. I hope you'll be careful around the child."

"I'm not exactly a chickenhawk. I just know how she's suffering in that *funny* little heart of hers," Paris said, remembering her own frightened bewilderment when she'd first realized she wasn't ever going to be like other people. That life was going to be a climb up a staircase that no one had prepared her for. She dipped a fork into her mashed potatoes. "I came out at seventeen. My salvation was the university, where I helped organize the gay student group. If I'd been stuck at home I would've been scared to tell anyone how I was feeling, just plain powerless in an adult world."

"So you're going to reveal her inner self, you brave and foolish crusader? You're so much like my nephew it's uncanny."

"Did Bubba have kids?"

"No, my other brother's son, Thor. He directs the community action program, V.O.W., Valley Opportunity Watch. Much to my brother's disgust."

"Sounds like your brother ought to be proud."

"Martin ought to be many, many things he's not. He followed Father's footsteps into the bank, but he's been huddled there ever since. He never had Father's vision, only his conservative nature."

"And Thor's got the vision?"

"In spades, if you'll forgive the expression. He's

out to conquer poverty and crack and illiteracy and crime — you name it, he's probably got a task force working on it."

"That looks so good," she said when Elly brought Venita's blueberry pie à la mode.

"Have a piece."

"My fat cells don't need to be indulged tonight. Besides, I don't want to linger so long that I'll run into anyone."

"I hate to break it to you, Paris, but I think Anyone just walked in."

Peg wore a herringbone tweed suit with elbow patches. She stood, legs slightly apart, hands in her pockets, in such a caricature of a dyke of a certain class that Paris felt fated to fall in love with her. But she was damned if she'd give in to destiny without a fight.

"You know, Venita," she said as Peg talked with her friends at another table, "sometimes I wonder if geography isn't everything. I never would have loved the women I did, some of them might never have come out, if I hadn't come into their lives like a blazing lesbian comet. And now here I am in Morton River, my appetite whetted twice over." She hadn't brought up Peg or Giulia to Venita.

Then at her elbow Peg said softly, "Paris," making a barely perceptible bow as she spoke, as if Paris were a goddess she approached with muted reverence.

Paris caught her breath. Peg strummed some chord in her so deep it had never before been touched. She desperately sought a lighter tone. "Evening, Peg Jacob. Care to join us?" She made the introductions. Venita concentrated on her dessert, but Paris caught the curious glances at Peg.

"I've tried to get you all week." Peg smelled like damp wool.

I'll just bet you have. Surreptitiously, she dried her palms. She said, "It's been one busy bitch of a week at school, hasn't it, Venita?"

"Aren't they all?" She could see her appraising Peg. Venita would throw her to that wolf in a matchmaker's second.

"And I've been spending extra time on the Hillside."

"That Sophia you told me about?"

"And her daughters. One of them plays softball on the Diner team. Do you know Maddy Scala?"

Peg's face took on an affectionate warmth. "The scruffy one in left field? I've noticed her."

"She's so isolated. I'd swear she's not out yet, maybe doesn't even know what to call herself, and I'm debating whether I should let her know she's got someone to talk to."

Peg nodded sagely. "I've run into that dilemma. It's dangerous. Maybe not as much for an adult ed teacher."

Paris felt herself flush with anger. "I think it's more dangerous not to offer some insight to gay kids. Look at their suicide rate. And AIDS. What are we weighing? A job against a life?"

Peg compressed her lips. "I've only run across two that I know of and I gave them every other kind of support I could. It's a hard one. One was a frisky basketball player. She came back a couple of years later and thanked me for encouraging her to go into P.E. She said sports kept her sane while she was dealing with 'personal issues.' I read between the lines. We still exchange Christmas cards. The other one disappeared."

Paris pushed vehemently on, ready to shake Peg, shake the world of cautious people. "Maddy's in trouble right *now*. She's a truant from a single parent home where the mother treats herself like a shut-in and the older sister thinks she's Cinderella's stepsister."

Peg and Venita exchanged glances. But Paris wasn't asking for permission.

Peg said, "The Reverend Minister was hoping we'd see you again this weekend."

"If you'll excuse me," said Venita, "I need to visit the powder room."

Paris made a mental note to compliment Venita on knowing when to take a powder. She threw herself into high speed to think of a safe response to Peg. Of course she wanted to spend time with her, but not this soon. She played with a packet of sugar, shaking the granules inside the paper. Peg's little lisp, though, was irresistible.

"I want to hang out some with Maddy this weekend," Paris said.

Peg played with the crease in her pants, unsmiling, those fingers so sure and slow. Yes, this woman was very good at reading between the lines.

"Listen, Peg. I'm a little gun-shy for some reason." How was she going to say this? She laid down the sugar when she noticed her hand trembling. "I know you don't have designs on me, but my poor little head can't quite take that in. Could the Rev wait until next weekend?"

"Actually, that would be even better. I was going to ask you to come to my work party Saturday. Introduce you to some women who live in Upton and Brockett Lake. They're going to help me insulate those back rooms. Next week, though, the fall colors should be perfect and I'd be free to go leaf-peeping."

She'd put Peg off out of fear of intimacy when the woman had been offering the safety of a crowd. "I'd love to help you work, though. Maybe Maddy and I could stop by?"

Peg gave her a look. "Hey, darlin', you're coming out to the young thing and then bringing her to meet all those closeted dykes at my house? I don't really think so."

There was that cowardice again. "Damn, Peg. It'd be so good for her."

Peg was firm. "You can be all the role model you want. There was a time I'd have been out there with you, but I was burnt out long ago on saving the world. And if *I'm* not up for it, I can guarantee my friends aren't, either."

Paris liked a woman who was willing to disagree, even if she was dead wrong. She also liked Peg's calm certain manner. Venita came out of the bathroom.

"I'll let you get back to your friend," said Peg, suavely polite.

First Peg talks about investing in pulling down some of the little green left on the east coast, mused Paris. Her closet was strike two. Paris had learned long ago that she should never start a relationship with expectations of changing a lover to suit herself, but then, she wasn't planning on being lovers with this woman, was she? And, she told herself, knowing it was only partly an excuse, couldn't Peg have influence on the fate of some rare forest land?

"Say hi to the Rev," she told Peg. "And call me about that scenic drive." Peg waved a gracefully nonchalant hand. Dirty pool, thought Paris, who read promises in that hand.

CHAPTER 6

Giulia gave Paris permission to pick Maddy up at noon. Paris, trying to keep her adult role clear, suggested the Upton Zoo, but the younger Scala had other ideas.

"I've never been in a Jeep before!" Maddy exploded, bouncing onto the seat. Her dimples could not have been deeper. No girl Maddy's age would be immune to those looks when Maddy got going.

"As a matter of fact," Paris answered, sweating in frustration as she jammed the clutch into reverse three times before it worked, "I haven't been in one all that often myself." It finally lurched backward.

"She got a name?"

"Not so far. What do you have in mind?"

Maddy squeezed her eyes tight in concentration. "I don't know. Give me an hour." Her eyes sprang open and she crossed her legs on the seat. "Are we really going to the zoo?" Her tone was not quite a childish whine.

Cautiously, she replied, "I've never seen it, but I'm open to suggestions."

"Good, because my elementary school teachers were always dragging us there. I *hate* to see animals in cages."

"You're the native, you tell me where to go."

"Somewhere I can take pictures."

She held up a Kodak box camera. Paris remembered her father positioning one just like it at midriff level when she was a kid.

Maddy reached above her head to the canvas top. "Does this come off?"

It was a hazy October day. The frostiness of the night had cleared the air for a true Indian summer Saturday. She doubted, though, that the leaves would last until she saw Peg the next weekend. They'd been battered by too much rain this fall. She'd better learn to make the Jeep convertible by then. They pulled over and for twenty-five minutes wrestled the top down.

"Now what?" Paris asked with a sneeze, dust lodged in her nostrils. Her hair was itchy from sweat. The kid looked cool and unusually neat in black jeans and matching jacket. Still trying to be the one in possession of herself, she pulled the left side of Maddy's shirt collar out to match the right. Maddy didn't act like a kid, though, moving toward her hand, eyes aglow with anticipation. Paris jumped behind the wheel. She'd forgotten the intense and unrealistic hopefulness of kid crushes.

"How about New York City!"

Paris just looked at her.

"Upton maybe?"

"Do you know it enough to give me a tour?"

"No. But I know where that land is, where stupid Peter's going to make his first billion. Dad used to take me to Bromsberrow State Park fishing."

As it turned out, Maddy didn't know how to get there, but between her memories and a map, they managed to find their way out of threadbare Morton River and through the orderly suburbs of Upton. The park wasn't exactly wilderness, but it was lovely, with a large pond, well-hiked paths, tall yellow goldenrod, clusters of the last blue chicory of the season, nodding thistle and the fresh smell of country. There were three carloads of teenagers and accompanying radios in the lot, but that late in the season they had the rest of the park to themselves and the trees muffled even those sounds.

Being with Maddy brought out both the kid and the grown-up in Paris. She felt free to frolic and ramble and laugh at Maddy's silly antics, but she tried to make it clear that she was nothing more than a pal.

"Where'd you get that accent, *paisan*?" Maddy asked as she climbed to the top of a rock outcropping overlooking Upton.

"Why, Texas," she answered from the distance of a few feet, hunkered down on a safe flat rock anchored to dirt. That iron stair nightmare had become recurrent and she was taking no chances on feeling panic in front of this child. The gray slab under her was hot. She warmed her hands, cold from the ride, against it.

"Oh, I thought you were a Southerner. We have a ke-jillion Southerners around here. Did you ride horses in Texas?"

"My Dad did. He grew up country and keeps his old ways to this day right down to the cowboy hat. We actually lived in a neighborhood in Austin not much different from the ones we rode through today. Only hotter."

"Did you play softball?"

"I wasn't athletic."

"How come you didn't get married?"

This was her chance. Hyperactive polliwogs circled in her gut. Had she maintained enough distance to pull this off? "Some women just aren't inclined that way," she answered, ready to go on.

"I'm sure not," Maddy announced, emphatically setting her hands on her thighs, elbows wide. Maddy leaned toward her. "Do you think I'm gay?"

Paris was so taken aback she almost lost her balance on her rock perch. She sank down and leaned into the tangle of weeks behind her, grabbing at roots. Here she'd been all psyched up to gently broach the subject and control the conversation. "I —"

"I mean, I guess I am. The idea of girls and boys — it's disgusting. But I don't know if that means I'm gay or if it really *is* just a stage I have to go through." Maddy dug at her bra and Paris imagined the fights at home to get her to wear one. "I watch all the shows on TV, but they're about men, and I looked at all the books in the library even if I didn't dare take them out. The best book is for parents, but it keeps telling them don't worry, be happy kind of stuff about how they shouldn't kill themselves for making a gay kid. *I* know that. But what about *me*? I need to know what to do when I can't think about anything but kissing the girl on second base. I mean, here I am trapped in the 'burbs when all the action is in the cities. What am I supposed to do, have my own gay parade?"

Paris sat nervously tugging at the grass roots, darting into the recesses of her mind for some simple answer. She kept her voice low, level and matter-of-fact. "What do you want to know?"

Maddy's curly head snapped up. "Everything."

"Do you know anyone at all who's gay?"

"I'd take bets on the whole damn softball team," she said, curls bouncing as she stabbed the air with an accusing finger. "And practically everybody at Dusty's Diner except my sister. But none of them will *talk* to me. Even Dusty won't go that far." She pounded her knees with her fists in frustration, looking near tears. "It's like when I look for a job. Nobody will hire me without experience, but I can't get experience unless they hire me!"

She nodded sagely. Fidgety sparrows bathed in a puddle several yards from them, chortling with joy over their tiny arcadia. In the sky the white trace of a silent jet slowly faded.

"There's even an after-hours club in Morton River that people come all the way from Upton and New Haven for," Maddy said, indicating the distant steeples and a few tall buildings in the larger city.

"It doesn't serve alcohol, but do you think they'll let me in? No way, José, I'm too young. Sometimes I feel like I'm too young for life and ought to bow out."

That kind of talk pushed her buttons. "Except for New York, there's not much for gay kids even in the cities, Maddy. There's not much even for gay adults in a town like this. I've lived in towns where I've thought I was the only one." What could she say?

She was frightened by Maddy's vulnerability. She could only offer herself as living proof that being gay wasn't all suffering. "But I wasn't. All of a sudden the world would open up in a supermarket aisle or at the library."

Maddy leapt to her feet and did a wild little victory jig that involved twirling her hat on one index finger while her other arm whirled like a propeller and her feet kicked and flew with amazing dexterity atop her narrow rock. "I knew it! I knew it!" she crowed. "You *are* one!"

Paris grinned to see the kid's joy. She decided it might have been prescient of Peg to refuse them an invitation to her party. After all, Peg was the one who knew teenagers and this one's excitement, always extreme, was even less containable now. She couldn't imagine what a roomful of lesbians would do to Maddy's energy level. Still, Maddy's joy at finding kin filled her with relief. Maybe that was all she'd needed, one adult saying *you're okay.*

Cross-legged on her rock again, Maddy, as usual, came right to the point. "How do I get a girlfriend?"

"Sugarplum, there are forty-one-year-olds out there who can't figure that one out."

"Are *you* forty-one?"

"And gaining."

"I thought you were younger than that."

"It's having babies and serving men that ages women."

"*Yeah.*" Maddy was pitching pebbles into the woods. "So how do you find other lesbians?"

"You figured me for one. Like I said, it just kind of happens in the supermarket aisles." She admitted an ulterior motive to herself when she asked, "Doesn't your sister have friends who might be?"

Maddy looked at her as if she were asking if Giulia ate babies for breakfast. "Are you shitting me? That yo-yo thinks gays should be shipped to a desert island. She's going to kill me when she finds out."

Paris winced. Someday she'd tell the painful story behind her discovery that the most rabid homophobes are the ones so queer they scare themselves. "Haven't you met anyone who's interested? Fifteen isn't all that young these days."

"No one will come near this fifteen-year-old."

She thought of herself hiding at the top of her iron steps, longing for and fearing the woman of her dreams. She had needed a Paris to come along and shake her up. "You," she said accusingly, "don't go to school, and you play on an older team, and you hang out in your backyard making things — and you wonder why you don't meet anyone."

"Don't tell me I'm going to meet somebody at Valley High," Maddy shot back, scratching under her bra.

"Ten percent of those students will eventually be gay."

"You have to be kidding."

"That's the statistic. And they tell me at the Center that there are six thousand kids in the Valley schools — how many in your high school, maybe six hundred? All you have to do is look for the thirty or so gay girls." She looked at Maddy over on her rock, an Italian elf with strong hands and back, raging hormones and hungry eyes. "I'll bet they're just waiting for you."

"Dream on, this is the Valley."

"I've found love in more backward towns."

"Okay, then give me your strategy. What should I do? How should I act? What should I wear?"

Wouldn't it be a kick in the butt if Maddy got interested in an education this way. "I'm telling you, sugarplum, just show up at school. You look the part fine already."

"So I go back to school Monday morning. And this ravishing blonde bombshell —" She caught herself, blushed and cast her eyes down, "— I mean, this girl my own age starts making eyes at me or whatever. What do I do, run over and sweep her off her feet?"

"You've got it. Only don't do it like a caveman. Just be yourself. Talk about class, or La Toya Jackson, or what she's wearing. One thing will lead to the next. It's natural."

"Okay, so now I've got thirty girls following me around."

She couldn't help laughing at the vision of Maddy as Pied Piper. The heck of it was, with her looks and gamin charm, she might well collect such a retinue. "Go to the movies together, but don't pay for her. Take a walk by the river. Go to the diner for an ice cream soda. And you know, sugarplum, nothing says you can't return to school in a blaze of gay glory."

"Come out to everybody? I want to *live* a few more years."

Paris tried to be proud, not self-righteous, when she said, "I've never been in the closet."

"You never lived in the Valley." Maddy went uncharacteristically still and silent. Then said, "What about privacy for — you know."

"Hey, no fifteen-year-old gets that, gay or straight."

"If we did manage," she mumbled. "I mean, I don't know, you know, the stuff that's not in the books. How do you do it? Like after you make out."

"I never took lessons either, Maddy. The best lovers use their imagination. Trust me."

"Just whatever —"

"You have fantasies, don't you?"

"Well, um, I mean —"

"It's okay, everyone does. Just act like you do in fantasies, but listen to what she wants too."

She heard Maddy's big sigh, but couldn't tell if it was from frustration or relief. Perhaps it was only embarrassment; Maddy picked up her camera and played with it. A warm breeze reminded Paris to enjoy the outdoors. Leaves rustled down around them. She could hear a trail bike on the other side of the park. Paris let out her breath. English was a whole heap easier to teach.

"Hey, *paisan!*" Maddy said after a while.

"Hey what?"

"What's all that stuff?"

She peered in the direction Maddy was pointing the camera. There was something yellow through the trees, but she couldn't quite make it out. "I'm up for exploring."

They scrambled down the short cliff, Maddy like a dashing doe, herself cautiously, slipping on pebbles, trying not to look scared as she grabbed the flimsy branches. They leapt a little glittering string of a brook, Paris refusing Maddy's help. She'd leave that part of baby dyke training to Dusty Reilly. The earth was spongy, the paths ragged.

"This is the hermit's property," Maddy said. "It was okay to use it, but you had to be very quiet or he'd pop out of nowhere and run you off. If you hurt an animal or a flower he'd know about it." She tiptoed along, twisting to avoid even the scrubbiest weeds. Birds chittered, squirrels berated them, and other critters, maybe dogs, but just as likely raccoons and skunks, had left their paw prints. She felt excited and apprehensive to see the wildlife clinging to the edges of the cities, not letting the developers take it all — yet.

Then she saw the yellow CAT. "Shit."

"What a mess," said Maddy.

Someone had already uprooted a number of small trees and there were stumps where chain saws had cut the mature trees. A shack had been razed. Very recently. The whole area smelled of chain saw oil and bleeding sap. She wanted to throw up. "What *is* all this?" she asked.

"I hate to tell you," Maddy answered slowly, "but I think somebody's got the jump on the city."

"I thought tearing up the hermit's property hadn't been approved yet, that the Land Trust appealed because the judge was paid off by the family."

"You mean because Mike bribed him?"

"Is that what happened? I wonder how we can stop this." Could Peg help? No wonder the wild critters were so noisy. They were watching their homes fall. She felt another twisting pain in her gut.

"You look so sad," Maddy said. "How did you turn into one of those crunchy-granola bag-savers anyway?"

"How could I not? Even ordinary folks like me want someone else to clean up our messes. Heck, when I smoked I threw cigarettes out my window so I wouldn't have to empty the ashtray. How many birds did my filters kill?"

"I never thought of it that way."

"And I don't understand men lying, bribing and stealing to cement another seventeen acres under."

"I understand that one, even if I am failing economics. So Mike can make that first million. So Peter can marry Giulia and go to bed with her."

"Obscene," Paris said, raking her hair back from her face, adding another reason to fight the pillaging of these little woods, of Maddy's big sister. But she'd only been in town two months and already she wanted to revamp the vocational education situation, restrict urban development, be a lesbian big sister. Someday she was going to get herself run out of one of these whistle stops she landed in. Then it hit her. "Wait," she said. "Are you telling me that Mike and Peter are the hermit's sons?"

"Grandsons." Maddy had lifted her camera and was snapping shots of the birds and squirrels amidst the machinery. She was obviously trying to capture the rays of the sun through the taller pines. Then she closed in on a small frog bathing in pools of water that had gathered in the rough deep tracks of the CAT. "I thought you knew."

"I can't fathom how someone's own family would want to desecrate what their grandfather fought to preserve."

Maddy turned and snapped her as she raged. "Take a picture of me driving this thing, would you? It's awesome." The kid pulled herself onto the earth-moving machine.

She did, but asked, "You don't really want to operate one, do you?" Maddy looked gleefully guilty up there, enjoying herself. "There are better ways to feel powerful," Paris said, indicating the destruction.

"Naw! I just want to ride around on it! Or use it up at the house, to flatten the dirt — it's already stripped bare — to put down my sidewalk."

"Oh, sugarplum, you don't need a sidewalk. Your house is great the way it is."

"I wouldn't want to bring a girl up there."

"Your house would be the farthest thing from her mind, believe me."

"You think so, really?"

Maddy jumped down. Paris led them back toward the parking lot. "I think she'd be so silly in love with you, she wouldn't see anything besides your big brown eyes."

"Aw. Follow me, there's an easy way back." Maddy picked up a stick and twirled it in her hand like a baton. "So you're really into keeping nature around." They moved along a faint path. "Watch out for poison ivy," said Maddy, pointing to a patch.

Paris squeezed by. "Life's going to get pretty strange down here on earth if we don't stop the

Peters from bulldozing their way through the universe."

Maddy hung her head. "It's funny, but when Giulia started talking about this whole setup, the crazy grandad, the courts, Peter's plans, I thought it was kind of weird. *I* don't want to kill any trees. And there's so many junked buildings right in Morton River, why put up more? But you grown-ups are supposed to know what you're doing. I figured I was being a jerk kid. Maybe I *am* right once in a blue moon. Maybe I should listen to me now and then." Maddy walked silently beside her for several yards. "So," she said then, her voice dogged, as if she'd made a grave decision, "we have to stop Peter." She hurled her stick into the woods like a spear.

"You're a quick study."

"It's not like I don't have a *brain*, you know. I mean, I made a solar panel last week. I just couldn't figure out how to get the energy to run through a wire."

"Maddy!" she exclaimed, stopping. "You actually made a solar panel?"

Maddy turned and glowered at her. "I can *read*, you know. I found these old hippy back-to-the-land do-it-yourself magazines in the library." She motioned with her head for Paris to follow.

"If only school felt like fun to you."

"Hey, now that I know about those thirty other girls waiting for me, maybe, just maybe, it will." Paris laughed as they reached the Jeep. "I think," Maddy suggested, "you ought to call your car Sugarplum."

"Why?"

"So you stop calling me that!"

Paris hugged Maddy. Oh, to be Maddy's age, to start out in life side by side with a fresh young companion, to stay with her forever — why hadn't she done that? What would life do to Maddy? What had it done to her that she'd left all her Maddies behind even while she searched for new ones? "Tell me where that after-hours joint is and you have a deal."

CHAPTER 7

Venita's building was a red brick factory just the other side of a secondary bridge over the Morton River. The bricks had been sandblasted, fitted with new windows and converted to retirement housing with limited support services like housekeeping, laundry and shopping. The renovator hadn't made enough profit, Venita explained at the door, to keep going. It was one of a kind.

Paris took in the crowded one-bedroom unit with a tiny windowless kitchen in a corner of the living room. One wall was covered with books. The furniture was cluttered with student papers and news magazines. Drapes decorated with autumnal bouquets hid the windows. Venita excavated half of a little round table and set out flowered china.

"Tomato soup and grilled cheese sandwiches for Saturday dinner," Paris said, sniffing the air. "This tastes like my childhood."

"Mine too," Venita said with her ripply laugh. "Although we didn't get the soup from a can then."

"You look exhausted."

"I hate to admit it, but I am. Worry does that to me."

"Worry about what?"

Venita set down her spoon and plucked at the crusts of her sandwich. Her face was somber, voice almost inaudible. "That's why I asked you over. I had dinner with the Picarris last night. Mr. P. told me what he learned at City Hall Thursday."

"Uh-oh."

"Are you sure it's all right to ruin your weekend?"

"You're not exactly putting a damper on a hot social schedule."

"The proposed budget for the Rafferty Adult Education Center for the fiscal year 1990 was cut in half."

She forced herself to swallow. "Sounds like I'd better start packing."

"Me too." Venita shook her head. "I don't understand. It's not as if we have any duplication of staff, or high overhead. You know how old our equipment and texts are. Just the same, they want to eliminate whole subjects."

"What happened? Are they lowering the boom just like that or has Mr. P. had warning?"

"He's certainly been aware of the trend. First there was that referendum for a tax increase that failed. Then we had the cutback in state revenue sharing. The final blow is this Finance Board study, looking for areas to cut. It showed that very few people who come through Rafferty become employed immediately or increase their wages."

Paris protested. "Wages have to do with lack of skills, and prejudice, if you ask me."

Venita nodded, stirring her soup. "If they do this to us we'll have almost nothing left but the income from the Rafferty Trust Fund and contributions."

"*Money, money, money, money,*" Paris sang softly, trying to capture a melody from *Cabaret*. "I wonder where I'll go next, or if my legacy from the Reagan years will be to watch the collapse of adult education." She nibbled at the crusts of cheese that had seeped from her sandwich. "Will any place be safe? Oh, Venita, what if I have to settle down and teach regular school?"

"Heaven forbid," teased Venita, her voice stronger.

She felt lightheaded from shock. "It's more than just the job. It never occurred to me that I wouldn't have a choice, that I'd have to stop wandering because of economic insecurity." She shifted on Venita's chair, imagining her bleak future.

"The other schools won't be hit quite as hard," Venita continued. "They can't cut other education programs because the state could take them to court and cut aid further, but the Center doesn't fall under that protection." Venita slammed her sandwich down. "They've really got my goat. What about quality of life? I suppose that doesn't matter in this day and age. Like Ed Klein, the history teacher, said, 'I never claimed world civ would get them jobs.'"

"Didn't Mr. P. have any solutions?"

"He suggested Ed look at his syllabus, turn it around so he's teaching more social studies and economics. Giving them vocational information."

"Well —"

Venita was ranting now. "What about the whole picture they used to preach, the whole person? Things have gone nowhere but downhill ever since Kennedy was assassinated."

"Everything's a bottom-line business these days. I've seen other towns adapt. Can you teach electronics math?"

"I could learn, but I'm not sure I'd want to. I teach mathematics as a life skill. I wouldn't want to leave out the whys that challenge minds. Look at —"

"I know, I know. All your students who go on to college."

"I mentioned them. Mr. Piccari said that's one of the problems. These students are going on to college and leaving the Valley."

"We're messing with their cheap labor supply. That's a no-no for sure. That whole person we want to teach is just too damned expensive in this day and age."

Venita gave a weak smile. "Your soup's getting cold."

There was no sound except their spoons on the bowls and cars splashing across the bridge in the

October rain. She peered at a small gallery of photographs on the wall. "Bubba?" she asked about an old black and white of a young man with a certain thrust to his chin and marcelled hair.

"And my mother and father," Venita said, a richness coming into her voice as she pointed out and named the rest. "The one in cap and gown is Thor, my nephew at the community agency. He graduated from Yale. I should remind those uppity-ups who want to fire us all that not every educated person leaves the Valley."

"The ones who stay want more than some measly old job soldering and dipping and crimping."

"Thor doesn't get paid much better than them, I'll tell you. We need to talk to that man, though, Paris. He'll have kittens when he hears they want to cut the Center. It's the last hope for a lot of people around here."

"But the uppity-ups are right. It shouldn't be their only hope."

"What else can we give the students?"

"Something to take to an employer."

"What employer? They're leaving the Valley as fast as the young people."

"Trained workers might make them stay."

"Trained in what?"

She was remembering her first day in Morton River, the old woman on the Hillside. "What do the new factories make?"

"There are three of them now — a medical instruments firm, one that makes those household plastic milk crates, and a small calculator manufacturer. They're scattered on the edge of Morton River, though. No buses go out to them and none of them will hire anyone without reliable transportation. If they do take anyone from town, the first cold morning when those old car batteries die they fire them, especially if their faces are black or if they speak Spanish or Vietnamese. They'd rather hire white housewives and kids from the suburbs part-time."

She tasted the tinny hot anger that had started in college when she'd first clearly seen the inequities of the world. They spooned soup in silence. "I feel so helpless, Venita. I suspect Mr. Piccari doesn't have it in him to find a way to make the statistics look better."

"Numbers don't lie."

"Statistics need interpretation. What kind of follow-up does he do? Maybe the figures look better six months after the students get out, or nine."

Venita opened a package of Fig Newtons, offered them to Paris and took one for herself, but seemed too tired to eat it. Her posture collapsed and she stared into her empty bowl. "I feel so tired. It seems like life is just one big struggle. I suppose I was lucky to have this job for a few years. I should settle for living on my retirement and volunteer as a tutor at the Center. Then Mr. P. could use my wages for you, or Hattie or Ed."

She couldn't stand to see Venita look frail. It made her feel hopeless, and like Venita was abandoning her personally. At this rate she'd be a bag lady by the time she was Venita's age. "Don't be ridiculous. You earn that money as much as we do."

"Eventually," Venita whispered, eyes glazed, "they'll switch the lot of us for people who can teach schematics and keyboarding."

"No," Paris said weakly. At age forty-one she'd have to return to Austin and let her parents support her while she got a secondary certificate, champing at the bit, craving her old freedom. So much for lavender hot tubs and romance in new places.

"They'll find some way to pervert the Center's charter to use the cultural money for computers." Venita pushed away from the cookies. "Oh, Paris, teaching has been my life! Education is getting more watered down with every decade. No wonder kids like your little friend Maddy don't want to learn. Where's the fascination, the glory of it? Why bother if school only leads you to an assembly line?"

"I ought to get out of here, Venita. We're both tired. Things always look better in the morning." Resolutely, she carried dishes to the clutter in the sink. It dawned on her that for the first time the stick had been passed to her. Venita's generation was running out of steam for saving the world. Stranger in town or not, Paris might have to take more responsibility for Morton River's ills than she wanted. Maybe she'd help, but she would not get invested in this Valley, would not, damn it, plant seeds she'd want to see grow, would not get attached to the outcome of any plans she laid, or contributions she made. "What about Thor? You said this would piss him off. Maybe he'd have some ideas."

"My firebrand nephew? I'm sure he's got ideas, but he's not always the most practical man."

"Maybe that's what we need, a dreamer to take the leap from can't to can." *To take the stick from my hands.*

Venita wouldn't let her wash the dishes, but

Paris was too riled up to go home quite yet. Out in the nippy mid-October air she considered driving the half hour to New Haven to find the bar she'd read about in *Places of Interest*. Then she recalled the after-hours club Maddy had told her about. It was only two blocks from her apartment. She parked in the Pizza House lot and walked through the puddles down Water Street toward the river.

She was cold and totally spooked by the long sad dark line of buildings that had probably once belched smoke by night and workers by day. Except for an occasional car back on Railroad Avenue, there wasn't a sound other than the river flowing at the bottom of the street. She stepped across the railroad tracks where the freight trains didn't stop anymore. One side of the street was a gaping vacant lot. The buildings opposite had either been boarded up or converted to contractors' equipment stores and shady-looking warehouses. Right smack in the middle of them was a brick two-story with a small sign that read, "The Sweatshop." For courage she imagined entering with her arm under Giulia's, the younger woman stately beside her, quietly ecstatic that Paris had brought her out. She pushed the door open.

A disco it wasn't, but then this was almost 1990. The room was enormous, dwarfing the cluster of tables and chairs huddled at its far end. Dark, cavernous, it felt damp, but it smelled of fresh popcorn. Her way was lit by long parallel tubes of orange and blue neon suspended from the ceiling. She could barely hear the jukebox from the door, though she could see it next to the disk of light which flooded the pool table. *What a strange building.* Though she should have expected a gay night spot in the Valley to look like this. A handful of people watched as she walked toward them.

Then a round-faced man with thinning light hair, probably in his late twenties, called, "Come join us!"

Her speed increased despite her attempt at composure, and she slipped onto a wobbly stool at the bar. The other customers turned back to the pool table or to each other.

"It's great to see a new face," said the man. "I'm Jimmy O'. You want coffee, pop, a sandwich?"

"How about a seltzer on the rocks?"

"You betcha, girlfriend. Hey Jimmy Kinh, come on over and meet our new friend."

Jimmy Kinh took a long time. When he came out of hiding, wiping his hands on his apron, she saw why: he was Mr. Kinh from her 2:00 class. He grinned at the floor.

"He doesn't speak a whole lot of English."

"I know," she said and held out her hand. This would make one class more fun. Jimmy Kinh shook it, then stumbled over his own feet all the way back to the kitchen area.

"Hi, Paris," said a soft voice at her shoulder.

"Peg! I didn't see you." The image of Giulia by her side, always fickle, immediately dissolved. Peg was no fantasy.

"I was in the jane."

"All the amenities, girls. Ask and you will receive," said Jimmy O', sliding a seltzer toward Paris. His face looked much more relaxed now that she was a known quantity.

"Isn't this a school night for you?" she asked Peg.

"Sometimes I'm wild and reckless. I needed a mental health day so I told them I'd be too sick to

107

go in tomorrow. Do you play?" Peg asked, holding out a cue stick.

She caught Peg's eye, looking for any inferences she might be making, but Peg really just wanted her to play pool.

Peg looked so debonair shooting the balls, the length of her bent in her vest and slacks, her white shirt sleeves rolled halfway up her forearms. Those hands held the stick lightly, confidently, manipulating it like a sculptor. Her limp looked like a pool player's stiffness as she straightened and moved to the next ball. When Paris's turn came, she rolled the little black ball right into a pocket. Peg looked at Paris, one eyebrow raised.

"Okay, so I played maybe twice back in Austin, but I thought I did pretty darned good. Do I get a second chance?"

"Darlin', you look so fine with all that silvery hair hanging over your face, you can get away with dropping them in the pockets by hand if you want."

She normally never blushed.

They played a game and then sat at the bar. Jimmy O', after serving up coffee for Peg, a diet cola for Paris, made himself scarce. This comfort with Peg was unnerving, uncomfortable in itself. It was as if they'd been lovers for fifteen years. Peg knew how to come on without being heavy-handed. "Are you still available for next weekend?" Paris asked.

"I've been looking forward to it." Peg drank her black coffee, her second cup since Paris arrived. "How'd your outing with the kid go?"

"Outing is right." She told Peg what had happened.

"Things ain't like they used to be," Peg said. "At

that age I thought I *couldn't* be gay until I was grown up. It never even occurred to me to look at other little girls."

"When did you figure it out?" Peg looked so dykey she couldn't imagine that Peg hadn't known forever.

"That I could be with someone my own age?" Peg laughed, her frank gaze never leaving Paris's eyes. "When I was a college senior my best friend since freshman year pounced on me."

"Pounced on you?"

"She was in track and made the high jump into my bed. She said she'd been holding back three years and decided it was then or never."

"*She* wasn't too young," Paris said with a laugh.

"She knew all the right moves and she wasn't interested in arguing."

"But it wasn't something to last a lifetime?"

Peg inspected her neatly clipped fingernails. The fingers tapered slightly. "No. Only nine years."

Why did that hurt so much to hear? "Wow. What happened?"

"She decided to pounce on someone else."

"And you?"

"I found a woman who wanted me for ten years."

It was disturbing to see a lesbian who had so much to offer lose relationships. Paris had always assumed that she could make a marriage work if she chose to. "So the next one will be eleven?"

Peg's lips were narrow, her eyes still downcast when she answered with some bitterness, "I think I've mentioned that there won't be another one. I'm not one of these women who can do this over and over. I want all or nothing. I'm not willing to try for all again. I don't believe in forever any more." Peg wrung her hands. "When I had my accident I couldn't do sports any more, but I was so grateful that I at least had teaching left. After the second breakup, I don't know exactly what happened to me, but lately I'm so empty I feel like I'm cheating the girls in my classes."

Paris let it rest. She sipped seltzer, squeezed her lime dry, smiled at Jimmy Kinh. After a while she said, "Maddy and I went to Bromsberrow State Park."

Peg looked up again, her eyes cool. She steepled her fingertips.

"The hermit's old shack is down. So are some of his trees. There's equipment at the site. I wondered what you'd heard about the industrial park."

Peg looked surprised. "Not a thing. I thought it was still sidelined, waiting for the courts to settle it."

"So your brothers haven't mentioned —"

"Brockett and Ned don't exactly share their innermost secrets with me. And money is their innermost secret. Now and then they make an investment recommendation, but they don't trust me to be able to think these things through."

"Because you're a woman?"

"A very queer woman."

Paris sighed, then sighed again. "First the woods, now my job. I'm not at all sure Morton River Valley was a good decision for me." She explained about the projected budget cuts.

Peg sat thoughtful and silent, sipping coffee. "Well, I can't do anything about Rafferty Center, though it'd be great to save your job if that would keep you here. I can try to pump the siblings about the park. It certainly sounds like something underhanded is going on."

"I'd appreciate that a whole lot. Morton River Valley feels like it could be a real special experience. The industrial park could help kill it off, and losing the Center as it is now could finish the spirit of the town." She looked around. Several more people had come in. "What's the lowdown on this funny old barn? I've never seen anything like it."

"Jimmy O' got hurt at Rafferty's about five years ago. He bought this building — they used to make playground equipment here — dirt cheap out of his settlement. He says he's giving it two years to sink or swim. There aren't enough of us in Morton River and the little towns around here to support him, so he's trying to draw customers from New Haven and Upton. If he can't make it as a gay night spot he'll lease it out, or rebuild old cars in it, his second love. He's been open seven months."

"But why after-hours?"

"They knew he was gay and wouldn't give him a liquor license." Peg drained her coffee. "Want to dance?"

"Dance?"

"Yes. I won't win any marathons, but this warped pelvis of mine doesn't make me a wallflower either."

"It's not that, Peg. It's just your anti-romance mindset. Dancing's made to lead to what you call trouble."

"Oh darlin'," she replied. "I'm not at all anti-romance. I'm just a marrying kind of woman who's permanently mateless. It makes me a perfectly safe partner." Peg held out her arm. "Come on," she said, raising her voice. "Maxie just put her evening's pool winnings into the jukebox and we're guaranteed some oldies."

Even bitter, Peg was fun. Paris hoped she'd be able to dance chastely, but before she could accept the invitation Peg slid one hand behind the small of her back. Was there a more intimate feeling in the world? The day had been hard enough — she was going to let loose. "I don't know what to think about you, Peg." She couldn't help but smile. "But I don't believe I've ever turned down a dance in my life."

CHAPTER 8

Valley Opportunity Watch occupied a storefront on Liberty Street, in the heart of the ancient rundown mill housing clustered on the north end of town. The agency was short on furniture, but full of people who looked so busy they'd never set their bodies down anyway. Even those lucky enough to work at desks stood as they spoke on the phone or rushed across the room to consult with other staff members or directories.

Thor was tiny. Tiny limbs, tiny close-cropped head under a crocheted red, black and green cap, tiny hands, tiny feet in sandals. He wore a business suit. If his face hadn't been a darker, miniature version of tall, large-boned Venita's she never would have guessed they were family. Paris tensed when his eyes seemed to look everywhere but directly at her. It had taken two weeks for his aunt to get an appointment with him.

"Okay. Aunt Ven, come in here or we'll be interrupted before you start. Quickly," said Thor, brusquely motioning to them. "Okay. I guess you're Paris Collins, the teacher," he said, pointing to chairs. His voice was definitely Ivy League, but in his brief perfunctory glance there was an anger she remembered from her student days when "I have a dream" rang fresh in her ears while rioting erupted in the cities. She felt a wariness about him that might have been a reflection of the color of her skin. Or was he one of these men who could sniff out dykes?

They sat grouped on one side of a table that looked like it'd spent its youth in someone's kitchen. A three-paneled torn screen did nothing for the noise level, but at least blocked the sight of all the bustle. "What's this about the Valley going to hell in a handbasket, Aunt Ven?"

"I'm alarmed, Thor. If it weren't for Paris I'd think I was just a senior citizen nostalgic for the good old days, but the forces of evil do seem to be winning out."

"Now you sound like Cousin Hell-and-Brimstone."

Venita explained, lifting her voice above the hubbub. "We have a very large and multi-talented family. Hell-and-Brimstone has the Right Hand Christian Church a few blocks away."

"Powerful preacher," said Thor, shaking his head, looking caught between admiration and disapproval. Paris realized that she'd been aware of Thor's cologne for some time. Funny, he comes on all business, but douses himself in sex appeal?

"In any case, we've been informed that the Center's piddling budget is about to lose half its weight in gold."

"What?" Thor stared at Venita. "What are they thinking of? The Center is our biggest hope. Adults can't be busing to Upton or New Haven to school. And I've been talking for two years with the district about developing an alternative school at the Center for dropouts."

"I suspect," Paris answered, "they're thinking about bottom lines, not people's needs."

"Not bottom enough," Thor shot back. "The bottom's going to fall out if we don't start treating people like they're more valuable than money, okay? We're busting our butts here trying to get some shelters together for the winter. Neighborhood complaints made two churches back out of the Homeless Project. As if we're not all neighbors. The daycare facilities can't handle all the kids they're having to take on. Both parents are commuting to Upton for work and not getting back to the Valley till seven at night."

He looked, for a fleeting moment, desperate. She wondered if he'd ever contemplated chucking it all for the Valley Savings Bank, or work with one of the Hartford insurance companies. The anger in his eyes glowed brighter. She wasn't afraid of Thor, but he seemed to be one of those people who directs his anger at the nearest vulnerable object. Was it presumptuous of her to think she had something to offer? If that was the case she'd back out, but meanwhile being Thor's whipping post wasn't exactly her life's ambition. She gripped the smooth arms of her wooden chair.

"I've been in adult ed for a lot of years now," she said, trying to sound like an ally. "We can't stop administrators ignoring everything but the bottom line, but we can make that line more attractive."

"How?"

"They want people to get jobs. We need to make sure they do."

"Do you think I haven't tried to get vocational funds around here? We have a part-time gal who works harder than God to match the educated folks with the non-existent jobs."

Venita leaned forward, that discouraged look back on her face. "Between the homeless and the jobless they'll be setting up Hoovertowns soon."

"What do you call those cardboard shanties under the bridges?" asked Thor. His voice was impatient, just short of rude. "Okay. Ms. Collins, tell me what you have in mind."

"The bigger picture. We won't get anywhere begging for nickels and dimes. If all they can see is numbers on paper we need to put it in their language. Other towns have intact adult ed programs. What are they doing right?"

"They have community colleges, programs hooked into the school systems. There's carry-over. A classroom full of computers can serve a lot of populations. Okay. Funding is based on graduation, ethnicity, employment, and a host of other factors.

The figures can be spread around, a weak link supporting a stronger one."

"But in the Valley," said Venita, "the Center is everything."

"The whole ball of wax," Paris echoed. Thor looked thoughtful. On the wall behind his head were poster-sized black and white enlargements of what looked to be Valley people: little kids in a pool, a group of men painting a house, teenagers in caps and gowns. On the next wall he'd taped up two photo posters, portraits of a group so large it couldn't all fit in one lens. "More Valeries?" she asked Venita with a smile.

Venita lit up. "Just about all of us. We had a family reunion two years ago over at the State Park."

"Bromsberrow?"

"The same," answered Thor, biting off his words as if this distraction were beyond his patience.

"I wonder if you'll be able to have your next reunion there. Or want to," she said to him, baiting.

"Why, you planning to persuade the city to sell it and give us the proceeds?" Thor asked.

"They may already have signed its death warrant."

"You're talking about that old hermit's land and his kids selling it off."

"Right on the edge of the park."

"It's always been a refuge for me," Venita said, "I can walk and think better under the trees. Do you remember, Thor, the walk we took there —"

"When you persuaded me to apply to Yale?" His face softened for a moment. "You reminded me about that kid's storybook you used to read me about the little engine that could."

Venita's laugh splashed out. "You'd sit there, such an earnest boy, taking that train's part. *I think I can, I think I can,* you'd huff, your little arms going like pistons."

"If the Admissions Committee only knew what inspired me."

Paris never had been able to leave well enough alone. She took advantage of Thor's lowered defenses. "What will kids and adults have now? Where will the wildlife go?"

"Don't give me that environment crap," Thor said. "You think I care if the possums eat well when our people are hungry?"

"Now who's being short-sighted? There won't be land to put shelters on, cardboard, brick, anything —"

"Don't mix issues. Okay. Let's talk the Center. Let's plan a statement. We can do a Save the Center Rally, let people know what's going down."

"Cousin Hell-and-Brimstone can speak," Venita said.

"Rub people's noses in that vote against the mill rate. The Board of Selectmen is only cutting where it won't hurt the property owners directly. The white middle class has said no more money for the poor folk, so these public servants are going to make damn sure only the helpless suffer."

"Those aren't the people who'll be at your rally," Paris pointed out.

"*I* know who'll turn out and I also know I can get media coverage. We've been putting our message across all by ourselves for some time now." Thor definitely didn't like her aggressiveness. "Okay. What do you suggest, Ms. Collins?"

She forced eye contact, loving the challenge. "A more pro-active tactic. Let's not assume the Board is hostile. Politicians around here don't seem very creative. If we lay a solution at their feet, they might just snap it up."

"Where are you going to buy a solution? At Caldor's?"

She wanted Thor as an ally, but his sarcasm was stupid. "That might be as effective as butting heads with you," she said with disgust.

Thor rose and looked down at her. His voice was contemptuous. "Okay. I appreciate your concern about our little crises, Ms. Collins, and if I can use your help I'll let you know through Venita. I may well need a white liaison."

White sounded like a four-letter word. Venita stood at her full height. Her swift voice lost all trace of breathiness. "You're your father's son as much as your grandfather's, Thor, and all that education didn't clean your father's bullheadedness out of you. Paris is not some do-good volunteer from the Hillside. She's spent her adult life teaching people like these." She swept her hand toward the chaos beyond the folding screen. "We need a breath of fresh air in this town and I have a feeling she's going to do us as much good as any of your big-man-bullying-the-establishment-campaigns. You may be too young to graciously accept help, but I hope you're young enough to learn." She swept out of the office.

Paris loved Venita at that moment, for appreciating her, for standing behind an uppity woman. She stayed with Thor a moment more. Perhaps she didn't belong there, but she wasn't trying to take over his show. The phone on his table rang and he picked it up. She slipped into her jacket and turned to go.

"Ms. Collins," he said, punching a button. "Why don't you find a city that's 'doing it right' and translate their strategy to the Valley?"

She was quick then. This might be all the recognition she'd get, but it was enough. "I wasn't intimating that you were personally doing anything wrong, Mr. Valerie. I thought we were dealing with a new problem here."

"The haves versus the have-nots is nothing new to us. If you've just discovered it, I hope you enjoyed your age of innocence."

She shook her head and left. Whatever the man was picking up on from her, it really had him going.

Venita was already installed in Sugarplum. "I apologize for my nephew's behavior. I am sorry we can't join forces."

"If it's black separatism he's into I can understand not wanting to hang out with the enemy. Some lesbians think men are the root of all evil."

"That they might be right about," said Venita with a closed look that intrigued Paris even more. What was this woman's story? "Still, I'd had high hopes for ideas from Thor."

She pulled out onto Liberty Street and headed toward work. "I wonder," Paris said as they crossed the river, "if Thor didn't give us something after all."

This time they bypassed the Diner for a coffee shop right next to the Center. "We have a few minutes," Venita said. "Can I buy you a cup of something?"

The restaurant was cluttered with firemen from up the street and hard hats who were shoring up the banks of the Morton River across Route 34. They were laughing as they told stories about how the cops had rousted the people who were living under the bridge.

Venita led Paris to a booth. Paris grabbed the well-read copy of the *Valley Sentinel.* "Looks like I'd better subscribe to this rag to try to keep up with all the machinations going on." This darn city defied her history of detachment. It was just large enough to pique her interest and just small enough that an individual could make a difference. She'd never subscribed to anything but *Off Our Backs* in her life and was annoyed with her hunger for news of this area.

"What did Thor give you?" Venita prompted after a man in an apron rushed over to give them coffee. Venita ordered a blueberry muffin. "Their specialty."

"He liked my idea about consulting other towns that still have funding. I wonder if they'd talk to me. I wonder how we could find the right model."

"Mr. Piccari goes to all sorts of meetings around the state. He might have some suggestions."

She folded the paper to its front page. "Ow!" she said, burning her tongue on the coffee, but too excited to care. "Look at this. *Zoning Board Pushes Hermitage Park.*"

"What's it say?"

" 'City Fathers Renew the Valley, a newly formed alliance of local business and governmental leaders, has proposed developing seventeen acres of woodland into an industrial park. The Planning and Zoning Commission listened to arguments by CIFRV that the park would attract industry and much-needed employment into the area. The hearing was closed to the public, but three members of the Morton River Watershed and Land Trust stood outside the hearings room and accosted Board members, pressing for disapproval of zoning changes.' So, now we know for sure that land shouldn't have been cleared," Paris concluded with an angry satisfaction.

"Those Trust people get pretty active on their issues. Between them and V.O.W., City Hall gets a lot of traffic."

"I've never been the lobbying type myself," she explained. "Battles can be avoided with enough slick moves." Yet she felt frustrated and powerless enough to want to do something. "I don't know, Venita, in the sixties I believed with my friends that we were changing the world and it hasn't changed. I wonder now if I can change even the piece of it I live in."

As always, teaching swept everything else from her mind. That day and in the weeks following she read the paper and talked to the other teachers, but drifted into a holding pattern where she wouldn't have to make decisions. She kept conflicts and people at a distance.

She also got to know the Morton River. Every day she crossed it to get to work. She could hear it flowing two blocks from her on the other side of the Sweatshop. In time she learned that it relaxed her to walk a couple of miles up to the dam to watch its waters rush in constant uneven curtains down the concrete slab. She had no idea why she found moving water so fascinating, but she'd never met a human being who didn't. Watching the old stuff, feeling its spray against her face, was a gift she gave herself when she was down in the doldrums.

By November she'd politely declined or cancelled all of Peg's invitations. On yet another Saturday she found herself at the dam instead of with Peg. Fallen leaves around her were rotting by now, soaked and trampled. The tree branches were empty, waiting for the cold winds and ice of winter. Someone was using a woodstove. The smell reminded her of northern California. Should she have stayed there near the ancient redwoods which had awed her? Should she have stayed with Teal, the woman who cleaned houses two days a week and canvassed the forests the rest of her time for mosses, mushrooms, fern and other non-flowering plants? No, Teal was always around, but never there for her, emotionally burnt-out, spacey from a marijuana habit.

Again, Paris felt stuck, confused. The water just kept noisily plummeting to its next level. She watched it for inspiration until a late afternoon chill set in.

She got a spinach pizza from downstairs, devoured it, then put a Gershwin tape on. Listening to the romantic lyrics, the graceful music, she dreamed for a while, worrying the subject of Peg.

She had spent *some* time with her. They'd gone looking for fall foliage that one Saturday afternoon, but another heavy rain had stripped the trees. Since then she'd seen her at the Sweatshop at least twice a week. They didn't arrange to be there at the same time, but always seemed to be. Of course, the fact that she could see Peg's car parked on Water Street from her windows made planning a little easier. She tried not to look. It had been exciting to entice Peg, but that game was getting old. Tonight, she was going to read some Marion Zimmer Bradley and go to bed early.

Then Giulia came.

She heard footsteps clanging up her stairs, rushed yet at the same time tentative, definitely the light steps of a woman. Peg? Venita? Maddy? Giulia was a complete surprise. It seemed so unlike the personality she projected, to be seeking Paris out a second time.

"Come in, come in," Paris said, feeling like the spider greeting the fly. Giulia smelled of cigarettes — had she just come from Peter?

"I didn't want to bother you. Maddalena told me you live over the Pizza House."

"It's no bother. Can I give you some coffee?" *Please,* she thought, *don't tell me Peter will be right by to pick you up.*

"No. Peter will be here soon to pick me up." Giulia eyed the living room and Paris sensed in her appraisal a curiosity she wouldn't have expected.

"Come out to the kitchen where it's warm," she said. "I've been grading papers." Giulia perched on the edge of a chair looking refined despite her coat, one of those bulky mauve quilted affairs that everyone had worn a few years back, this one darkened around the cuffs from long wear and washings that never got all the grime of the Northeast out. Paris waited for Giulia's excuse.

"I wanted to talk to you about my sister, but not in front of Mama. Since you've been coming around I can tell she understands more English than she ever let on."

Uh-oh, thought Paris, feeling pulled from the safe nest she'd been hiding in. The light of the wall lamp over the table enclosed them. Giulia's eyes were strangely light themselves, as if there were a fire burning behind them. Concern about Maddy was not what Paris saw. It was a desire she couldn't name. Not for Paris, not necessarily for anything sexual, but stark desire that was close to going out of control. She could even see it in Giulia's lipstick, a purply bruised-looking color that made Paris think of a stunning drag queen.

"She's a good kid," Paris said, though Giulia wasn't there to listen to her opinions. She stopped herself from nervously playing with her split ends, but a minute later caught herself feeling for them again.

"You've helped her — she went to school for a while."

If you only knew why.

"And she has a friend now. They whisper in her room for hours, half the night."

What a fast worker! She tried not to sound defensive. "Just what teenagers are supposed to do."

"Yes," Giulia replied, leaning back with a shrug of her shoulders as if to cast off an insistent spell. Then she shook her head. "No. They're too close.

They play hookey together, not as often, but who knows where they go, what they do? At least before Maddalena spent most of her time around the house with her junk. Now if she's home it's behind a locked door."

She was damned if she'd say the kid was going through a phase. She kept quiet, fingering her hair.

"She's listened to you before. Can you find out if that girl is making her a lesbian? It would kill Mama."

Cold poured down her body and goosebumps popped out on her arms. She couldn't tell if she was reacting to the word *lesbian* on Giulia's tongue or the trouble the kid might be in. Had Maddy implicated her at all? Then her mind cleared. This was not the romantic butchy woman she'd made of Giulia in her imagination, but a real woman, controlling and scheming. *It would kill* you *is more like it,* she thought, wanting to assure her that Peter would marry her anyway.

"What makes you think it's the other girl?"

"Because," Giulia spat, "there's *nothing* like this in our family."

"There doesn't have to be, Giulia." You'd think in the nineteen-eighties they'd talk about more than birds and bees in sex ed.

Giulia covered her face with her hands. "Why does she do these things to torment us? If Mama finds out, I don't know what will happen."

"The girl is only trying to find her own path. She's not doing anything because of her family. She's hell on wheels, but she's okay inside. If you and Sophia could just love her for who she is, she wouldn't have to be such a rebel."

"How can we love a . . . a . . . *queer?*" she sneered.

"She's your sister."

"I can forgive talking back to Mama, dressing like a street person, smoking, coming in at all hours, but this, in her own home, in the next room! It's her father's fault." Giulia looked at her hands on her lap, the same perfectly applied deep purple on her nails. "He taught her so much, all man things, all unfinished. It did more harm than good."

"You don't know that yet."

"She'd be happier if she were more like me."

Paris wanted to come out to the woman so bad she ached, but Giulia was a viper. Paris stung first. "You're happy?"

The question seemed to dismay Giulia. She realized that the woman's eyes were sixty, seventy years old, but without a shred of peace. Giulia knew every last question and lied to herself about having the answers. She knew there was something she wanted besides Peter, besides money, but was convinced she couldn't have it all. Tonight she was daring, looking at herself under Paris's kitchen light. It was safe, Peter would save her soon.

"I want a home of my own. Children with futures."

"You've got it all planned."

"How else can I be sure to get what I want?"

Just like in the movies, their eyes locked. She was one hunk of a beautiful woman, all ivory and ebony with those thrusts of passionate color on her lips and fingernails. Paris wondered if Maddy's secret adolescent sexuality had awakened something in Giulia. She knew with a queer's instinct that no

127

man had ever seen her like this. She'd be contained, calculating and purposefully seductive with Peter, her ticket to the future. There was a wildness about her, though, that made Paris doubt Maddy's claims of virginity. Or perhaps Giulia liked temptation, liked pausing at the brink.

If Giulia had wanted to tempt her, Paris was having none of it. She gave Giulia the Scala shrug, but unplanned words came from her lips. "Are you that sure about what you want?" Whoops. Maybe she *was* having some of it.

"This is so comfortable — and private," Giulia said, indicating the apartment. "This freedom. You don't have anyone to take care of."

Was she after a secret formula to single life? "Right. Freedom of loneliness, it's guaranteed in the Constitution. Freedom to eat takeout pizza. Freedom to go out into the cold to find human warmth."

"I couldn't." Giulia twitched her shoulders, as if a light shudder went through her under her puffy coat. "Is it worth it?"

She laughed. It was all so obvious. She let Giulia get under her skin because there was no way she could have her. "We're so different, yet so alike. We're on opposite paths, but we have the same fear inside: the grass may be greener on the other side." The iron stairway quaked under heavy feet. "That's the trouble with men," she said. "They're so darned big and loud."

Giulia's eyes widened. How many times had she seen that look? Without trying, sometimes when she opened her mouth to let out the most everyday lesbian truths, she found that she'd said something dangerous and unthinkable. On her way to unlock the door she imagined the horror of Peter's size, now that it'd been shown to her, haunting Giulia until she could live with it no longer.

He filled the doorway, blonde, blue-eyed, smelling of tobacco and a popular aftershave. "I'm here for Giulia," he announced in a rumbly mutter.

Too late! she wanted to announce. *She's in my clutches now.* Instead she gave him a witchy cackle.

"Ready?" he asked Giulia.

Giulia was buttoning her coat.

"Come back any time, Giulia," she said. "I get hardly enough visitors."

Giulia's eyes had gone flat. "Thank you for all you're doing for my family. I hope you'll talk to Maddalena."

"I suspect I'll be seeing her around."

Peter flashed a hasty minimal smile toward her as he ushered Giulia out.

"Oh, Goddess," she said when she'd locked the door behind them and heard feet clattering down as fast as they could go. "All that woman. What a waste."

CHAPTER 9

When someone straight brings a friend home, the friend is the focus of attention. Because she and Peg were dykes, Peg's family subtly but firmly herded them together, interrogating with their eyes, assuming and judging with their careful but ignorant words.

What good was it to get angry? Paris imagined how they looked to the Jacobs. The picture the two of them made together, the family would think, told the whole story. Peg, ravishingly handsome, dyke hands hidden in the pockets of her perfectly creased charcoal flannels, a white button-down shirt under her matching vest, with short, thick waves starting to gray at the temples, lounged on the couch. Paris had chosen a grey wraparound skirt with her favorite lavender turtleneck for the occasion. They complimented each other. Peg, of course, didn't touch her, yet Paris felt touched, embraced by the acknowledging, protective curve of her friend.

"Do you ever get back to Texas for Thanksgiving?" asked Ned Jacob, the younger of Peg's two big brothers. He looked a fit fifty and talked with the same trace of lisp Peg had.

The house smelled like turkey stuffing. Outside the window was an acre of lawn, not a worn patch or a path in sight. She laughed, but didn't say aloud how she'd hate to be required at these family gatherings. "My folks are travelers with a capital T. If I get to see them on a holiday it's because they're breezing through my neck of the woods. We've done elegant restaurant Thanksgivings, a Christmas picnic in the Redwoods, and once they came to my little cinderblock shanty in Arizona. I served them turkey with barbecue stuffin'." But her parents were always traveling when it came to her gayness, choosing to ignore it. "No," she concluded, "I never go back home."

"Texas!" breathed Darcy, Ned's wife, as if savoring an exotic name.

The rest of the family smiled, shifted in their chairs. These were not hearty New Englanders, these brothers. They ran more to the pinched-mouth Yankee type. Their wives looked enough alike to be sisters: well-dressed empty-nesters with brand new tinted hairdos and camouflaged love handles. The brothers had both chosen plumpness after childhoods with a mother whose wasting disease, according to Peg, had been terminal hypochondria. But they wouldn't talk about that.

Ice clinked in the men's glasses. Now and then she heard one of the sisters-in-law sip something sweet and frothy through a straw. Sighing, Paris plunged into the game. She complimented Marilyn, the elder brother's wife, on the decor.

"Oh, I'm redoing the whole room come spring. I get so bored looking at all this white and shiny chrome. It was *de rigeur* at the time."

"I'm thinking of it too," Darcy said. "Maybe Peg could use the furniture?"

Both brothers scowled at Darcy.

"Peg doesn't need our castoffs."

"We're glad to see Margaret fix up the old homestead," Brockett commented, trying to keep a pipe going. She wondered how hard he'd worked to banish his own lisp. "Dad wouldn't let anyone in there once Mother died. The house got pretty shabby."

She set down her cider glass and looked around, pleasantly startled by this new perspective on Peg. "Margaret!" she exclaimed. "I've never heard you called that."

Peg dipped three fingers into her vest pocket and leaned to take a canape with her other hand. "Brockett doesn't like nicknames," she said with a grin. "Do you, Rocket?"

He gave her a swift annoyed glance. "The only one that ever fit was yours, Pegleg." Peg's eyes went stony and her lovely hands turned to fists.

"How about your name, Paris?" Ned asked. He

was never still, moving from window to hearth where he neatened a small fire with a poker and gently kicked at the andirons. "There must be a story behind that one."

Staying gracious was becoming tedious. Was something burning? "Just more traveling. Mom and Dad got the twinkle in their eyes in Paris. Nine months later I appeared in Texas."

"Very unusual," murmured Ned's wife.

There was a crash in the kitchen. "That *girl!*" said Marilyn. "Excuse me."

Peg looked at Paris. "They import South American help, then don't understand why they get rattled learning to cook pilgrim food."

"There's nothing difficult about a Thanksgiving dinner," Brockett said with finality.

Peg laid her head against the back of the couch and looked at the ceiling. The family obviously deferred to the eldest. Darcy darted after her sister-in-law.

"Can I help in the kitchen?" Paris asked. She felt a little less protected without the additional female presences. That's why, she thought, all over America women fled to kitchens on holidays.

There was no answer for a moment, as if the brothers had to think through protocol. Brockett polished his glasses.

"No," said Peg, taking her hand briefly. "You stay here by me." Peg's normally dry cool palm was clammy, but her eyes were tender and amused, as if to acknowledge the awkwardness of the situation. *Perfect,* Paris thought. It would take a lot of effort not to appreciate this woman.

Peg sipped at her own cider. The brothers

relaxed, taking seats. Their sister was obviously the "man."

Staying put rankled, but she did so. The silence thickened with unasked questions. *You're not mannish, why are you a lesbian? What turned Margaret this way? Is there something in our genes? Should Dad know so he can change his will? How long have you two been together?* They may have feared confrontation, but she was here for more than a homey afternoon with her friend's family. She showed a claw.

"What do you fellas know about Hermitage Park?"

They looked at each other, then at Peg. Her face stayed motionless this time. Ned cleared his throat. Brockett, cool as a cuke on ice, said, "Whatever the newspapers say. Why?"

Just as casually she answered, "Folks like you, owning department stores, I thought you'd have an inside track."

"Looking for some investment recommendations?" asked Ned, as if he'd just figured her angle and wanted to encourage her.

Her mouth was dry with nervousness, but she refused to hide behind whatever convenient ruse the men offered. The cider tasted all too sweet, but she drank it. "No, actually, I was out there a few weeks back and noticed someone's acting like the court has decided in the developer's favor."

"The court!" Ned snorted. "That's just a formality!" Brockett glowered so briefly at him she almost didn't catch it, but her silence seemed to unhinge Ned more than his brother's warning.

"Besides, it's still private property. The sale is contingent on a zoning variance."

"So as long as the Zoning Commission or the court ties this thing up, the current owners can do whatever they please?" She tried to keep her voice cool, academic.

"Unless someone gets a restraining order against them too, yes."

"Which no one will do since the land's out in the boonies and won't be noticed."

"You noticed," said Brockett. "The owner doesn't have a thing to worry about unless you're part of the Land Trust."

She laughed. Only her recent paralysis had kept her from looking the organization up, but Brockett's attitude made her wonder if she wasn't more valuable as a free agent. "I'm not much of a joiner," she said, sidestepping the question.

"I wonder," Peg mused, carefully brushing cracker crumbs from her palm into an ashtray, "if Dad will be glad to see us today." Paris wanted to hug her. She'd gotten what she wanted from the brothers.

Obviously just as relieved as Paris to have the subject changed, Ned stood and crossed to the window. They were all going to the Living Center after dinner. "Or, if he'll be cursing," said Ned, "the bother of Thanksgiving."

Brockett's eyes touched her. *If he'll know who you are,* they seemed to be saying.

You bet he will, big brother.

What the men didn't know was that Peg had already told her dad who Paris was supposed to be. Peg, in creased jeans tucked into shining high boots, had talked about him that day when she'd shown Paris the family land: rocky meadow, pine-strewn woods and major lawns.

"Dad thought girls got a raw deal," Peg had explained, stretching her arms up as she walked. "He made Brockett and Ned teach me to ride, to play sports, use a hammer and saw, anything I wanted," she continued. Inside Paris's head a dykey little Cupid was singing "I've Got A Crush On You." They entered Peg's favorite pine grove, her limp giving her a dashing look, like a wounded hero. Sun streaked through the branches, hazily lighting the trail. "He told me once — when I was so young he probably thought I'd forgotten — 'I don't know why anyone would choose to marry a man, Margaret.' I even remember his sigh. 'We fight and lie and bully women.' "

They'd paused, pine needles thick, slippery, fragrant, making the slightest crunching sound under their feet. "Maybe he wanted you to stay home and take care of him," she'd suggested, wanting to rest a hand under Peg's elbow.

Peg touched her arm and they moved forward. "Whenever Dad had dinner parties he'd invite single women. Mother had fits. She thought he was eyeing the ladies, but I don't think so."

"You think they were for you?" Somehow it seemed possible in a family of this class. They didn't seem filthy rich, but there'd apparently been comforts and privileges for generations.

"In a sense. I think he was showing me my options." Her voice was thick, eyes pained. Because, options or not, father's approval or not, she was alone? "I believe some of the women were lesbians. But I could be wrong about all of it."

Another time when they met at the Sweatshop, Peg had just been to see her father.

"He was there and he wasn't," said Peg, stirring cream slowly into her coffee. Paris nodded in understanding. "I just talked to him, told him about never being drawn to men, about falling for women, about remembering the direction he'd pointed me in."

"Did he understand?" She thanked her stars for the siblings back in Texas who would take care of most of this aging parent business for her when the time came.

"I'm not sure." There was that thickness to her voice again. "He said, 'You never brought one home.' That was all, but I lost it, just started crying like a little kid." Peg's eyes got moist as she spoke. Her hands fell open on the table as if pleading for understanding. "How could I have guessed that he'd want me to? How could I have brought home first one, then another woman? Brockett and Ned managed to stay married, but I was always getting left or leaving someone, just like a damned stereotype of a dyke."

Another reason not to get involved, Paris realized. She might be safe from the messiness of her own family, but it'd be all too easy to take on someone else's. "And now that you've given up, you're upset that your father'll never see you settled," she guessed. Could she help? *Down, Paris, down!*

Undemonstrative Peg slapped the table with the

flat of her palm. "I'd rather die than go through another breakup, Paris. But he'll be gone soon. I'd love to have given him that peace about me."

"We need to whip up some instant lover soup to bring him, sweetie." She didn't know any way to comfort Peg except to hold her hand, to smile into her eyes.

Peg had withdrawn her hand, laughed, patted down her hair, but then they'd both grown quiet. Their eyes met. "If only —" Paris finally said, but Jimmy O' had come to chat and she'd swallowed her own confused longing.

Until today. The Jacobs' South American help served Thanksgiving dinner, the table talk was of nutmeg squash and the vintage of the wine. Peg was attentive, appreciative, treating her much more lovingly than the brothers did their wives. She saved the meal from being totally boring, with her stories of students and teachers. Paris couldn't get over finally finding a woman of the old school. She probably knew how to dance to Gershwin tunes. And she wasn't available.

After dinner she and Peg followed Brockett's car to the retirement village.

"My father's not the man he used to be," said Peg at the wheel of her Z. "He's shrunken and disagreeable. Last year we were able to persuade him to come home for dinner at least, but this year he insisted that he wouldn't be able to stand all the confusion and noise. He's just not much interested in life a lot of the time." Paris dreaded Peg's pain, but mostly because of what it would bring out in herself: the comforter, the partner, the way she'd be with a lover. As they parked in the lot next to Brockett she sighed. It was inconceivable that she could pat Peg's hand in sympathy and turn away.

They gathered in the old man's small suite. Trim, fastidious-looking Brockett haltingly escorted Mr. Jacob, on a walker, in from a lounge where the father had been playing cards. The old man looked minuscule next to his son. His scalp was freckled, and his pale knobby fingers picked, when he sat, at a plaid lap blanket. She tried to see Peg in his face, in his angry eyes.

Darcy shouted at Mr. Jacob, trying to kiss his cheek. "You look so well, Dad!"

Mr. Jacob brushed her aside, but accepted Marilyn's shoulder squeeze.

The two couples began a marathon chat, never letting their words stop as they discussed business, the weather, sports and the grandchildren — all of whom had grown up and moved far away. Only Peg was still and contained, watching her father who stubbornly refused to participate except for an occasional irrelevant or caustic comment.

"Why isn't Margaret here?" he interjected in a low growl.

Paris tensed. She could feel the trembling of Peg's hand as it covered her own. "I am, Dad." She paused till his eyes took her in. "I want you to meet someone. This is Paris."

His eyes moved to Paris. "What kind of name is that?" he challenged in a disapproving tone.

As she explained, Paris reminded herself that it was age, or medication, or anger at his situation talking. She told herself not to take his tone personally. She wanted to run. Run from his rejection, run from his mortality, run from the image of her parents in his place. She felt as if she were at the edge of a chasm and losing her balance. She teetered forward, terrified, and pulled herself back. Mr. Jacob was still appraising her. She forced a broad, winning smile, turned it on Peg and back to Mr. Jacob.

He looked in her eyes for a long moment. She kept her smile, trying not to make it a promise. Finally, he leaned forward and took her hand in both of his. "I'm glad to meet you, Paris," he said in his growly voice, pressing her hands.

Then with a shock she realized, as he searched her eyes, where her fear came from. This meeting was not the sham she'd planned with Peg. No matter how hard she tried she was not just a friend volunteering to stage a gentle lie to comfort a dying parent. Peg was a woman of substance and stability who, too hurt to try again, deep inside wanted exactly what they were pretending. And now Paris had the father's blessing.

Great, she thought, a tremendous churning inside her. It was all she could do not to bolt from the nursing home.

CHAPTER 10

She lay low again after Thanksgiving. When Peg sent roses, delicate pink fragrant blossoms, she wrote a brief thank-you note. Maybe the Goddess was throwing her hints right and left about supposedly safe Peg, but she wasn't taking her up on them. Giulia made a safer fantasy, but, next to Peg, was hardly adequate. The passion for Giulia had been silly anyway. The woman was in an ice age of denial.

She spent more time with Sophia Scala. Maddy was either going to school or truant with her girlfriend. Paris assumed the girlfriend was a latchkey kid with the run of the beds in her family's home all day long. Was fifteen too young to be wallowing in sex twenty-four hours a day? She imagined that she wouldn't have turned down the chance had it been offered to her back then.

She'd begun to give Maddy's mother homework. Today, over strong black coffee, with the art deco clock ticking cozily above the stove, Sophia read aloud a composition about her pious childhood. Though Paris was pleased with Sophia, she didn't give herself credit for bringing her this far this fast. After Giulia's hint she'd pressed and found that Giulia was right: Sophia really had a lot more English than she'd let on when they started. It had been the usual fear and embarrassment that had kept her silent.

The composition, written on a wide-lined pad Paris had brought for that purpose, was full of errors, but the gist of it was that Sophia felt trapped. She'd written about the promise of her days in school with the nuns.

"Do you go to church?" Paris asked in the slow way they talked. She forced down some of Sophia's coffee. Almost espresso.

"In here," Sophia said, hitting her chest with a fist. "And on the TV."

"That must be hard on a believer like you."

"Hard?"

"It hurts that you don't go to church."

"Yes." The brown eyes looked down, then seemed to bring buckets of sadness from a well inside her. "I once was —" Sophia curved her hands in the air like a man shaping the figure of a woman. "No one wants me now. *Grassa.*"

"Fat."

She nodded, looking at the floor, face dark red.

"It's not the end of the world, you know."

She squinted at her without understanding.

"You're not the only fat woman in the world," Paris said extra slowly. "There's no shame."

"In my heart," Sophia answered, pointing at herself. "I have shame. If I go to the convent I am not fat."

Encouraged by Sophia's restlessness, she suggested, "I think it's about time to start your lessons where you're going to use them. And," she added, "to put your body out there so you get over that fear of being fat in public. Want a ride in a Jeep?"

Sophia's eyes widened in the same way Maddy's had.

It was strange to see Sophia in the hermit's Jeep, knowing her daughter was marrying the son of its past owner. Twenty minutes later they were at a little white painted storefront down the hill, next door to the Congregational church. It was December cold out, but sparkly bright. Sophia struggled from the Jeep under her own steam and they went inside the store.

It smelled of cold cuts. There were only two aisles and they walked them, spelling out the names of products. The owner spoke Italian and Sophia couldn't contain her excitement when she showed Paris cans and boxes of goods imported from Italy. Sophia still loved best to teach her and coached her on the canned tomato label. Paris bought paper-thin provolone for lunch and Sophia asked for a chunk of hard salami.

"Next week," Paris promised when she dropped her at home, "we'll go Christmas shopping."

Sophia seemed to catch her breath. "Good! Good!" she said. "I can surprise the *figlie*."

"What?" she prodded.

She scrunched up her face in concentration, then got tricky. "My three," she said, counting on her fingers. "Giulia, Maddalena and Paris!"

Warmed to be included, she let Sophia get away with using the Italian and drove Sugarplum to the Diner.

"Long time no see!" said Dusty, who was leaning on the counter talking football with a customer. It was 4:00 pm on Saturday afternoon, a slow time. The ice cream vendor came through the kitchen with a bill. Dusty, joking easily, paid him from the register. Paris looked around for Giulia.

"Don't you ever go home, Dusty?"

"Sure," Dusty replied, her air of assurance like a promise that life was as it should be, hers, Paris's, everyone's. "I take Sundays and Mondays off. I like to have one day when the rest of the world is playing, and one day when I have Elly all to myself. This Sunday we'll go to the rally."

"Rally?"

"At the shopping center out on Route 34."

"For what?" The ever-smiling waitress Rosa brought her coffee. Paris took a stool.

Dusty ticked off causes, tugging at each finger as if for emphasis. "To increase funding for the

144

homeless, restore money for M.O.V.E. and for Rafferty Center. V.O.W. put it together."

Diner coffee tasted like water after Sophia's. "No, I didn't hear a word about it at the Center. This town gets an F on coordination. We could have gotten our students there."

"Thor Valerie's pretty good about that. He has a way of reaching into the poorest sections of the community."

"And he's a one-man band."

"Mister Ego we call him, but he gets the job done."

"If you say so. What's M.O.V.E.?"

Enthusiasm lighted Dusty's face. "For a while we had a really good transit system, Morton River Valley Express. You could call in your location and they'd pick you up. You had to qualify for a pass: disabled, poor, old, anything like that. The cost was really low, but guess what?" Dusty softly kicked at the counter. Her tone turned disgusted. "The funds got cut completely. We lost business out of that. The older people up on the Hillside would hit the few old stores downtown, visit the bank and the post office, then come in for lunch. It was a big outing for them."

Paris had noticed that despite the numerous hills surrounding the Valley, there was only one Hillside, an informal district which housed the majority of homes put up by the European immigrants who'd built and worked in the factories.

An affectionate grin stretched across Dusty's face as she went on. "There was even a bunch of employees from the rehab program, people with

145

Down's Syndrome or whatever, who'd come in after work and raise a ruckus. Did we ever freak when they discovered us! But we learned that we were being ignorant and made some good friends. Now they have to go straight home in the rehab vans."

Dusty, so calm and steady, should have been dull as dishwater, but instead her wide-open enthusiasms were exciting. Paris could see why Elly would have grabbed her and never let go. She was like a good-looking favorite old jean jacket, a pillar who wouldn't fall no matter what the odds. And Paris could see that she'd wage a fierce battle if anyone tried to keep her down. Dusty restored her faith in her own future. Paris understood Venita's obvious crush on the woman.

Taking a stool, Dusty began to talk again. "That's when the Diner became a Special Olympics sponsor. We financed a trip up to New Avon. What great spirit that town had. We lost miserably, but had too good a time to mind. New Avon has programs coming out of their ears: MRDD, retraining, a clean air council."

Paris's interest was kindled. "Where is this place?"

"It's just a little burg in southwestern Massachusetts, another old river town. It's near Sturbridge Village."

"I've always wanted to see Sturbridge." She filed that for future reference. No one else had come up with a city Morton River could use as a model to lick its late-century malaise. "What time is your rally?" she asked.

"Two P.M.. They figure to catch mobs of

Christmas shoppers and give 'em a bad case of the guilts, then push petitions under their noses. The shoppers won't even have to part with spare change to feel better." Dusty lifted the round, see-through pastry cover and took out a frosted prune Danish.

"Petitions to whom?"

"Whoever's holding this Valley hostage. We were doing so good until Reagan's policies took hold."

Out of respect for Dusty's business sense, she leaned over the counter and whispered, "Do you go as a gay group?"

"Not officially." Dusty grabbed a napkin from a dispenser and wiped her mouth. "We're so unpopular no one'd be willing to ally themselves with us. Being flaming queers hasn't cured society yet."

"Even after all you've done for the Valley?"

"Hey, this is my home town. They let us be. I didn't do anything to win a popularity contest."

"Maybe you should have," she challenged.

Dusty rose again, face closed, stepped behind the register and broke open a roll of quarters. She looked up. Paris fully expected to be told to butt out. Instead, Dusty grinned. "So you're one of those go-get-'em libbers like Peg used to be," she said, teasing.

"Peg?" Paris said with surprise.

"Didn't she tell you about her checkered past? Her and Annie Heaphy and Victoria — Oh, I can't remember all of them. Even Elly was involved."

"In what?"

"You'd have to ask Peg. That was twenty years ago. I was still drinking through most of it. But they had a women's center and Peg was always dragging some libber in granny glasses to the bar. Got hitched to one of them for a while."

"I can't believe it."

"Take my word. Peg wasn't the firebrand some were, but her teacher's pay bankrolled more than one of their escapades for sure. Not me, though. I'm a businesswoman. Doing my bit just gets me the right to live here and run my business in peace."

Paris put a dollar on the counter. "On the house," Dusty said, pushing her hand away. "I like somebody to shoot the shit with. We'll see you at the rally tomorrow?"

"*We'll see* is the operative phrase," she answered, still reeling from the new image of Peg she had to digest. Maybe Peg would even appear at the rally, whistling along with "I Shall Overcome." She'd considered boycotting any project of Thor's, but now it sounded as if the whole community might be there.

All night she stewed about Thor, and had sweaty nightmares about him behind her on the disassembling steps. Come morning she decided she'd be more valuable on the barricades than sulking in her flat over the pizza parlor. She called Venita to see if she wanted a ride.

"Thanks, dear, but Thor called last night to tell me about it. He's arranged to have someone pick me up. There was no answer at your phone. I don't know why he didn't let me know sooner, I would've passed the word at the Center."

Some people are Vietnam veterans, some are disengaged yuppies, Paris considered herself a rally vet. Back at the U. of Texas she never had membership credentials in anything except the gay campus group, but she knew her value as a body. It was a skill she'd kept: showing up, yelling and singing, getting counted, swelling the ranks of the Against factions. She'd protested against racism and war, against Nixon and Reagan, against hunger and homelessness, against non-union grape growers and deforestation, against abortion law repeal, against queer-bashing and against cutting AIDS funding. Going to Thor's rally brought back the lightheaded excitement she always experienced along with her illusions of power.

Thor had done the job, she had to admit. By the time she got to the vast parking lot every kind of rattletrap stationwagon, gospel choir bus, business van, sedan and rusted-out pickup was letting people off. The morning freight train sounded as it passed across the highway.

It was sunny, but still cold enough at 2:00 pm for her to see her breath. Hands under her arms for warmth, she read signs for a while, a little uncomfortable at rattling around alone in this quiet, expectant throng. The gay crowd was unofficially bunching up on the fringes and she moved to join them. Elly hugged her, explaining that Rose had been left in charge of the Diner.

"How's that old Jeep behaving for you?" asked Louie. He was all decked out in tight K-Mart designer jeans. John's lanky body curved down toward him. Jimmy Kinh, with an armload of popcorn in paper bags, came loping across the lot from the Mini Cinema. A group of people she recognized slightly from the Sweatshop looked dazed, like this was their first demonstration.

149

Peg wasn't there, nor, as far as she could tell, were any of her closeted friends. But Maddy was. Her face was flushed as she steered a little gal in dreadlocks to meet Paris.

"*Paisan!* This is Tyna!" Maddy said breathlessly.

"You two look like you've been living in the Garden of Eden lately." It was true, their faces shone with a satisfied sensuality. They were careful not to touch but it was an obvious sacrifice. She envied them their newness.

"You the teacher?" Tyna asked.

Paris looked at Maddy who narrowed one eye and nodded. She was learning the signals already. Tyna knew she was gay. "I teach at the Center."

Tyna chattered. "You have to get us in up there. At Valley High the kids know something's going down with us. It's not that I'm scared, but —"

"But you're scared," Paris said. "If it's that bad — maybe you need to keep a lower profile at school."

"It's not too bad in some of the classes where we're split up," explained Maddy. "But in study hall, and in girls' gym?"

"You can't leave love in your locker," Tyna said wisely.

"Then confide in a safe teacher." She wanted to gather them up in her arms and protect them. "If the bullying starts you'll have someone to run to — and someone who'll know what's going on if you don't run fast enough."

"Oh, I can run all right," Tyna said.

"She's the fastest girl in school, won every race last year at field day, even against the seniors," bragged Maddy.

"Hush, you," Tyna said, shoving playfully at her. "But isn't there a way we could get out of there?"

"We shouldn't have to run," Maddy said. "We're not hurting anybody. One of these days I'm going to push Ruggiero's face in."

"Ruggierro?" she asked.

"This geek who used to be my best friend. Now I'm gay and he follows us around calling us names. If he gets one of us alone he gooses us or grabs at us."

Tyna nodded. "He's getting his friends to join in. What if they all —"

"You have to tell somebody," she said. "If you don't, I —"

"How can we? Then they'll tell our mothers and the real shit'll hit the fan."

They were caught between legitimate fears and she didn't know how to counsel them. Yet she was loath to see first love blow up in their faces.

Venita joined them wearing a perky royal blue hat not too different from Maddy's fedora. Paris asked if she'd heard of any progress on an alternative high school at the Center.

"So far the Center doesn't even know if it'll survive," Venita answered with her rapid-fire words. She looked twice at Maddy's lover. "I know you, child. Your mother's the student who —"

"She's at the college on a PELL grant. Honor roll every term!" exploded Tyna.

Venita explained. "Brilliant woman. She left school to have Tyna, then registered at the Center when you were, was it eight? Your mother can run circles around my math."

"She's going to be an engineer."

"Then," said Maddy, "when she has her own company she'll hire me as staff inventor."

"Two months in school," Paris teased, "and you've got a job?" She'd had a lover like Maddy once, a slight Peter Pan of a woman who thought she could do anything, and intended to.

Teasing didn't trip Maddy up. "I'm not letting some bunch of men manufacture my inventions." She looked over her shoulder and lowered her voice, curls catching the sun. "I'm working on this idea I had about solar sidewalk panels. Every house on a street could plug into them. You know, if you're cementing over the earth you might as well help the ecology."

Venita and Paris nodded solemnly. Dusty ambled over.

"Listen," Maddy said, looking around her again. "We hitched a ride with Peter down to that park again, Tyna and me." She moved as if to take Tyna's hand, but stopped herself. "They're still at it. They've got a road into the land now and survey markers all over. They've marked the trees that're going down. Peter's such a ding he showed us around and never guessed we were spying."

"Where's this?" asked Dusty.

Maddy went into a stage whisper. "The old hermit's property by Bromsberrow State Park."

Dusty frowned, crossing her arms. "They don't have the go-ahead on that yet. You mean they started construction?"

"Destruction is more what she means," Paris answered.

Dusty waved Elly over. Elly was brandishing a hand lettered sign: KEEP M.O.V.E. MOVIN! "They're

152

monkeying with our courting ground," Dusty told her lover. "That park'll be ruined if they build so close."

"Isn't anything sacred anymore?" asked Elly, slipping an arm through Dusty's. "Who's behind this?"

Dusty looked at Maddy. Maddy looked at Paris who sensed that it was a little much telling on Peter himself. "The developers," Paris supplied. "I spoke with a gentleman I suspect of being an investor and he seemed to feel the Zoning Board would approve it without any problem."

"Damn," Dusty said. "Do we have to fight for every little thing these days? Why does it feel like men are trying to gobble up the earth?"

Paris said, "I feel so helpless sometimes I want to stalk right out of this town. I'm hesitant to get active in the Land Trust — I'd be called an outside agitator."

"Which," said Venita, "would give them even more ammunition against the Center since we brought you here."

"Doesn't anybody besides us little people care about that land?" asked Elly.

"I care," Maddy said. Tyna had slipped her arm through Maddy's and they stood hip to hip, thigh to thigh, shoulder to shoulder.

"You're as impotent as the rest of us," Paris told her.

"Shit," said Maddy, "another word to look up." One-handed, so she wouldn't have to let go of Tyna, she pulled a slender dictionary from a deep pocket inside her jacket. "My English teacher says she'd give me an A if I make up all the work I missed plus add two hundred words to my vocabulary. Tyna's going to college so I'm going to get in too." She paged through the dictionary. "Impotent: weak, powerless, useless, feeble! No way! We'll stop them. I'll come up with something."

"That reminds me," said Paris. "I've got a couple of books over in Sugarplum I thought you'd like. She's unlocked."

"Our kind of books?"

"None other."

While Paris dashed to the Jeep and back for the books, Thor began his speech, a short one outlining the problems facing poor people in the Valley. He gave instructions about the petitions that were being handed out. Then he let Cousin Hell-and-Brimstone loose on the crowd. His loud exhortations rang across the lot and seemed to rise to the hills behind. When he told them to gather signatures, the rally broke up, protesters, Paris among them, racing to positions through the mall.

CHAPTER 11

When the Goddess and I plan my next life, Paris decided, *I'll check the box for a non-Christian country.*

Christmas in New England, she found, was everything the movies and the picture books promised except for large warm households taking in strays. And, except for rare patches remaining from a half-hearted storm the week before, snow. On Christmas Day in Morton River she found herself walking to the dam in a spitty drizzle just short of freezing with nothing for company but "Singing In The Rain" on her walkperson. She was not inspired.

Her parents had sent a gorgeous wool sweater from Peru and she was walking to test it. By the time she'd reached the dam she was still dry, warm and slightly more chipper than when she'd set out, enveloped by the smell of lanolin and soggy wool. Her brother's family was spending the holiday at her sister's, back in Austin, and she'd talked to all four nieces and nephews about the new cousins they were producing to extend the Collins clan. She rewarded herself with one See's chocolate per relative, since brother Don had sent the box. That had also done duty as breakfast. She'd crashed badly afterwards and spent the rest of the morning crying over her holiday cards.

Most of her old lovers sent them, and a few of her old students, and all of her old friends. She didn't want to be back in Montana or Wisconsin or northern California or South Dakota or Florida or Texas or anyplace else, but sometimes, like on Christmas Day, she missed having some kind of family she could see and touch.

Peg's invitation to Brockett Lake had been offhand, but had hit her as hard as a marriage proposal. She was not going to spend every holiday with the Jacobs. She was not going to fall into a liaison with Peg out of expedience. It would be all too easy to let that woman get to be a habit.

The river ignored Christmas, lazing along, deceptively placid as it approached the dam. It didn't even speed up until the last second. Then it quickened, rushed, surged over the embankment, and plunged into twisting, silvery ropes of water seeking their level or perhaps the excitement of the fall. Why did it rush to the churning cold ocean? There was no peace there, only movement and change, yet the vast agitated waters must feel like home.

As if water felt. She'd check that box too — mineral, not animal, so she wouldn't be constantly buffeted by conflicting emotions. What was she after, a feeling of home? So far home was pretty close to being a wave that slapped the shore over and over, happy in its agitation.

Directly across Railroad Avenue was one of the ubiquitous red brick factories. The upper windows were gaping, but the whole front of the structure, empty last time she'd been by, was now a used book shop. Instead of looking dingy in this foul weather, the bricks seemed to glow, all scrubbed up and housing a new venture.

She crossed and peered in the windows. Who'd been smart enough to think of this? Why, some other enterprising low capital business, maybe a used clothing store, could move in upstairs. All the way home her mind churned like the river with dreams of renovation and full occupancy. She wanted to buy some old building like that and make it a social hall for the Vietnamese students who said they had nowhere to do their kind of music, or for the Valley women who had nothing but a battered women's shelter for their own. The Learning Center could use an annex, for that matter, to teach car repair, or even vegetable gardening, survival skills for these days of runaway poverty.

She'd been dreaming so hard she hadn't noticed that, sweater or no, she was chilled to the bone. She was about to climb to her lonely lair when she noticed another glow a few blocks up. Was the Diner open today?

"Later for you," she told the cold, dripping iron steps. The Diner windows were so fogged that she couldn't tell until she was right on top of it whether the place was open or someone had left hot water running. Then she saw Dusty's shipshape old green Dodge Swinger parked up the street.

Inside the Diner Elly cried, "Merry Christmas!" Paris's glasses were full of steam, but she recognized Dusty, sprawled in a booth next to Elly. There were two other women she didn't know.

"You're open! And it smells like you're brewing vats of hot chocolate."

"Honey, don't say we forgot to tell you!" Elly's voice was horrified. "We always open up Christmas Day and serve free hot chocolate. Dusty and I both know what it's like to be alone today. Pluck off those headphones and join the human race. I want you to meet our best friends in the world. Gussie Brennan, Nan Heimer, this is Paris, that new teacher in town." Elly lowered her voice. "We're trying to influence her to settle in the Valley."

Paris slid her glasses halfway down her nose and could just barely make out two old women grinning at her, one half-raised in her seat to shake her hand. "You're just as pretty as Elly told us," said Gussie, with the gaze of a cruising dyke right out of *Beebo Brinker*. That look touched clear down to the soles of Paris's feet.

"This little town gets more and more interesting," she parried, holding Gussie's dry soft hand an extra second or two. She smiled at Nan. "I guess you discovered that long ago." Nan gave a shy grinning toothy nod. "Now that I think if it," Paris told Dusty and Elly, "I should've known you'd be here. You two are more reliable than heat in Texas."

"Hungry?" Elly asked. She'd been doodling on a napkin.

She confessed to her diet of See's.

"Sounds like you need a real breakfast, hold the chocolate," said Dusty, pushing herself up. Paris knew not to argue. The Diner door opened again.

"You started something, hon," Elly said.

Peg, of course — and with her hand on another woman's shoulder. "That's a first," Dusty muttered and stomped off toward the kitchen.

Elly arched her perfectly drawn eyebrows and said in a bristling voice, "I've never see her before." She'd admitted that she wasn't above matchmaking to keep Paris in town and now spoke as if Peg had no right to be parading strange women through the Diner. Paris could feel Gussie and Nan watching the whole scene. She heard Dusty smashing pots and pans as if to trumpet her disapproval. She broke eggs onto the grill, but Paris's stomach wasn't interested. Did she look like a jealous lover? Did she feel like one? She was mostly annoyed. Peg had, after all, invited her to the family get-together. Peg also had every right to all the lovers she wanted — except that she'd claimed celibacy. What was her game?

Peg steered the woman over. She was shorter than Paris, top-heavy, and wore a parka in one of those blindingly repellent new combinations of colors, fuchsia and violet. Paris felt dowdy in her hairy-looking brown wool and her navy watch cap.

The woman had bright red cheeks puffed around a smile.

"Jennifer!" the woman exclaimed by way of introduction.

"Hi, Nan, Gussie. Happy holiday, Paris," said Peg, her eyes as clear as she'd ever seen them. Paris gave her a grumpy smile. "We escaped from the family feast —"

"Right after apple pie!" Jennifer said.

Finishing each other's sentences already?

"And mince pie," added Peg.

"And plum pudding."

"How could I forget?" Peg patted her stomach, gently rotating her hand. Paris averted her eyes.

It looked like bringing her home for Thanksgiving had broken the ice for Peg. The sisters-in-law were probably complaining that they never knew who Margaret would drag to the family functions next, yet relieved it wasn't that brassy Texas tree-saver.

Before she could stop her mean-spirited peeved mouth she was asking, "Is Jennifer one of your *students?*"

"I'm older than that!" protested the girl, who looked no more than sixteen.

"No, no," chuckled Peg. She peeled off her tweed Chesterfield and hung it on a hook at the end of the booth, brushing off dreaded lint. "What are you to me?" she asked Jennifer with a teasing tone.

"Not half what I'd like to be," Jennifer teased back.

The little flirt.

"This is Brockett's daughter," Peg said, "the proverbial gay niece."

"And," Jennifer interrupted, hands encircling

Peg's arm and tugging, "this is the legendary gay auntie."

Peg laughed and shook the little twerp off. "They grow them up fast these days," she said and sat beside Paris in the booth, briefly covering her hand. Jennifer was abandoned to fend for herself. Gussie and Nan looked as relieved as Paris felt. She'd embarrassed herself by getting so bent out of shape.

"You look fine enough to be a Christmas present," Peg told her.

"After walking in the rain all morning? You are gallant," she replied and dug into her eggs and hash browns.

The Diner really started to fill up then, mostly with old singles and adolescents who couldn't wait to show off their new clothes or portable Nintendos. Two boys spent half an hour dunking new diving watches in glasses of water. Elly refused to serve them colas for fear they'd experiment on them too.

Christmas dinner at Dusty's Queen of Hearts Diner had obviously become a tradition for many people in downtown senior housing as well as for odds and ends of folks: a young couple whose stove had broken their first year together and who'd come back every Christmas since, hospital staff on lunch break, a cab driver, the guy who kept the paper store open Christmas morning, and a monosyllabic woman trucker named Jody who brought Dusty, Elly, Nan and Gussie presents from different parts of the country every year and ate in silence, averting her eyes and blushing every time she was addressed.

Venita arrived in a flurry, unpinning a dark hat with a long iridescent feather. "That family of mine," she exclaimed with breathy eagerness. "They didn't want to let me go. But I promised Elly I'd make it this year."

"Have you met Nan and Gussie? This is Venita," Elly said.

Once settled, Venita looked at Paris, a shy question in her eyes. "Right," whispered Paris under the general conversation. "They're not the marrying kind either." After that, she caught Venita staring at the women with interest.

Members of the softball team came in intent on loud horseplay. Three of Peg's closeted friends dropped by, two together, another, an extremely well-groomed woman with salt-and-pepper hair, lingering a while, engaging Paris in small talk. This was a family gathering, Paris thought, unable to stop smiling. When Peg and Jennifer got up to go she wanted to keep them. Gussie and Nan had asked Venita back to their house just across the river. Elly and Dusty were too busy to hang out. Paris felt like she was facing exile at the top of her stairs.

"Come to my flat for a while," she said to Peg, keeping her desperation under wraps. "You and your niece." The perfect chaperone.

Peg looked at Jennifer. "Excellent!" the niece said. "I like to see where other people live."

They got the Reverend Minister from the Z and walked up Railroad Avenue arm in arm, singing carols into the empty street, saluting the liquor store flag. The rain had stopped, but it felt much colder. She could see a car fishtail on ice around a curve. Jennifer clung close to Peg, pretending to slip on the sidewalk. Paris's mind raced ahead, planning hot cider, choosing a mug for Peg, getting a roll of toilet paper onto the spindle.

She handed her key to Peg and motioned the two of them to lead. Behind, she wouldn't have to hide her halting progress, or how she white-knuckled it all the way along the rail, waiting for the stairs to fall apart under her.

The steps had iced. "Careful!" she called.

She climbed tenuously, finding her footing on each coated rung. Halfway up the second flight the dog next door started to bark. The Reverend Minister about-faced, trying to pull Jennifer down the steps. Jennifer slid and slammed into Paris's arm. Paris lost her grip on the rail. She swung back from Jennifer, lost her footing and fell with all her weight hard on one knee on the next step down. She felt nothing but the pain for a minute, five minutes, an eternity? She tasted frozen iron, smelled her own perspiration through the woolen sweater. When she could see again, the sidewalk below looked closer than her pillow at midnight. She held back a scream, afraid to move a millimeter, shaking and hyperventilating.

Above Jennifer, Peg was crying, "Paris!"

Jennifer was still struggling to hold onto The Rev. The leash had Paris trapped against the rail. She couldn't straighten her leg. She heard a moan and clamped her lips closed before she realized that it had been a freight train moaning its way through town. She lifted her head. Peg grabbed the leash, handed Jennifer the key and hauled in on the dog. "Go to Jennifer, Rev," Peg ordered. "Up, up!"

They were alone on the steps. Paris felt as if

she'd narrowly escaped death. Now her mouth tasted like vomit. She swallowed, wanted to cry for a month, from the initial loneliness of the holiday, those warm lesbians at the Diner, her crazy jealousy around Peg, and her knee which she would have donated to science in a nanosecond right about then. "I'm fine," she said curtly. "I'm fine. Let's get inside." This was worst case scenario numero uno. How could she let Olympian Peg, who'd never shown a weakness in her life, see her now?

Peg's steady hands guided and supported her up the steps without pushing or squeezing. Lifting that knee each time was like setting it on fire. What if she'd done permanent damage? Oh, Goddess, she thought, too near tears to laugh: matching limps! Peg guided her to the couch. Jennifer came out of the bedroom with an old afghan, then disappeared into the kitchen. "I'll make tea!" she called back with that annoying exclamation point. At least she knew enough to take herself out of the way. Paris sat there listening to the last of the train whistle and getting over the shakes. Her little apartment had never felt so good.

Peg felt for her pulse. "I think you're in shock, darlin'," Peg said as she eased her onto her back and piled pillows at the foot of the couch. She relaxed into the familiar feel of her little home and wallowed in Peg's protectiveness.

When Peg helped her to swing her legs up, the right one made Paris cry out. "Let's see it," ordered Peg. The jeans were torn. Peg tried shoving the material up, but Paris gasped in pain again. "Just take down your jeans. You're covered with the blanket." That wasn't quite true — the afghan stitch was too loose for her to feel covered, but what else could she do? So there she was, completely helpless, lavender French cut bikinis for all the world to see. What did she care? Peg's solid arm was around her, hand soothing with caresses. "It's a grisly gash," Peg noted and asked Jennifer for first aid supplies.

Peg washed the open wound. Paris bit her lip and swallowed every whimper. As she bandaged the cut, Peg said, "I have to do this now and then for my students. You're a good patient." Peg smiled and leaned so close Paris could feel the heat of her. Those gray eyes were gentle and reassuring. Had Peg's own pain begun to leave them? "And you've got great legs."

That did it. She felt like the Morton River dam. The tears just exploded out.

"It's okay, Paris. It's okay," Peg said. She felt Peg motion Jennifer back to the kitchen. "It's going to be fine," Peg soothed. "That was a nasty blow. You're doing great."

"I'm sorry," she finally sputtered. Peg had produced her blindingly white handkerchief. "It's been a rough day."

"Christmas is like that. The tea is ready. Want it?"

She nodded. The Reverend Minister had sidled up so close to them she was leaning against the couch. Her mournful eyes seemed to apologize. "It's okay, Rev," she said. "I know you're just an old hound-dawg with no more sense than a politician."

Jennifer arrived with the tray. Paris sipped some tea, hot and aromatic. "Help yourself to chocolates."

"No," said Jennifer. "That ice cream sundae already wrapped an extra ten pounds around my hips!" She wandered off to the record collection. "You *really* like oldies, don't you?" she asked Paris.

The knee throbbed now. She still felt trembly all over. Glad of distraction, she said, "I grew up on big bands and forties jazz. It's all I heard at home."

"Can I play some of this stuff?"

So there she was not only with her pants off, reclined with Peg at her side, but a rap era kid was spinning discs of her magic music into an afternoon concert. Though she never wanted to move again, she felt too vulnerable. "I'd better get some more clothes on," she announced and tried to rise. She couldn't stop the wince.

"Slow down, girl. Tell me what you need." Her lisp was so endearing.

"I don't know. Maybe just another blanket."

"Do you want us to put you to bed? It's probably time we got back anyway."

"No!" she said too fast, too loud, too urgently.

Their eyes held. Peg fell to her knees. "Oh, Paris," she said, putting her arms around her.

"Whoa. It's just Christmas making me cry," she said, feeling absurdly safe in those arms. "It's just the fall shaking me up."

"Yes," Peg agreed quickly, holding her even tighter, her hands like magic wands lightly massaging her back.

Don't kiss me, she chanted in silence as she pressed against Peg's warm cheek. Jennifer, damn her, was playing "Embraceable You." Peg was so strong, so gentle. It was true, sometimes she longed for a comforting presence to lean on, longed to let down her own careful guard, to be taken care of.

Her tears stopped, but Peg held her anyway. She could hear Peg's ragged breath in her ear. "This must be hell on your pelvis," she whispered, her knee like pulsing flame.

"What pelvis?" Peg asked.

It took a while, but by staying perfectly still like that Paris finally got herself under control. " 'S Wonderful" came on and she laughed self-consciously. "The silliest song Gershwin ever wrote."

Peg disengaged. Paris saw her take a deep breath, as if relieved at a narrow escape. The concern in her eyes was gone and they looked more haunted than ever. Her amazing hair hadn't budged. "I'm sorry The Reverend Minister got so out of hand. I should have left her in the car."

"We didn't know the other dog would bark, or that the stairs would ice. If I hadn't been embarrassed to go up first I wouldn't have been an accident waiting to happen."

"Embarrassed?" asked Peg.

She took the deep breath this time and hid behind her hair. "I'm afraid of heights."

"Then why do you live here?" Peg asked, tender fingers pushing Paris's hair back.

She explained about the Center renting it for her, about the housing shortage. Peg shook her head and said, "So every day —"

"— at least once a day —"

"— you make that round trip petrified."

"It's good for me. I'll get over it this way."

"Maybe. Maybe you'll break a leg next time. Is the knee any better? I'd like to see if we've got more than a cut there. You might want an x-ray."

"You've got such good hands," she said as Peg twisted the knee just slightly back and forth, then bent it.

"Who knows?" Peg concluded about her examination. "See how it is tomorrow and think about getting it checked out." Peg managed to mask with her efficient bedside manner whatever feelings their intimacy had unearthed. "We really need to get back. You'd be welcome, you know."

She felt really helpless on that couch. "Let me try walking. I think I'm ready for a long nap, but I want to make sure I can hobble around here on my own later."

"It'll be pretty stiff." Peg pulled her up and she leaned on her to the kitchen, then took off on her own.

"That's one sore son-of-a-gun," she said, "but I'm okay now. "She made it back to the couch. "Are you going to see your dad today?"

"That's why we need to get back. We're due there at four for dinner with him."

Her heart fluttered, her mind said no, but her mouth said, "Will you give him a hug for me?"

That stripped the cool from Peg's face as she lit up like the only Christmas tree Paris would have that year. "I think I can manage that. He's asked for you. I told him you've got people of your own to see. Maybe you'll come back sometime?"

She remembered that scared feeling she'd had at the nursing home, the feeling that she was getting sucked in. It hadn't been much different from the fear on the stairs. What was the worst that could happen? No bones had been broken in either case. Maybe. "Sure."

Peg put her coat on. Jennifer tore herself away from the stereo. "I never realized how cool those old songs are."

It was so hard to let Peg go. For a very fleeting moment she wished Peg lived right here, with her. "Peg —"

"You need something?" Her hands reached out to Paris.

How about a home, companionship. "Have you ever been to New Avon?"

"I've been through it, why?"

"I hear it's a pretty together town. I'd like to talk with them about how they did it, maybe bring something back Morton River can use." Her shyness was another surprise to her this Christmas. "And I've never seen Old Sturbridge Village."

"Would you like company?"

"I'd have to arrange to be there on a Friday when people were available and it'd take a while to set up. Could you get a day off?"

"We could go up on a Thursday night."

There are such things as motel rooms with two beds, she reassured herself, shivering in the cold draft that hit her as the door closed behind Peg.

CHAPTER 12

"The x-rays," she said caustically, "show that I still have a knee." She'd called Peg to thank her for a bouquet. "The doctor prescribed anti-inflammatories and pain killers, but I didn't fill the prescriptions. Life is hard enough without muddying up the old gray matter."

On Peg's suggestion she began work with a chiropractor in New Haven who was all the rage with the local dykes. He'd found arthritis that had been in her knee before the fall, probably an old injury aggravated by immoderate working out. She'd likely have a permanent limp later in life. She kept her mouth shut about matching limps and parried with thin excuses Peg's offers to visit.

Almost two months had passed and she felt more stuck than ever. Her love life was mired in confusion, her job was threatened, and in the damp and cold her knee was such a misery she didn't even want to go out. One round trip a day on her stairway to heaven was bad enough. If this was middle age, she told Venita, no wonder so many people wanted to find the fountain of youth.

She'd kept putting off the trip to New Avon, feeling powerless to affect her own fate, much less the Center's. Finally, halfway through February, when it began to look as if she might be able to travel without an ice pack and a heating pad and could lay off her exercises for a day or two, she called New Avon for an appointment.

She chose a Friday at the start of a long weekend for her social debut, limping the Sweatshop gauntlet toward Jimmy O' at his station. He came running over.

"Jimmy Kinh told me you'd been hurt," he said, jutting a firm thick hand under her elbow. Leaning on other people, in every sense, upset her balance, but she was so glad for company, for the sound of the cue against the balls and the blender whirring behind the bar that she let him guide her onto a stool. "Peg's dog knocked you down?"

"It was a little more complicated than that. More like your Yankee winter sabotaging my steps."

"I've heard about your staircase. Did you ever think of using a rope ladder?" he joked. "It sounds easier."

"I'm getting rope burn just thinking about it," she said, swiveling her stool around to see who was there. Dina, a tall skinny chatterbox who was guaranteed to ask her out for the seventh time, was playing pool with the ever-present Maxie, but that was it for gays. "Who *are* all these people? They look straight."

"Are you kidding?" he asked. He whooshed canned whipped cream into her cappucino. "On week nights for the last month or so this spot has been turning into breeder city. They'd ruin it for the gay crowd, but weekends the hets pour out of the Valley for excitement and leave the place to us. Still, sometimes I want to put up signs. *NO displays of affection between breeders. NO staring.*"

She turned her back on them, comforted by being with one of her own for the first time in a while. "They can't help it. I think it's in their genes."

Jimmy O' laughed. "Some kind of sick craving for opposites?" He went to help Jimmy Kinh prepare sandwiches.

She lapped at her whipped cream, fretting about the approaching — limping — years when she wouldn't be able to indulge herself in this luxury of calories. That led her to thoughts of other kinds of lapping she might enjoy. It might not, she concluded, chuckling to herself, be a bad idea to have someone to lap in her life as she aged, just to keep her weight where she liked it.

She jumped when she felt a hand on her shoulder.

"Welcome to the social highlight of Morton River."

"Why, Thor Valerie. Don't you have to be up at the crack of dawn to save the world?" Even this late at night he looked fastidious in his choker-tight tie, suit jacket and shoes so highly polished dust would slide off them. He looked like a black Ken doll. He was so civil she tensed in wariness. And he still smelled of his pungent cologne. She wondered if straight women actually liked that odor.

He even laughed. "I've delegated saving the world. But only for tomorrow morning. I had a late meeting with the Board of Selectmen."

"I didn't notice anything in the paper about that."

"Once in a while I convince them to meet with me behind closed doors. I do have some influence with the disenfranchised voters." He looked her up and down. "What happened to your leg?"

"An angry crowd accused me of being white and middle class. I fell fleeing their censure."

He studied her face, then smiled. "Okay. You think I was hard on you. Don't take it personally and I won't apologize."

She shrugged. Why had he even come over?

"May I sit down?"

"If you're not planning to hit on me."

"I guess you're as up-front as they come. Don't worry, I'm not into converting white women of unnatural tendencies."

"I'll take that as an insult."

"That I'm not interested?"

"*That's* the best news I've had all night. No, your judgmental attitude about my natural tendencies."

He squirmed onto his stool. "I do want something from you."

She lapped at the last of the whipped cream. "Why aren't I surprised?"

"I need information about that little patch of land you set so much store by."

"That's the last thing I'd imagine you'd want information about."

"It occurred to me while I was talking to the alleged town fathers that I have no club to hold over their heads, nothing to make them listen."

"Except your constituents."

"They don't count for that much with those men," he said with sarcasm. "No, I need something that'll make them sit up and take notice. When I saw you tonight it occurred to me that the park may be just the little bomb I've been looking for."

The earth was no bomb, and damned if she'd be part of letting a man use it as one. "And what, as they say in the movies, do I get out of this?"

"You get to save your precious trees. If I play my cards right, you also get to keep Rafferty Center."

"Let's up the ante a bit."

"Hey, I'm not asking you to share your lily-white body with the enemy."

Anger spurted through her veins and out her mouth. "Someday someone's going to smack you right across the chops, you know that, Mr. Ego?"

He smiled again. It almost made him personable. "And you, Ms. Dyke, are a worthy adversary. What's your ante?"

"I don't care about statistics, but the town fathers are on the right track. The Center is a gold mine. Mr. Piccari is a fine office manager, but he has no vision. The Center needs to grow, not shut down. It keeps the spirit of this town going and it could do so much more."

"Like what?"

"I only know we can do something. I don't know what. That's what Venita was hoping for from you. Morton River is stuck. With a little prying it can get back on track."

"Or fall off into the river." A man passed and slapped Thor on the back. Thor turned to shake his hand like an incumbent politician certain of a win. "No, Ms. Collins, I think *you're* on the wrong track. That's been my thrust with M.O.V.E. If we can get our transit system operational again we can take people to training and jobs in Upton."

"And they'll be commuting half their lives, working down there, straining the daycare facilities. Not to mention the tax base Morton River's losing every time an employer chooses a larger city. You're giving away the town's biggest resource with your worker shuttle."

"Listen, Morton River's ready to *throw* these people away. At least I can help them live someplace with a slightly better quality of life than the big cities. And my plan is possible, I have a shot at getting those buses back. After all, the politicians have mothers. Old people were half the ridership."

"I guess they wrote that song for you."

"What song?"

" 'My Way.' "

He stood and straightened the tie that looked as though he'd recently checked it with a leveler. "I know this town a whole lot better than you. How long have you lived here?"

"Consultants make millions for their bird's-eye views. I've lived in a whole heap of towns like Morton River and seen them go under with more or thrive with less."

"I notice you're not living in any of them. What do you do, hit and run? Maybe your interference wasn't welcome elsewhere either."

She held her anger. This wasn't the first time she'd been accused of the same thing. It was true, she was mighty tenacious for a butterfly. "I'll tell you what. I've got appointments to meet with some folks up in New Avon the first week of April. You've probably read about what a great job they've done turning a ghost town into the seventh best small city for quality of living in America. I'm planning to pick their brains for ideas. Between now and then I'll keep my ears open for more dirt on Hermitage Park and I'll call you right after I get back. You can at least listen to what I come up with."

He pursed his lips in skepticism. "What does that give you, a little over a month? Okay. If I don't get any further with these crackers in that time I may be open to your input."

From the corner of her eye she followed Thor's progress to a rear table where a woman waited. The woman looked peeved.

"He's cute," said Jimmy O'.

"Maybe till you get to know him. He reminds me, if you'll excuse the expression, of an ambitious wasp, with a very sharp sting." Still, she appreciated Thor's challenge. She needed something she could sink her teeth into right now.

At the Scalas she felt like a spy. It would have been easier if, while chit-chatting with Giulia at the Diner, she could have gradually gleaned tidbits of information about the Park, but Giulia had no chit-chat in her. So she waited for another invitation to one of those maelstroms the Scalas called a meal. It came early in March.

"How's Peter's business going?" she asked before Maddy joined them.

Sophia served her a mound of kale beside a spicy-smelling steaming casserole. "Dragging the feet!" she complained before Giulia could say a word.

"Those Land Trust jerks," Giulia confirmed, her voice high and annoyed, "don't care about people. Now they say some bird will go extinct if the park is built. What are we supposed to do? Stop the world for some dumb bird?"

Paris held her tongue.

"How is a man supposed to make a living?" Giulia asked. "Mike's been talking to the politicians, trying to get the go-ahead, but they're telling him the deal is too hot right now. Wait till it's out of the papers and some other bird is endangered. Then they'll make their move, they promised."

Paris looked as innocent as she could. The main dish was rich with ricotta cheese. "How can they promise? Don't they have rules to go by?"

Giulia laughed. "The rule is, make money. At least Peter works hard for his. These politicians are so greedy for a handout they'll approve almost anything these days. When you're in a big prosperous city, with lots going on, you can make a mint in city hall. But here?"

She could have kicked Maddy for coming in at just that moment, but the girl dropped quietly into her seat, sulking. Giulia went on. "Peter's starting to talk about moving to Upton where there's more building."

"Make my day," grumbled Maddy.

Giulia squelched her with a look. "But his connections are here. It'd take years to start over down there."

"She," Sophia struggled for words, "wants much, my Giulia."

"Yeah," Maddy said, mashing kale into her casserole, "she's so ambitious she'd cut her own sister's throat to shut her up."

"That had nothing to do with Peter's plans," said Giulia quickly and viciously.

"Sure, sure," Maddy said, jabbing her fork into a cooked tomato. "Like he's so important his fiance's family has to be locked in the closet." Maddy turned to Paris. "You know Giulia's never even brought Peter's parents to visit? They won't be seen on the Hillside. And you say *I'm* ashamed of her," she accused Giulia, pointing her fork at Sophia.

Sophia blasted them in Italian. "Sorry," she apologized to Paris. "Fight, fight, fight!"

The table fell silent except for glasses thumping down and silverware grating against plates.

Paris plunged into the opening. "So whose palm *do* you grease around here? The mayor? The Board? The zoning people?"

Giulia offered seconds, set down the casserole cover with a clang and shook her head. "No. It's still got to be through Judge Malley. He's the one who ruled for Peter's family in the first place. You start involving too many of these politicians and they're all looking for a handout. They get you at the dinners, the luncheons, twisting your arm at a United Way, even a Land Trust fundraiser between the salad and the entree. That way no one sees them do anything wrong. It's all out there in the open. I've seen them at work when I've gone with Peter."

How could men live with themselves? "Then the judge passes his cut on to the politicians?"

"And to the loan officers." She looked at Paris, those deep brown eyes haughty but hesitant. "They're all crooks. I don't like doing it their way, but it's the only way. The American way."

Paris faked a laugh, but felt lunch lump in her stomach. No wonder Thor was so bitter. It would take an ego like his to assault the Valley's corruption. Sophia's eyes were following every exchange. "Was it like this in Italy?" she asked Sophia.

"Over there just as little gets done over the table."

Maddy leapt up and hugged Sophia. "You're so cute, Ma. You mean everything's done *under* the table."

"All the time now Maddalena studies," said Sophia, nodding, approving.

Maddy glanced at her over her pastry, a flake clinging to her chin. "Tyna says it's my only ticket out. I'll get trained, move far away and send for Mama and Tyna. I'm not leaving her in that one's hands," she said, pointing her pastry at Giulia.

"Cut it out, Maddy," Giulia said. "She was bad for you."

Maddy's voice was heavy, full of choked tears. "Tyna was the friend I always wanted."

Paris felt herself go alert, like an animal in danger. What had happened to Tyna? Maddy said, "She's awesome. Also, smart and pretty. She'll go far,

179

you'll see. Tyna's got more brains in one earlobe than your Peter'll ever have."

"And you had intellectual discussions in your bedroom all night long?"

"Yeah. We did. I shoulda taped them?"

"I heard enough."

"Shut up!" cried Sophia. "This is not company talk."

"Sure it is, Mama." Maddy hit her knees with her fists. "Paris knows the facts of life. What do you think of a sister who rats to her best friend's mother? Tells her all kinds of stuff moms have to be protected from? Mrs. Lewis used her aunt's address to put Tyna in school in New Haven so we can't hang out any more."

"A white friend is better, yes?" Sophia asked Paris.

So Giulia was telling Sophia she objected to Tyna's race. Paris wasn't going to tackle that can of worms in front of the whole family, but she couldn't watch them paralyze a gay child.

"It was just something you went through. You'll forget all about it," Giulia said. She got up to clear the table.

Paris helped to dry the dishes, then said goodbye.

The world outside was still with cottony snow clouds against a white sky. She shoved her mittened hands deep into the pockets of her wool sweater. The dampness made her knee ache deep inside. As she'd expected, Maddy followed her to the Jeep. She handed back the books Paris had loaned her.

"Thanks," Maddy said. "I never knew there were books like these. I really liked *Patience and Sarah.*"

"Not *Happy Endings Are All Alike?*"

"It was def. Like real life." She watched Paris pull herself into Sugarplum. "What happened to your leg?" Maddy asked, jumping on and off the running board as she talked, like a boxer warming up.

"My steps were icy."

"It's dangerous living up there. Why don't you and me get an apartment? I could get a job and pull my load. Spring is almost here. I'll bet I could land a job with a landscaper, digging holes or something."

"Whoa, Maddy, that wouldn't help, believe me. I'd be arrested for fooling with a minor before you'd moved in your first teddy bear."

"How do you know about my bears?"

She started Sugarplum. "We all have bears."

"Even you?"

"One or two."

"Can I bring mine to meet them?" Maddy's eyes were beseeching.

Poor needy kid. The world was stomping on her love life now. "We could go to the park again. Take the bears with us."

"No way. Someone might see us. I don't want more hassles. I can hear the kids now: *Scala's queer for bears too!*" She clung to Paris's door, head down, swallowing tears until she was red-faced. "Can't you talk Tyna's mom out of it, Paris? Tyna changed schools Monday and I don't know if I can hack it at Valley High another minute. I thought it was bad when the two of us were there together, and now, by my lonesome, I might as well be a walking pink triangle."

"Do you get to see Tyna at all?"

"No." It was an angry shout. "I got a letter from her through a little kid on his bike. That's how I found out what happened. She's grounded when she's in the Valley. The only thing she's allowed to do is Girl Scouts. I'm thinking about joining up. At least we'd be together a couple hours a week."

The tears in those tough, hurt dyke eyes were so sad Paris wanted to cry too. "Maddy, I don't know what I can do that won't make it worse. You don't want to hear this, but time is on your side. Things will ease up as you get older. And I've got to get to class."

"*If* I get older. I've got to get out of this town. I know! I'll hotwire that CAT at the hermit's land and drive it to New York. That'll keep them from tearing down the woods a little longer and give me wheels. I'll be outta here before they know what hit them."

"Right, Maddy. The cops will look the other way when they see a sixteen-year-old girl, who's probably been reported missing, on a CAT on the New England Thruway."

Maddy jumped off and ran toward the house as the first snow flakes drifted down. "I'm going to do something!" she yelled with baby dyke bravado, fists in the air. "I'll make Giulia Scala sorry she was ever alive. And none of you will ever see me again."

CHAPTER 13

During the first few days of April Paris felt as if winter would never end. The land was bleak and lifeless, the river black-grey and monotonous, the sky laden with stagnant clouds. She couldn't get warm no matter how far she walked, or how close she snuggled to a heater. Spring seemed like a myth, a false promise someone had made to a world locked in everlasting doldrums. She'd do about anything for a glimpse of sun or a change and was ready for the trip to New Avon, even anxious for its dangers.

Still, packing for the trip was a new height in

the scatters for her. She put her toothbrush in her backpack, turned around, folded a blouse, then tried to find her toothbrush again. When she'd finished emptying the backpack a second time she knew with certainty what a big deal a weekend with Peg was for her.

Venita stopped by and Paris assailed her with hypothetical situations. Would the motel have a pool? If so, should she walk around in her bathing suit in front of Peg? Should she wear makeup to dinner? What would move the woman's hands to touch her? What would send them scurrying into pockets?

"Young woman," Venita said in her clearest, most dignified schoolteacher voice, "your future isn't being decided this weekend. Why this fussing over a little pleasure jaunt?"

"I'm *not* fussing."

"It must be because you haven't let yourself have a girlfriend for so long."

"You should be my model, Venita. You've been celibate all your life. What am I carrying on for?"

"It may have to do with the flowers."

Peg had sent yet another bouquet, this time early daffodils, with a card saying she was looking forward to the trip. "She says she's not interested."

Venita had only smiled and, slicing another piece of Sarah Lee German chocolate cake, murmured, "Your frenzy is really quite appealing. Did you know that Nan Heimer, the woman I met at Christmas, didn't become gay until a few years ago?"

Paris was too distracted by her dilemma to answer.

When Thursday came Peg picked her up right

from the Center at 7:00 pm. Peg put her overnight pack in the trunk with a fate-sealing thunk.

"You're sure you don't want to take the Jeep? It's convertible, remember," Paris teased, though her palms were too sweaty to maneuver a steering wheel.

Peg laughed, her eyes as clear as they'd been when Peg and Jennifer had come to the Diner on Christmas Day. "I'd rather travel in a World War One tank."

"Humph," she said, stowing her small pack behind the seat. "Where's the Rev?"

"Ned took her for the weekend. She gets along real well with his spaniel. She'd be uncomfortable in the Z on a long trip. And the motel didn't want pets. You, however," Peg added, caressing Paris's hair in a way that made her shiver again, "anybody would want."

As they zipped onto Route 8 Paris felt like she'd pulled the cord on her parachute. Winter was no longer a vile season, but sharp and chill, giving her shivers like excitement, its long nights dark to hold that many more mysteries.

Peg wore a white down vest over a plaid Pendleton shirt and Levi cords, with impeccably clean white sneakers. Where she'd originally been amused at Peg's old-fashioned neatness, now the sight brought a very pleasant tingle to Paris's more sensitive parts. She'd stayed in her teaching clothes and felt frumpy — they were friends, that was all — but Peg's compliment, and the flowers, and her own sense of anticipation, confused her.

No wonder her level of anxiety was still major.

She couldn't think of a thing to say as the Z hummed through the dark north along the Morton River. "It's so kind of you to drive," she murmured, letting herself doze. When she woke they'd stopped. Neon light flooded the car. She looked sleepily at Peg.

Peg walked around to open the door. She grinned. "I thought you might like to see another landmark diner." She offered a hand to Paris and drew her up from the bucket seat.

The Olympic Diner was larger than Dusty's, newer yet shabbier, not as snug and a great deal noisier. "This is the seedy old Berlin Turnpike — motel row," Peg explained, leading her in by the elbow. "When I was a kid it was the main drag to Massachusetts. I always wanted to stop at this shiny, busy hotspot, but the Jacobs didn't go to diners, don't you know."

Once in a booth Peg laid two neat rows of quarters on the table and used the first to punch in every Supremes record in the directory. She offered Paris the second row.

Paris didn't need the kind of stimulus her kind of music would provide. "Yankee jukeboxes don't have my kind of music. There's nowhere backwater enough to want to hear the old oldies around here."

"Not true," Peg said, flipping cards and jabbing numbers for Sinatra tunes.

As Paris's sleepiness abated she could see that Peg was barely containing her excitement. Was this trip also a big deal for her?

"Yah?" asked the waitress, a scrawny officious woman who scowled at the dark window, never meeting their eyes.

"Breakfast for two," said Peg. The waitress kept staring at the window as she wrote the order. After she turned away they both peered into the darkness.

"Nothing but a parking lot," Paris said.

"Maybe it's her dream screen," Peg suggested. "Knights on white horses."

"Actors in Rolls Royces."

"She's definitely not dreaming of dykes in Datsuns," Peg concluded.

They laughed and exchanged stories about their fellow teachers. The waitress brought plates of eggs and fries and toast, then ice cream sundaes. All that food, and the laughter, delighted Paris. She was immune even to Sinatra's "All Or Nothing At All." By the time Peg got the hiccups Paris had let her guard way, way down. She'd certainly never started a relationship by being this silly, therefore she couldn't be starting a relationship now.

Peg hiccupped all the way to the car, then was fine until they reached Massachusetts. The state welcomed them with a gun control sign. "You'd better chuck your six-shooter out the window," Peg joked, and the hiccups began again. "I'm glad *you're* enjoying it." Her tone was aggrieved, but she smiled.

"To think," Paris said, "perfect Peg Jacob, not a hair out of place, her lifelong major cool betrayed by her body."

"Her glottis, to be exact," Peg hiccupped, covering her mouth.

"It figures you'd even know what causes hiccups, Doc."

"A lot of good it does me."

Paris was so reassured by their laughter that she forgot to worry about what would happen next when they pulled into the motel lot. The row of room lights made it look cozy and safe, under a canopy of pungent pines. Peg unlocked their room door and Paris threw herself across the nearest bed. The room was fairly large and had the cardboard, unsettled smell of motels.

"Excuse me," Peg said, dropping her bag and collapsing beside Paris. "Don't you know the butch always sleeps on the outside?" This close, Paris could smell a very faint spicy cologne. Peg's eyes were tender and amused, then nervous-looking, then in control again. Her proximity, the nearness of those idle hands, threatened to sober Paris right up.

Keep talking, Paris told herself. "Are you still playing that butch game?"

"It's no game."

"In that case, is it chivalrous of you to make me move? I'm so wiped I may pass out any second."

Peg propped herself up on an elbow way too close for Paris's comfort. "And if a large bear comes to the door during the night, darlin', then what? This is the country."

She didn't move away. She could feel herself trying to draw breath, watching the hand whose silver and onyx pinky ring was as constant as the delicate blue veins. "Not only are you fossil enough to believe in femmes, you think femmes are dumb. I'd lock myself in the bathroom, of course."

"And leave me out here?" Peg asked.

She reached to feel Peg's bicep. "You butch, me femme?" She loved it when Peg smiled into her eyes like that, but grabbed her hand back when she felt the telltale tingle. "Okay, okay," Paris said, rolling to a standing position and amazed at herself for doing it. "You sleep near the door and protect me. Imagine," she teased, "for the first time in my life I'm going to get a carefree night's sleep. I wish I'd known about you butches years ago."

In the morning Peg's travel alarm woke Paris from somewhere centuries inside herself and nowhere near any stairs. Had she really felt safer with Peg around? Was there a part of her that believed in this butch nonsense? She expected Peg to go off on her own after that, but she stayed near all day long, making Paris laugh, pointing out old New England architecture.

Despite Peg's nervous eyes and her own reluctance, this weekend kept all the airy excitement of a true beginning. She loved really getting to know someone new, loved the point at which a woman can't be read yet, was still unpredictable. It made every decision, every comment, just a little bit risky. Being Paris Collins, Adult Ed Teacher, in front of Peg Jacob wasn't so much uncomfortable as challenging.

The temperature was in the high forties, almost springlike at last. Peg wore a trench coat with slash pockets over a loose-fitting suit with no vest. Paris would have spotted her for a dyke in a second, and the two of them as a couple, but they didn't seem to ruffle anyone's feathers as they explored New Avon. It was larger than Morton River, though only slightly, and flatter. Small working dairies surrounded the industrial center. They visited the branch of the local community college that had set up shop in an abandoned shoe factory — how unique, Paris commented to hide her envy — and talked with the adult ed people at the local school system that supplemented what the college offered.

From there they went to a liaison who coordinated referrals from social service agencies and the school system to the programs. Her office was in City Hall, a beautifully ornate classic of white granite, sandblasted clean on the town square.

"Welcome!" said the liaison. "I'm Trixie Onofrio."

Her desk sat before a huge arched fanlight window. The room was cold, though they could hear the old heating system labor in the walls. The woman, in contrast, was warm and welcoming. Stocky, she wore plain brown slacks with a yellow v-neck sweater over a checked blouse. When Paris introduced Peg she tapped her large desk with an eraser.

"I thought you looked familiar, Dr. Jacob. I started out in P.E.," said Trixie, both hands clasping Peg's a little too long. "Didn't you teach a course at Springfield College in geriatric recreation?"

"Under great pressure," Peg answered smoothly. There was a confidence to her professional persona which impressed Paris. "I was already teaching high school full-time and trying to finish my thesis."

"You were brilliant. My, uh, housemate was so inspired she specialized in it. Now she's a consultant in the subject. Always running to Beacon Hill to talk to some committee on senior citizens."

This was another side of Peg that surprised Paris. Peg nodded her modest thanks and pulled her hands away. Paris wanted to hold one, demonstrate possession somehow. "It's always been a special area for me, but there's nothing like that where we live. I'm not built to fight city hall for money."

"I understand that's exactly what you want to do, Paris," said Trixie.

Paris smiled and turned on her accent to its broadest. She wanted to win Trixie over and even more, she wanted to do it in front of Peg to prove her disinterest in Peg. "I'm here to pick your brain if you'll let me. I don't have any hopes of getting a coordinator like you into Morton River Valley. All I want to do is save what we have. And I think the key is in expansion."

"You're absolutely right. Don't limit yourself to the status quo. I did that for too long. Think big, talk big and the pols will treat you like you are big. Why not a liaison person? My job saves us tens of thousands in duplication of services. With someone who has an overview you can plan more efficiently. And you can attack in strength. I'm this town's best political activist and they pay me to rattle their cages. Pay me to shake money loose from their pockets."

All afternoon Trixie regaled them with tales of her battles with the city government. She showed them statistics on costs, savings and growth. She taught Paris the language the politicians spoke and the way their minds worked.

"Sounds like I have to stop expecting that there'll be even one understanding person among the powers that be," Paris concluded. She'd been reminding herself all afternoon not to get wrapped up in Morton River's solutions. "I'm just the messenger," she explained to Trixie, who'd exchanged glances

191

with Peg. Out the arched windows the sun headed for the hills.

Trixie switched on another lamp. "I can't count on anyone but myself and my staff. I'm in charge of preserving the bureaucratic life that provides the services."

Paris looked at Peg. "I can't let Morton River depend on me. When I go they'll be back where they started from."

Trixie asked, "Where are you going?"

"Somewhere else. I'm not a permanent settler."

"You don't like Morton River?"

She'd never asked herself that question. "I do. I like it very much, but I make it a habit to move on every couple of years."

"How awful," Trixie said, then stopped herself. "I'm sorry. I'm such a hometown girl I can't imagine anyone living like a nomad." Trixie looked at Peg. "Can you?"

"There's nothing I hate worse than filling out change-of-address cards," Peg answered.

"I'm not saying I still like it," Paris said, feeling defensive. "I —" Did she still like it? Did she like it as much as she liked the Valley? "In any case," she went on, "it sounds as if I should expect the holders of the purse strings to be pretty dense."

"Send them up here for a field trip. I'll see if I can get a motel to donate rooms and give them a fancy meal or two. We'll show them how it gets done."

"Speaking of fancy spreads, where's the best restaurant around here?" asked Peg, rising and perching on the edge of Trixie's desk.

Trixie tapped her eraser and thought for a

minute. "Some of the fanciest-looking eateries are microwave city. I wouldn't miss the Publick House." She looked at her watch. "Especially if you get there before the bakery closes. The best peanut butter cookies anywhere."

Paris laughed. "That's a mighty strange referral for a New Avon booster."

"My, uh, housemate and I treat ourselves up there regularly." Trixie went to her window and pointed south. "Now, New Avon can offer you the best Italian food in Massachusetts." She looked at Peg. "Except, of course, for Ciro and Sal's in, uh, Provincetown."

This otherwise articulate woman was having such a hard time signaling them Paris wished she'd worn her double women's symbol necklace, though it probably would have freaked Trixie totally. She'd been around closets enough to know that covert communication can be more comfortable than a good healthy dose of honesty.

Peg saved the woman's day. "Great restaurant," was all she said with words, but Paris saw the way she lifted her eyebrow, the conspiratorial tilt of her head, the half-smile and half-wink that were punctuation to her silent lesbian sentence. She'd seen Maddy use the same facial language. She'd never thought of it as a butch thing before, but they seemed born to know how to do it. There was certainly something inexplicably exciting about it.

Trixie could have beamed in acknowledgment, but that wasn't in their dictionary. She sucked in her cheeks and nodded, returning Peg's gaze from the corner of her eyes. It had all taken no more than a few seconds. "Follow the railroad tracks toward

Sturbridge," Trixie went on, as if she hadn't just exchanged life stories with Peg. "Take a right at the Hillside Spa and you'll see a dinky little edifice two blocks down." She tapped her fist on the window. "I'll warn you, though, if you go for dinner, eat a light lunch."

Since they'd skipped lunch they stopped at the Italian restaurant in New Avon on the way to the motel. It was standard fare inside, with huge murals of Italian hillsides and Roman columns decorating the walls and curtains drawn against the plebian world of New Avon. The smell, though, was of garlicked tomato sauce and frying peppers. They were the first diners. As they ate they entertained themselves with conjectures about Trixie's life and, uh, housemate.

"That hashhouse, darlin', is worth a trip back," Peg said as she held the door for Paris and they emerged into the just dark streets of New Avon.

"Not this weekend!" she protested. "I'm not sure you could stuff me into your car." She figured all this eating was a sign of sublimation. Could she keep it up?

The temperature seemed to have risen. Peg was eyeing her body. "With your shape? You can afford dozens of meals like that one. How about a walk?"

Paris put her faint-hearted hand in her pocket as they walked, but Peg drew it out and tucked it under her arm. Paris hadn't realized how hungry she'd been for touch.

One-story bungalows, windows shrouded in plastic, crowded the first street they walked. At the corner they ran out of sidewalk and veered around a partially dismantled Toyota on blocks. Three-family houses had five or six mailboxes hanging on their front porches. A shutter dangled from a once respectable colonial. Then they were on a main road obviously evolved generations ago to connect New Avon and Sturbridge. Several children stood bunched outside an old movie theater.

"*Bedknobs and Broomsticks,*" Peg read.

"Disney! I love it!"

Peg looked surprised and a little disapproving.

"This film is ancient," Paris explained, "early seventies at least."

"We really must be in the boondocks. Can't people rent it on video?"

"That's not half as much fun. It's a silly classic. Come on," she urged. It was better than the temptation waiting back at the motel. "This is one of the silliest weekends of my life to date. Don't poop out on me now." The children had gone in.

Peg sat, hands steepled, until the bed took flight and then she barked out her first laugh. By the time the armored knights took on the Nazis she was cheering with the kids. Paris was pleased and annoyed — this woman passed every test.

At the motel Peg read the *New York Times* and a local paper while Paris read a science fiction paperback. She felt like part of an old married couple in her separate double bed and basked in a harmony of energies she'd never felt before. Passion was some has-been actress playing in another theater. Or waiting to make her comeback.

The next morning the sun poured warmth into the streets that just a few days before had been wintry. Spring leapt into Sturbridge Village like a chorus line of pastel-clad dancers. A soft April rain had come in the night before on a warming wind. All of a sudden the tips of crocuses poked up through the ground and green grass returned to the world. On the forsythia bushes were noticeable buds. Jays loudly scolded at the tops of thawed trees. Iridescent starlings rasped at one another over food. She felt dizzy with the balminess of noon. Had the Goddess set the stage for them, wondered Paris.

They rolled along a dirt path in a cart, their feet resting on hay, alone except for the driver, horses and a het couple who were way up on the front seat. It was a time to hold hands, to look into eyes, to bask in the romantic perfection of the day, to lay her head on Peg's shoulder, the world smelling of sweet warm hay. She didn't. They climbed off the cart and meandered from exhibit to exhibit. Neither of them said a word for half an hour. A bonneted woman churned butter.

"So," she said, afraid to break the mood, afraid not to. She tried to read Peg's eyes behind her sunglasses. "Who wore the bonnet back then? The butch or the femme?"

"Please, darlin'," Peg answered, lifting her hands as if to a bonnet. "Picture it."

"You're so true to type," she said with a laugh. "You'd look ridiculous. That doesn't mean I'd be a knockout in a bonnet."

Peg turned and measured her head, her face, with her eyes. There was such mute affection in them she wanted to be looked at like that forever. "But you would be, Paris," Peg said.

She sighed. Where was the strife with this one? When they added sex would it come? She caught herself. *If* — not when. They moved outside.

"I'd like two female goats when I retire," said Peg, arms folded across the top of a fence. The sheep had backed off, but a lamb bolted from its mom and returned again, curious and scared of the two-leggeds. The warm sun heightened the less pleasant barnyard smells.

"Not a couple of these woolly little things?"

"They don't stay little. And they're not very companionable when they grow up," Peg answered, bending to stroke the black wet nose poking through the fence. "Goats are feisty and loving and funny."

Were those the qualities of a woman who could land Peg? Never mind, she told herself, she didn't want to know. The cart returned with a larger load. The horses clomped off and three families headed for the lambs, children filling the air with noise. Paris and Peg followed the cart back. A tinsmith assembled a lantern. A spinner spun sour-smelling wool with a drop spindle. A cooper up to his ankles in nose-tickling sawdust finished up a wooden bucket and handed it to them to examine. They stopped in the general store and bought penny candies. In her cavalier style, Peg offered a white bag of Boston Baked Beans.

"These could be addictive!" said Paris cracking open a handful of the sweet nutty bits.

"Never had them before?"

She looked at this real Yankee in her life and tingled again. Today, she just wanted to give in. She wanted to feel the falling in love that was going on inside her, not block it. They reached the parking lot.

She sorted through her bag and carefully set all the licorice jelly beans in the palm of Peg's hand, one by one. Peg smiled endlessly at her. The sweets, the Datsun's sweltering interior, made her sleepy. At the room she lay on her bed and watched Peg through half-open eyes. "I hate to waste the last afternoon of vacation napping." She let her eyes close and went out like the proverbial light.

"Paris." She was so groggy she couldn't open her eyes. "Paris." Peg's hand firmly gripped her shoulder.

She didn't want the hand to leave. "Mmmm. Peg," she said. She felt the sweet smile wash over her whole body and soul.

"You looked so peaceful, I decided to try it," Peg said. "We slept for an hour." Peg stretched and yawned, her shirt drawing tight over her chest. For once she wasn't wearing a vest, jacket or sweater. A current coursed along Paris's spine and goosebumps rose on her arms. Breasts, the woman had much more substantial breasts than she would have imagined. The nipples poked against her shirt like that little lamb's nose through the fence. "We've got reservations for 6:00 P.M."

When Peg finished in the bathroom Paris bent over the sink, splashing cold water on her face. She smelled Peg's minty toothpaste. She couldn't banish the sight of those breasts from her memory. Her hands hankered after their warm curves.

She looked in the mirror. "The woman doesn't want you," she told herself, wishing she'd brought a lighter shade of lipstick.

There was something about applying makeup that felt like a rite of spring, and she hesitated, tremulous with fear and excitement. It was a rite she loved, even when, like this evening, it felt dangerous. Every stroke of mascara seemed to draw the night in around her like a glamorous black velvet cloak. The song "How Long Has This Been Going On" took up residence in her head. She'd brought her grandmother's tiny gold locket to go with her opal ring and they gleamed in the mirror as she worked on her lips. She dabbed rose essence behind her ears, at the base of her neck, thought of other places. But they were running late. And that wouldn't be necessary: "The woman doesn't want you, Paris." That wasn't how it felt.

The Publick House in Sturbridge was vibrant with activity even this early in the season. The personnel all wore costumes. A young Pilgrim led them to a booth. Peg stepped behind Paris to help her off with her wool sweater.

"Oh," she said, surprised. She smiled her delight at Peg. "No closets tonight?"

When Peg took off her white down vest Paris's heart stopped beating. She'd thought that never really happened until that moment. It was the Gershwin tune "Love Walked In" come to life. The tie was narrow, plum-colored and lay flat against Peg's pale yellow shirt as if she didn't have those breasts under there. But Paris knew she did, and noted how the tie lay, long and silky, exactly between them. When her heart started again it was with a thud. She wanted to stroke Peg's vest. Untie the tie with her lips and teeth. A hand in a pocket of those soft corduroy slacks, Peg was obviously waiting for her to sit first, but Paris couldn't move.

When she met Peg's eyes she knew the clothing was no mistake. Here was the lesbian Peg at her full sexual power, the woman who knew what she could give, willing to risk what she'd get. "You *are* Peg?" she asked aloud.

"Of course."

"How long has this been going on?" she sang, just softly enough that Peg raised one of those butchy eyebrows at her.

"Beg pardon?" Peg asked, handing her into the booth.

She sat, hoping Peg wouldn't notice the perspiration along her hairline. She couldn't *stand* their pseudo-courtship another second. What was wrong with her, with Peg? Was it a human trait to do exactly what one swore one wouldn't, didn't want to do? Or was it a lesbian trait, some kind of internal homophobia that insured self-destructive behavior — or happiness.

"You're lovely in makeup," Peg said.

"You're lovely in a tie."

Peg ran her tongue thoughtfully back and forth along her bottom lip. The lines to either side of her mouth deepened. She was so incredibly good-looking. Paris had known that all along, but it hadn't entered her solar plexus before; she hadn't been this profoundly physically affected by a woman since her first lover.

Had Angela been what Peg could call butch? As seniors in high school they'd borrowed each other's makeup, fixed each other's hair, smoked pot with college boys and caught all the arty films in Austin. They'd discovered the art galleries and scoured the newspapers for openings where they'd cop free wine and mingle with the adults, telling extravagant tales of fantastic adventures. Then they'd go parking with each other, not with the boys. Her fingers had been so eager to reach under Angela's dress and touch those drenched lips, slide up that silken canal. She could still feel Angela's hot mouth nipping at her neck.

She wanted to finger Peg's tie as she had Angela's genitals, smooth it against that valley of her breasts, slide the knot aside until she broke the plum circle, opened the butch gate, got at the woman inside.

The wine waiter hovered. "You don't seem to be much of a drinker," Peg said.

She could taste the wine of her days with Angela. She laughed. "No. It was always superfluous."

Peg was watching her eyes, and didn't ask superfluous to what. As if measuring the moment, as if deciding for or against the distraction of wine, Peg tapped her fingers on the table. She waved the waiter away.

Almost immediately someone in a gray starched colonial-style skirt brought a basket of hot breads, sweet and yeasty-smelling. Sounds became hushed. Peg's manicured hands broke open a coarse piece of cornbread. The crumbs fell to her plate. She slid butter across the opening. Paris fondled the baking powder biscuits, pulled a hot cinnamon bun from the basket. Peg bit into her golden bread, licked her lips of butter and crumbs. Paris's roll was sticky, crunchy with bits of nuts, full of hot cinnamon and sugar.

She offered Peg a bite. Peg held the cornbread out to Paris. They leaned across the table, eyes locked, and broke pieces off with their lips.

"Sweet," Paris said, closing her eyes. It tasted like the yellow afternoon.

"Sweeter," Peg said, pulling a stray nut from her lower lip with her tongue.

She ran her eyes down Peg's tie again, back up to her shining eyes, her perfect hair. Just then she would have sold state secrets to get her hands in that hair.

Even without wine dinner got fuzzy. It seemed as if they went from bread directly to the chilly parking lot. The bakery and gift shop were open late for the weekend. Peg got them a batch of the famous peanut butter cookies. She took Peg's arm this time and huddled against her, shivering.

"Cold?" Peg asked.

She squeezed tighter against her. "No." Peg's hand encircled her upper arm.

They walked up the dark country lane that led to their motel, the white bakery box which Peg carried by its string glowing as it swung back and forth. Paris ignored the ache in her knee. This was no time for pain.

"Crickets," Peg said.

"Tree frogs," she answered.

Their footsteps were almost the only other sound. Still leafless elm trees met over their heads, a branch creaking now and then in a breeze. She wanted the lane never to end. Peg stopped, guided her by the shoulder until they faced. She pressed her cheek to the front of Peg's cushioned vest. The top of her head met Peg's jaw. Her fingertips tingled with want.

Oh, Goddess. Peg pulled her face up with two soft fingers and their mouths met, open, hot, wet, breath ragged, then met again, until Peg's hand wide open against her back led her forward again. They walked faster.

"What are we doing?" Peg cried, when they got inside. The blood rushing through Paris's body all but drowned out the words.

She had Peg's tie in her hands, looking her full in those commanding, desiring eyes. She pulled at the tie, stroked it, separated the two ends. Kissed the valley of Peg's breasts, spread the tie further apart, wanting Peg's legs spread soon. She twined the tie around her hands, opened buttons. Peg stopped her, began to loosen the plum strands.

"No!" she wanted the undoing of her tie for herself. She pushed Peg to the bed, pulled off her vest, undid the buttons of her collar, pulled the shirt out from under her tie and off along with the vest. Her vision had become unfocused, but she made out Peg's breast-hugging short-sleeved undershirt. She pulled it over the tie. "Now," she said and began easing the knot down with one hand, kissing Peg's neck as she did.

"You've still got your sweater on," Peg said.

"Is it scratchy?"

Peg rubbed her bare breasts against the sweater and the strawberry nipples rose. Paris brushed them with her lips as she slid the tie apart, apart. At its tip she freed the other end. "There," she said, "you're open." She pushed Peg, bare to the waist, down flatter on the bed, and stood looking at her.

"Umm," she said, admiring. "Who would have thought?" she hefted Peg's breasts in her hands. "So much, so soft, the cream in those Yankee pewter pitchers." She pinched the nipples, each one, with her lips. "Strawberries and cream." Peg reached for her. "No." Paris stepped back, undressed quickly, lay Peg down once more, lay on top of her, kissed her face, her neck, her shoulders, those breasts again, kissed down to her belt line.

"Paris," Peg said, trying to rise, that tender amused look in her eyes, a slight smiling curve to her lips, her hands reaching.

"Hey," she said, pushing her down, pushing her again, a third time, unbuckling her belt as she did, unzipping her slacks, pulling them off with her underwear. "Umm," she crooned at the glorious sight of her and parted her legs like the two ends of her tie.

"This doesn't work for me," Peg said, her voice tight, but her telltale breathing a pant. One hand kneaded Paris's shoulder, the other had a fistful of her hair. "I need to make love to you first."

That lisp was a turn-on. "You're gorgeous," she told Peg and plunged to the knot in the tie of her legs with her mouth. "Butch," was the last thing she said before she took a faintly cinnamon mouthful of her. The word was a challenge.

CHAPTER 14

At 7:02 am Sunday she awoke stunned in a rumpled bed. It had happened. How Venita would laugh. Finally, it had happened. Her mouth even tasted like Peg. Hot damn.

She wasn't on a pink cloud, didn't feel consumed with lust, didn't need Peg in her arms then and forever. That was lucky, she thought, dragging her sore knee out of bed to find that Peg wasn't in the room, or in the bathroom. Her luggage was there, as was the unopened bakery box. She moved the curtain and saw the Z outside, but still no sign of

Peg in the misty gray morning. The last time she'd looked it'd been 2:00 A.M. Peg had been between her legs. *I'm too tired for more,* she'd whispered to Peg, surprised at how husky her voice sounded. Peg had laughed and kept on. They were good together. Not explosive, but very good.

She brushed her teeth smiling. *Finally,* she thought again as she got back under the covers, luxuriating in the feel of being well loved yet alone. Her whole naked body seemed to exhale. No more waiting, no more conflict. Now she'd find what cards she'd dealt herself. Could she retain her freedom and still have Peg without skipping town down the line? Maybe this time the terror that went with being loved, like the terror at the top of a flight of stairs, wouldn't pursue her. Maybe their maturity, their slow careful progress, would be a safety net for her. She wanted them to work. A shudder of pleasure shook her shoulders. She squeezed a hand between her legs and fell back to sleep.

At 9:30 she woke again. Peg's eyes were all worry and expectation. She held two Styrofoam boxes to her chest and over them she gave Paris that sweet bath of a smile, eyes keenly watching for the slightest response. "Want some breakfast, you sensational woman?"

It was a stumbly sunny Sunday, a little bit cooler. They made love once more then snoozed till checkout. They took a long route back to Connecticut through little old mill towns.

"Can we stop at the Olympic?" Paris asked.

"Are you hungry again?"

"All that exercising last night —" They laughed. Her hand was on Peg's thigh. Peg covered it with her own. They hadn't talked about how they felt, but after removing the will we/won't we suspense from the relationship she was even more comfortable with Peg. All she wanted at that moment was to enjoy her proximity.

"You really like diners," Peg said, moving her hand to the back of Paris's neck where it rested, firm and reassuring.

"They're pretty exotic for this Texan. But it's more than that. It's part of our history together now."

Peg looked over at her. The moving landscape framed her, forever setting Peg in the early New England spring. Her voice was dry and appraising: "Is that like my sisters-in-law and their wedding books, stuffed with pictures and souvenirs of everything from engagement parties to honeymoons?"

"Goddess, no." The thought chilled her. Was that what Peg wanted? "We're traveling together in a landscape. The geography we touch takes on different meanings as we pass through it. It seems fitting to start and end at the same point."

She heard the smile in Peg's voice. "The Olympic was the first time I woke you."

She leaned and kissed Peg's neck just above the lightly starched collar. "I feel *very* awakened."

Peg raised her eyebrows. "Good." Oh, those most lesbian of all eyes, beguiling those most lesbian zones in her with the slightest glance.

"It's been a long time for me."

Was Peg blushing? "Me too." Peg looked at her own hands. "I couldn't imagine not ever touching you, Paris. And I knew if I touched you once I might as well hang it up."

"You touched my arm in the woods at your house. That was the first time."

"I know. It took months to admit I'd lost the battle." She looked at Paris and smiled. "Or won."

Yes, she felt won. "Were you ready for it to happen this weekend?"

"If you're asking whether I planned it, no, but it seemed a pretty sure bet. I almost backed out."

"Did you?"

"I don't ever want to subsist for months on peanut butter and jelly sandwiches again."

"Is that what you do in new relationships?"

"No." Peg's voice was mournful. "After breakups."

Her throat threatened to close in panic. "If you're looking for promises, I flat out don't have any in me."

Peg raised her eyebrow and shook her head. "Yes. It'd be a little late for that now, darlin', wouldn't it? I flat out wanted you."

She hadn't realized how erotic that unexpected, irresistible lisp had become. "Touch me," Paris said, without knowing she was going to speak. She spread her legs and lifted her skirt to pull Peg's hand underneath, melting with sudden heat.

Peg didn't hesitate. Her close-clipped fingers were against her, stroking and slipping, while her other hand stayed on the steering wheel. She wanted to stop at the side of the highway, but Peg would have to shift then and she couldn't bear to lose those fingers. She smelled herself.

"Faster," she said. If she could come fast Peg would keep driving. She had to come. She slumped against Peg's shoulder, wanting to feel her, to smell her. The fingers kept working against her and she pulled her skirt up farther to see them. Don't let a truck go by, she thought. She dropped her skirt. The touch of those fingers became everything. She heard her raggedy breath and the start of her voice. "Peg." There was nothing else. "Peg. Peg, Peg, Peg."

"You're lovely, delightful," Peg said, sniffing her fingers and smiling at her.

"Peg," she answered, and laughed. Maybe she and Peg were hotter together than she'd guessed. She was shaking as she took Peg's fingers and wiped them on the inside of her skirt. "I don't remember that ever happening before."

"I never missed an exit before."

"Thank you. Your gear shift was my mortal enemy just then." The car was roasting hot. She pulled back to her seat. "I love your hands. I'm in love with your hands."

"I relish your body."

"It's getting so old," she said, checking her upper arms for flab.

"Maybe I've been looking for a mature woman all my life."

"Where were we?"

"Peanut butter. And how where we've been changes when we touch it. This highway will certainly never be the same for me." Peg drove in circles briefly, trying to get to the diner by an unfamiliar route.

"Where'd you go this morning?" Paris asked, not sure she should.

"For a long walk."

"To escape what we'd done?"

Peg took her time. "Maybe. Mostly to clear my head."

A tiny part of her wanted Peg to back out now before things got any heavier. "You're not sorry about last night?"

"And this morning? And this afternoon? You don't see me running the other way, do you?" Peg said, the smile in her voice again as she downshifted without a jar, trying to pass a Sunday driver. "Scared maybe, not sorry."

"Me too," she admitted. She touched Peg's hair. "Where do we go from here?" she dared ask, knowing there was never an AAA Triptik, yet wanting it mapped out.

"The Olympic."

"Good idea." She liked this woman so much. She was unusually temperate, consistently even, and prudent. When she thought of some of the crazy women she'd been with, rash rather than impulsive, unrealistic rather than imaginative, in lust but not considerate, drinkers and dopers and angry women, compulsively ambitious lovers, or women in care-taking careers that wrung them dry — Peg was a catch. She wasn't out to set the world, or Paris, on fire.

So she was surprised when, over fries and coffee at the Olympic, the Sunday afternoon crowd cheerfully loud, she found herself rearing in alarm like the stallions in old west movies.

Peg had turned somber, her eyes almost stern. Her hands were wrapped tightly around a cup. "There's something I need to get out of the way before I decide not to say it at all."

She sensed that this was big. Her heart raced with fear. Her knee was seething with pain.

"When I brought the Reverend Minister over to

Ned he asked if I was spending the weekend with you. Then he asked if you were a member of the Land Trust."

"Uh-oh." So it was Peg's family that would ruin this.

"He talked about the family, how we were socially responsible people who'd always supported charity and sponsored children's sports. He even reminded me that the store sponsored a girls' softball team at my insistence — and against Brockett's better judgment." Peg smoothed her hair back. "I told him I was going to be late and to get to the point. He reminded me that we'd 'proven' ourselves to the Valley for generations in our own way and that if I were ever challenged on the Jacobs' integrity I should remember all our civic contributions."

She'd hoped to like Ned even if she couldn't like the other brother, but his thinking was just as vile. "You mean he never did get to the point?"

"Somewhere in all that talk he planted one sentence that I didn't even hear till I went walking this morning. He said that our investments were our own business and that I profited from them as much as he and Brockett did." Peg looked at her, chin on her fists. "I wondered whether it was local investments he was talking about."

"Like a certain industrial park?" she asked, retreating to her split ends.

Peg nodded, tapping a finger against the cup.

"Then you're in it up to your neck too."

Peg raised her head and Paris saw layers of defense go up, clang, clang, clang, like gates. "Oh, no, I —"

"Come on, Peg. Your blinders are so obvious even you're starting to see them." It had been too promising. Well, better to find out now and get out before anyone had to revert to peanut butter sandwiches. "You were brave to tell me."

"Brave," Peg said with a derisive tone. "How could I keep it from you?"

"I'm serious. Your family thinks I'm dangerous. And you, Peg Jacob, care what your family thinks. Ned didn't want you to come at all, did he?"

"He has nothing to say about who I spend my time with," Peg answered, but her debonair confidence sounded thin.

Paris was steaming mad. Peg was nothing but a yuppie puff pastry from the Publick House Bakery. Another handsome shell. The disappointment tasted bitter. "But," she jabbed, knowing she was turning sarcastic and unable to stop, "you leave everything else to the boys. How butch. Just bumble on your merry way trusting them to do what's right for the family and screw the rest of the world."

"You say that like I'm committing a crime. Most people pay their investment counselors. I have savvy brothers."

Damn Gershwin. "Let's Call the Whole Thing Off" roared in her ears. She crumpled up a napkin. "Didn't you live through the sixties? Didn't I hear that you helped turn the world upside down in the seventies? All of a sudden social responsibility is the Jacobs contributing to the United Way?"

She could hear the stridency of her voice, but was too angry to stop. Giulia's comments about what went on at United Way functions came back to her. Peg might not have any more idea about what connivers her brothers were than an ostrich. "Did you stay out of geriatrics because Brockett and Ned wouldn't have approved of you getting your hands dirty in other people's problems?" she taunted. Peg wasn't handsome to her now. The only thing that looked the same about her was her expensive grooming. "Aren't you anything but a clotheshorse?"

There was no smile in Peg's eyes. "I knew better than to make myself vulnerable again." She pushed her cup away.

"Whoa, Peg, this has nothing to do with last night." *Am I overreacting?* Paris wondered. *Why?* She tried to be soothing, but she didn't feel very conciliatory, just unbearably warm. Between the musical warning in her head and the noise of the Olympic she couldn't think. She just wanted out, out, out and here she was dependent on Peg to get home and away from her.

"It does for me, darlin'," Peg said, rising and laying a bill on the table. "I'll be in the car."

If Peg believed in building industrial parks, okay, they might not be headed for forever, but she was willing to coexist pretty intimately for a while with some rousing disagreements. The ride home was going to be damned sticky.

Not to mention silent. She had a sneaking suspicion Peg spent the whole hour holding back tears. Paris's anger had such a hold on her heart and mind it felt like a suit of armor from "Bedknobs and Broomsticks." She *was* inside the armor, wasn't she, not a phantom warrior tilting at windmills? Confusion and uncertainty seeped through the cracks, but all the while she felt Peg's hands on her like bruises of love.

Oddly, the Valley hadn't gotten as warm as Massachusetts. There were no signs of spring unfolding. Peg's voice was sandpapery when they said goodnight. Peg stayed in the Z at the bottom of the steps while Paris, shivering in the cold, limped up the steps and unlocked her door. She'd picked up the *Valley Sentinels* from the last three days and was about to step inside when she heard a horn below.

It was Dusty's green Swinger. "We need to talk to you two!" called Elly.

She wasn't about to go down the stairs. "Come on up!"

They brought Peg with them.

"It's the kid," Dusty said, catching her breath, as soon as they were inside.

"Maddy?"

"She's disappeared."

"But I just saw her —" She thought a minute. "I guess I haven't seen her since last weekend."

Elly was wringing her hands. "She didn't come to practice all this weekend —"

Dusty interrupted, "— after pestering us about when we were starting up again, like softball is the biggest thing in her life —"

"— so I asked Giulia about her. At first she wouldn't say, just looked at me funny. Later she came up to me and told me Maddy hadn't come home since Thursday night."

"Did they call the police?" asked Paris. She found she was holding onto Peg's hand for dear life. Pride told her to drop it, but she didn't.

"Not till Friday. Giulia thought she might've been with some friend?" Elly looked to her for answers.

"There is a friend, Tyna Lewis. They were lovers for a while, but Giulia broke it up by telling Tyna's mother." To make matters worse her hand had turned icy cold and sweaty.

Dusty slammed one fist into the other. "That stuck-up bitch. I told you I didn't trust her, El."

"Shh, honey. She's reliable, that's hard to find. Do you think, Paris, she'd be with Tyna?"

"No. The mother reacted pretty strongly. Pulled Tyna out of school. I doubt Tyna's any sanctuary unless they've run off together. What did the police do?"

Dusty looked disgusted. "The usual police things. Maddy's not a major criminal, just a little girl lost in a big world so she's not exactly top priority, though they did put out a missing persons report and spent yesterday showing her photograph around. Apparently Giulia's trying to keep things quiet."

Elly nodded. "We offered to put flyers up and Giulia acted like we wanted her to walk naked down Main Street."

"Jerk. She doesn't want her future queered, so to speak, with bad press."

"But her kid sister's in trouble," protested Elly. "I tried and tried, but I couldn't budge her."

She hadn't thought about Giulia all weekend. The woman was a lost cause. Attractive, but oblivious to everything other than her tender obsession.

"Where's your phone book, Paris?" Peg asked, eyes cloaked. "I'm willing to call this Tyna's mom. Would I know the daughter?"

"I never thought of that. Of course! Maddy was bragging about how fast a runner Tyna is. You probably do know her."

"Tyna, Tyna," Peg said as she riffled the white pages, sitting on the arm of the couch. Her hands seemed naked. She looked up. "Is she a black girl in dreadlocks?"

"That's her."

"She is fast." Peg smiled, but only with her lips. Paris knew their battle weighed on Peg as heavily as it did on her. "And a gay prodigy too? Let's see if she's flown the coop." Peg, looking cool and graceful on the couch, dialed, listened. "Hello, Ms. Lewis? This is Peg Jacob. I coach girl's track down in Brockett Lake and we're trying to set up a special meet as a fundraiser. I wonder if I might speak with Tyna."

Was Peg really going to get involved in this and use her career for cover? Paris couldn't believe she'd risk it. She felt the muscles in her face relax a bit, as if she'd lifted off an armored face mask she'd donned back at the Olympia diner. Peg looked so perfectly composed on that couch, a study in androgyny.

"Tyna. I teach down at Brockett Lake. We're putting together a local field day to raise money for the Special Olympics and it just occurred to me that getting some of the super athletes from the county wouldn't hurt attendance. I wondered if you'd be interested in helping out?"

Oh, right, she thought, Peg's covering her ass good. Still, she clanked off another piece of armor.

"Peg's a sharp one," Elly said. "And fast."

"You have to be sharp when you live in the closet," she told her. The chest plate stayed on.

"Before you hang up, Tyna, I have another

question." Peg was drumming her fingers on her knee. "About Maddy Scala. Can you talk? Okay, do the best you can. We're trying to figure out what happened, where she'd go. Have you seen her since Thursday?" Peg listened for a while. "Do you have any idea where — Yes, I guess that would be a logical destination, but does she know anyone there?" Peg was quiet briefly. "No problem. I'll be in touch about the field day and please keep my number in case you hear from Maddy. Thanks, Tyna. And hang in there. Love's a good thing to feel, don't let anyone tell you different."

She gave in and dumped the chest plate. "Thank you, Peg," she said, going to her and hugging on her arm. "Thank you for telling her that."

"I know what she's going through," said Peg, her voice sandpapery again. She looked like she wanted to cry. "Tyna doesn't know where Maddy went, but she did know why."

"Tell," said Elly.

"Apparently Maddy showed up at Tyna's Girl Scout troop Thursday after school. She marched up to the leader and said she wanted to join, but Tyna's mother had warned the leader. When she was turned away, Maddy made a fuss, yelling about Constitutional rights and discrimination and stormed out. Tyna's blaming everything on herself for not walking out after her, but the child's no romantic. She said her mother almost threw her life away for love and she wasn't going to do the same. She said she won't trade away her future for Maddy, not when it's — how'd she say it? When it's so hard for a black woman to get a future at all."

They were all sitting down. Elly and Dusty still had their jackets on. "Want coffee? It may be a long night."

"No," said Elly. "We've got to get up early. Did she know where the kid might be?"

"Tyna's guess was Greenwich Village, unless she hitched all the way to San Francisco. She said Maddy was always dreaming them into apartments in one or the other."

"If only I'd been here," Paris said.

"You think she might've come to you?" Peg asked.

"It's likely she'd try. I knew what was going on with her and she knew that I'm gay." Her risk hadn't paid off then. She hadn't saved Maddy at all.

"You didn't see a note at the door?"

"No. Nothing but the papers." She still had them on her lap. "Do they put runaway stories in the *Sentinel*?" She scanned the headlines. "Whoa, listen! *'Park Site Vandalized.* Developers involved in planning reported that several pieces of heavy equipment at the proposed Hermitage Industrial Park site were disabled beyond repair. Vandals drove pieces of equipment over rocks or into other equipment. They slashed belts, tires and seats. The engines were partly dismantled. Parts were twisted and sheared with heavy rocks. A CAT was apparently driven off the site, but abandoned about a mile away, out of gas. Members of a local environmental group are being questioned.' "

The others looked expectantly at Paris. "You don't think Maddy had something to do with that?" asked Dusty, her words slow, thoughtful, a smile beginning in her eyes.

She didn't know if it was safe to smile back in

front of those two, but she was so proud of that crazy little dyke she couldn't help herself. This was Maddy's runaway note.

"Maddy understands how important it is to protect that piece of land," she conjectured. "We'd visited it; she loved it. She knew that once it was destroyed no one could do anything, whatever the court ruled."

She carefully avoided looking at Peg. Maybe getting hit in the wallet would open her eyes. "She also knew Giulia's fiance was counting on making a mint from that project and she's been plenty angry at her sister."

Peg asked, "You think she did all that single-handedly?"

"Sure as shit, Peg. She knows motors. And that's a disenfranchised gay child if I've ever met one. She's been getting dumped on at home for being herself since long before she could have understood what sexuality was, never mind homosexuality. She's poor. Her dad took off and her own sister wants to profit from tearing up a park he and Maddy used as their stomping ground. She's denied shop classes, her strong point. She falls in love and that's destroyed. Now she can't even join the Girl Scouts where she might fit in with the outdoor girls."

Dusty said with a kind of aching cry, "I remember. I remember just what it was like. I thought it was different for kids today. Hasn't Stonewall helped at all?"

"Not this town."

"Okay," Peg said. "What now?"

They sat in silence. Without explanation, Peg jumped up and rushed outside. For a moment Paris feared that Peg would want retribution, but Peg's car door slammed below and she clanged back up the steps amazingly fast for someone with a reconstructed pelvis.

"Cookies," Peg said, presenting the Sturbridge box.

She laughed. Peg hadn't brought back a cop, or her lawyer's phone number, just an irrelevant but welcome box of cookies. She could love a woman like this. They helped themselves. "That seems like years ago." She caught that sweet look in Peg's eyes. Investments or no, they grinned at each other over the cookie crumbs.

"What's with you two?" asked Elly. "Did we hear right that you went away for the weekend? Together?"

"El!" chided Dusty.

"Maybe congratulations are in order, lover."

Peg took Paris's hand. "Ask us in six months when we get sorted out," she told them.

"Six months! It'll be ten times that with our clashes."

"Or we may have fewer than we suspect. For example," Peg continued, waving her cookie in the air, "I think that hotheaded kid deserves a medal. She's undermined what hundreds of adults couldn't prevent."

"But —"

"Paris," Peg interrupted, eyes flashing anger, but briefly. "Just because I never bothered to think for myself before on some subjects doesn't mean I never will."

"Well," she confessed, swallowing her pride, "next time I pick a fight, you go ahead and ask me what I'm scared of. Tell me I'm pushing you away."

"Deal," Peg said and leaned to kiss her lightly. How could lips be so womanly soft and dyke-firm at the same time?

"What a good-lookin' couple. Aren't they, Dusty?"

Dusty just chuckled, arms folded, a look of approval blessing them, as if to say to Paris, "Gotcha now!"

"I guess this takes care of your wandering ways," Elly said with finality. "Thanks for making my job so easy, Peg."

"Ah —" Paris began.

"Meanwhile," Peg cut her off. This wasn't the time. "Meanwhile, I think we all agree that Maddy's got to be found. If it isn't too late."

Dusty looked at a loss. Maddy had left her territory. "How long can a runaway last these days without trying drugs or making money off them? Or worse."

"What do we do?" asked Elly. "There's no lesbian cavalry."

"Oh," said Peg, leveling a finger at Elly, "but there is. Don't you think our old pals would help?" She turned to Paris. "Annie Heaphy's a cab driver and puts on a lot of mileage in the Big Apple. Turkey's a sociology prof at CCNY and she wrote her dissertation on the gay street kids of New York. I'm sure she still has connections. And she grew up gay right here on the streets of Morton River."

"Start calling!"

"The numbers are home. Neither are listed. I'll try to get them tonight and report in to you, darlin'."

"Agreed. I'll call you folks with news up till —?"

"We have to get some sleep," said Dusty. "Drop by tomorrow. Breakfast's on the Queen of Hearts."

Paris unpacked after everyone left and ate another of those cookies as she waited for Peg to call. She wondered if Venita would still be up. *No, she thought, don't let it be suicide.* That hadn't occurred to her before. She wanted to talk to someone before the worry mushroomed in her head, but there was no answer at Venita's. She swept the kitchen and dusted the entire apartment, then dragged her phone into her bedroom. She undressed and rubbed salve on her knee.

Twelve hours after they'd checked out of the motel in Sturbridge Peg called. "Turkey's contacting her troops tomorrow. Annie's still at work, but Turkey will let her know. We've done all we can for now, darlin'."

"Thanks for calling, Peg. And thanks," she said with a warmth in her chest that was part gratitude, part affection, and part, she acknowledged a little reluctantly, love, "for the weekend. All of it."

CHAPTER 15

The next morning Paris stopped at Dusty's Diner on her way to the Hillside. The florist had already clanged up her steps to deliver a dozen deep red, almost purple, roses. Peg's courtliness hadn't let trouble overshadow what they'd given each other in Sturbridge. Paris arranged the roses on her kitchen table.

Giulia, as she served Paris's English muffin, looked glum. Her hair didn't shine, her face was sickly pale and anger pulled her mouth taut. At least for the moment her beauty had faded to a bitter hard look, lost in a silly battle against life. *Life's not your enemy,* she wanted to tell Giulia. *You'll get all of it you're supposed to.*

"How're you doing?" she asked, waving back to Dusty in the kitchen.

She got a Scala shrug, nothing more. She gave Elly Peg's report, ate and trooped up the hill. She needed Sophia's liniment; her calves were stiff from lovemaking.

The yard was just as she'd first seen it, except for the missing burly kid with the curls and the wraparound smile, and the first brave buds struggling for life on frozen-looking trees. There were scraps of snow left from weeks ago. Where was Maddy? Was this just a major sulk for her or a new life? She'd turned sixteen recently and seethed with her earnest, formless ambition. She had a flash of Maddy storming the mayor's office with the new group that was making headlines out in San Francisco, Queer Nation, roaring all her anger and pain into the streets.

She hugged Sophia tightly. Things must be bad — she didn't feel Sophia's usual girdle. The house was hotter and stuffier than normal and the curtains still drawn. "Shall we go out?" she asked.

"And look for Maddalena? The Virgin takes care of her." Sophia sat in a rocking chair and looked heavenward. "God forgive me, I want her to hurry!"

Except for the heavy accent, her English was darn good. *What a faker,* thought Paris. This woman had fooled her, even her kids, for so long. "I don't think there's much chance you and I could find her. I didn't even bring Sugarplum today."

"Sugarplum?"

She told Sophia the story of naming the Jeep in the woods, in Maddy's dad's woods. Sophia's eyes filled, but she tossed back her head and didn't break down. Paris wasn't quite family enough for that.

"There is something," Sophia said, a guilty cast to her eyes. "If only I tell Maddalena on time."

Not that Sophia's English was perfect. "You can't go blaming yourself."

Sophia looked at the floor, then from the corners of her eyes at Paris. She rocked. "Three months ago? No, four. Just after you come here, I have a letter from the girls' *padre.*"

"Mr. Scala?" Darn! What a difference that would have made to Maddy. "Why didn't you tell them?"

"Because why make trouble? He's in — how do you say it — Knee-brass-ka."

"Nebraska? Even I haven't been to Nebraska."

"There are not so many junk men out there. He says he's doing good. Here." She pulled a worn letter on yellow lined paper from her pocket and unfolded a money order.

"Twenty-five hundred dollars?"

"For the weddings." She patted her eyes again. "When Maddalena comes back, I tell her. Maybe she visits him?"

Paris looked at Sophia. This didn't sound right. Why would she hold back something so important? "Sophia, you need the money so badly. Giulia," she said with sarcasm, "would be thrilled to be able to buy a trousseau."

"Giulia!" said Sophia, her little bird hands flying, waving the letter and the money order. "She takes all of it! I know. Put it away, what's she say? For a rainy day. Only it never rains enough to use. She likes to make the interest. I like to give things to my girls. Maybe bus fare for the *bambino* to Nebraska." She picked up her rosary beads from the table. "The world is bad. Do you think Maddalena comes back?"

She was surprised at her certainty. "She'll be back. Sixteen is hard. Giulia is hard on her. But she loves you. We'll hear."

They went to the kitchen to drink coffee. At least the Scalas were letting light in here. Recently, this had been the extent of their English lessons, talking at the kitchen table. She'd told Sophia to register for the ESL class at the Center, but Sophia had put it off. Now they planned a time when they could secretly visit a bank with the money order. "Giulia looks so worried. Is it about her sister?"

"Yes. And Peter. Since someone breaks Mike's machines he tries to borrow money for new ones."

She fished a little, stuffing her guilt, pretending absorption in her split ends. This was important. "Haven't they got time to raise the cash? I'd think the vandalism would delay everything."

"No. Giulia says soon." Sophia leaned across the table, her hands working the rosary like worry beads. "This is why the boys have no money. They borrow to pay for the job."

"To pay the judge?"

Sophia nodded. "Everything goes bad at once!" She put her face in her hands. "My house is . . . is . . . cold without the child's messes, like when her father goes." She patted her face again with the handkerchief. "If the boys lose this money they get from other people? Then what?"

"They may not get it. A bank would be dumb to

sink cash into such an iffy project. It's been nothing but trouble."

"Iffy?"

"Uncertain." She fumbled. *"Incerto."*

"But *milliones* if it works, Giulia says. They don't go to a bank. They go to the wealthy men who give before."

"The investors?" she asked, angrily picturing the Jacobs in Brockett's living room, surrounded by their private preserve of trees and peace.

"Sure. Giulia says they give so much already they give more to save" — Sophia tugged at a sleeve — "their shirts."

Thinking aloud, she said, "So if the investors decide it's a bad deal they'll pull out. I wonder what would influence them. Maybe a better investment?"

Could they be lured away? Her mind sprinted ahead, crowded with schemes. The weak sun had moved into the kitchen window and lit Sophia from behind. She looked much more attractive than Giulia, robust with hope and a faith in life itself. "You should have a full life, Sophia. I wish you'd stop hiding up here on your hillside. I wish you wouldn't depend so much on Giulia. Please take the English classes. If Maddy doesn't come back welfare will find out."

She nodded into her coffee cup. "It's a bad world," she repeated. "If I don't have girls I go back."

"Back where? To Italy?" She thought of the frayed letter in Sophia's pocket. "I'll bet a box of pastries from Marena's Bakery this has something to do with Mr. Scala."

Sophia lowered her eyes. "I dream of going home.

He does too. Now he has money. In my village it's cheaper to live than here. He says he leaves us for shame when he has no money for rent. And," her eyes went down again, "there is no other woman."

"Sophia — you don't think Maddy somehow learned where her dad was and went to him?"

Her eyes went wide. "From my letter? No. I keep it here." She patted her pocket.

"While you bathed? Slept? She could have been looking for money to run away on."

"No. If this is so, I will hear from Patrizio."

His return address was in North Platte. She prevailed on Sophia to let her call information, but there was no listing for Scala.

They hugged goodbye in front of the kitchen window, Sophia a soft full bundle of heat. Paris could see down the ragtag, dwelling-choked Hillside and her stomach went queasy. She had a sense of sliding down the Hillside: house, Scalas and all, into change. She held onto Sophia for dear life.

Two weeks later Thor Valerie deigned to meet with her. She needed to accomplish what she wanted in one fell swoop so she conspired again with Venita. One of Venita's nieces was a security guard at the old Rafferty's factory and arranged to let them in on her shift.

It was a rainy day, yearning toward full spring. Thor whizzed into the parking lot in a tiny metallic blue Geo, parked in a puddle, slammed the door and reparked. He approached them, studying his watch. "I have to be back at the office in half an hour, ladies," he announced, shooting his cuffs just past his sleeves.

"That's a snappy new car, Thor," said Venita. Her voice was hoarse from a cold and she wore a glossy Russian fur cap with a thick scarf wrapped around her throat.

"Like it? I talked it out of Valley Motors for V.O.W."

"If you can talk a dealership out of a whole brand new car," Paris said, challenging, "you can do this."

Thor's eyes followed hers to the old factory shell. "Okay. What exactly are we here for?"

"Inspiration, dear boy," said Venita. "Inspiration."

He scuffed at the asphalt with his shiny shoes. "I've got all the inspiration I need, Aunt Ven. It's time and money I'm after." Venita's niece, taller than Venita and at least twice her weight, shambled out of the office in a drab uniform with a shiny badge, head down, sorting through keys. As she led the way Thor asked, "I see in the papers that industrial park thing's blown wide open. They got caught destroying the old man's land while it was still tied up. What do you know?"

He was going to pay attention even if she had to tie him down. She laughed, caught herself switching to her seductive mode. It was hard to be persuasive without it, but she wouldn't use that skill on a male. "This is my half hour. We can talk about your schemes on your time."

"They raise them tough down your way, don't they?" challenged Thor.

Venita laughed as they entered a huge empty room with ceilings dripping severed wires and now unidentifiable fixtures. There was a smell of mildewed plaster and their voices almost echoed. "That's why we import them, Thor. The women around here don't have a chance of influencing you."

"They don't need to, Aunt Ven. I do everything for them."

"Oh, barf, Mr. Ego," Paris said. "If I didn't need you —"

Thor grinned. "See?" he said.

"Is this guy putting me on, Venita?"

"Now and then, Paris, I think he is."

"Look around," she ordered Thor.

"Okay. An abandoned space station after a Klingon attack."

"Don't tell me *you're* a Trekkie."

He laughed. "Old generation. My one human weakness."

"I doubt it," she said, looking him up and down, alert to that scent he used, like an animal to danger. "I brought us all here so we could use our imaginations. This space and everything else we're seeing is lying idle." She motioned to the niece to lead them on. "This could be a major crack house. It's an eyesore, a danger to the city. Could we move the Learning Center here, or V.O.W? Could M.O.V.E. make it a bus terminal? Could you get some computers donated and a teacher to hold classes?"

"In this drafty old factory?" They were in some kind of shipping room now. Mice had left old packing materials in tatters. Their droppings littered the floor. A broken scale lay tipped over on the floor. Thor kicked at it and set its springs jangling.

She went on, saying anything that came into her head. "Couldn't we get some experienced shipping and receiving person to teach inventory and packaging right in a room like this with some donated used equipment?"

"Good idea!" said Venita. "I'd teach the same old arithmetic I've always taught, but we'd give the students calculators to use and call the course — let's see — Rate Calculation and Inventory Control." She coughed.

"You're catching on," Paris told her. "They like those fancy titles."

Thor looked disgusted. "That's been the problem all along with these programs. By the time the government identifies employer needs and gets bankrolled, the skills are obsolete. You teach them on old scales like this," he kicked it, "and the companies have digitals." He was looking around, though, and they went into a huge old office with rows of battered but serviceable desks. Thor slapped one loudly. "Where was all this stuff when I was looking for it? Damn. You saw what we're using at V.O.W. and my workers have to double up on that."

"What kind of rent do you think the city would charge to move V.O.W. in here?" she asked, looking around speculatively. It was an intimidating size.

"How do we heat the work areas? Are the bathrooms working? What about lights?" Thor snapped back. "Is the electricity on?"

The niece went over to a switch and fluorescence filled the room. "They left us juice so we can put on the heat and keep the pipes from busting in a freeze. Over here," she motioned, leading them to another space. She had caught Paris's eye a couple of times and now looked directly at her.

"The Sweatshop?" Paris whispered.

"I seen you there too," the guard said, flipping

another switch. Ceiling heaters roared to life as Paris wondered if the gay life was democracy's last stand.

"You mean to tell me all this shit's been sitting here for two years collecting dust? They told me they'd gutted the whole structure. But I don't know, ladies. It'd take a lot of work." He looked around. "Just cleaning the windows —"

Venita had her hands in her coat pockets and bore down on Thor. He looked like a captive male in the midst of Amazons. "What's the V.O.W. Cleaning Service for? They do industrial buildings, don't they?" Venita turned to Paris to explain, "It's a project that employs the mentally ill."

He pretended to ignore her, but his eyes took in everything. "I wonder if they'd lease us the property for a dollar year," he said, peering in desk drawers and file cabinets. "If they'd sell it to us for peanuts and if Dad would spring for a mortgage." He pivoted and folded his arms, glaring at her. "Okay. There's still all that equipment we'd need. Computers, software, maybe automotive electronics equipment. What else is big? Numeric control manufacturing? CADCAM? Robotics? It's endless," he whined.

"By God, I think he's got it!" she said, grabbing Venita's arm. "The possibilities *are* endless. Delegate V.O.W. to one of your assistants, Thor. This project is even bigger. It's *made* for your scheming, monomaniacal mind."

"Flattery, woman, is not going to bring me over to your way of thinking."

"But power will," suggested Venita, her head cold turning her laugh to a gurgle.

Paris told him with an intense rush of words about Trixie in New Avon and about her job.

He was attentive. "But she's got a community college backing her."

"Young man," said Venita. "I've dreamed for years of connecting with Upton C.C. Bureaucrats, just like Mr. Piccari, are well-meaning, but limited. All they need is a herder and they'll fall in line."

"With their funds —"

"There's more." She let her passion for the project show. This was the moment to fire him up. "Trixie is writing a pilot program. New Avon is trading space with the employers Trixie recruits for training facilities. They're not only teaching skills, but English right at the worksites."

"Morton River won't give anything away."

"It's not a giveaway. The city donates space to a batch of small companies in a useless eyesore like this. The companies fix their spaces up however they want and provide personnel to teach. The machinery is all there, they can purchase additional equipment or use slightly outmoded machines. Trixie has someone go into the plants to make sure the training is quality. The contract would trigger rent if it wasn't."

"How about tax breaks? What good is new industry if they're not paying taxes?"

"Thor," said Venita, "the workers would eventually be paying taxes instead of eating them up with services."

"You're right, though," Paris added, "there'd be no property tax. But the city could impose graduated taxes over time, or a time-limited break."

Thor looked at his watch. "Okay. I'm into my next appointment. How would you sell this?"

"Me? You're the wheeler and dealer around here. But if I were to try, it'd be on numbers, with a marketing plan and a projected budget," she smiled at Venita, "maybe something even more persuasive."

"Why do I think this is what I came to hear?" said Thor, cocking his head.

She shared what Sophia had let out about Mike and Peter bribing the judge, then going to the investors for more money.

"Okay. So the hermits' sons are blackmailing — don't I love that racist word — the investors into spending money to cover their losses." He paused, straightened his tie. "Are they threatening to mention the payoffs to the authorities?"

"I doubt it," she said. "They seem to be fighting pretty hard to keep their slimy little reputations. If they spill the beans now they'll never get another job in the Valley."

"So," Thor said, with one last push to his tie, "you think I ought to go do my civic duty?"

"Not yet. These investors have money burning holes in their pockets, remember." She smiled at Thor. "It seems to me we've been talking about a pretty good investment right here under our noses."

Paris loved how involved in the intrigue Venita was. "You can't just claim the park's crooked from the get-go, Thor. What proof will you threaten them with?" Venita asked.

"Don't worry, Aunt Ven. You know what a good bluff I am at cards."

"I surely do," said Venita with a laugh. For all his faults there was real affection in her voice.

"By the time they ask for proof you can throw them your pitch for the new improved Rafferty Center. Heck, Thor, why not toss in the old building as a cultural sop? Tell them it'll be used as an art gallery, for star-studded workshops, community events for the upper echelon."

"I wonder if there'd be support for this bizarre scheme."

"That's the real brilliance of it," said Venita, sneezing and resettling her hat. "I'm no power broker, but even I see what'll happen. It'll become *their* scheme. They'll push it and sell it. And as beholden to you as they'll be, you'll get to direct it all."

Thor snorted, his lips twisted in disgust. "I can't think offhand what profits I can tempt them with except luring new businesses, but I'll bet you're right. Once they bite they'll figure all the greedy angles better than I ever could."

"Well?" she asked.

Thor erased the excitement from his face. "Okay. I'll give it some thought." He looked at his watch again, though it must have been a vain exercise. He'd never make his appointment now. As he burned a considerable amount of rubber on his way out of the lot, she suspected he'd think of nothing but Rafferty Center for a long time to come.

"You got him going," said the security guard, clapping her hands together with a grin.

"And that's no easy task," agreed Venita. "See you at the picnic this summer?"

"For sure, Aunt Ven. I'm in charge of the little kids' entertainment."

"Now," Paris shouted over the clatter of a passing

freight train and the steady hiss of falling rain, "for some investing of my own — making sure the men Thor's trying to persuade are feeling shaky before he even opens his mouth."

CHAPTER 16

Something more than their fight kept Paris and Peg pretty much at a distance for the next few weeks. Maddy had been gone a month already and they'd let that crisis smooth over their differences without examining them. The price they paid was a nervousness when they were together, and the fact that they hadn't made love again.

"This is really strange," she told Venita on a warm evening in the first week of May. "The first six months of a lesbian relationship are usually spent keeping the sheets wet."

Venita blushed and laughed. Her cold had gone to bronchitis, and she still spoke in a husky whisper. "I suppose I really have missed out on something, but then, I haven't had your troubles either." Venita lowered her voice even more, though they were alone in her classroom. Outside the tall window streaks of spring light kept night at bay. "Tyna called me here. She feels like she betrayed Maddy and drove her away."

"Oh, no —"

Venita put up a hand. "I took care of that nonsense. Then the girl told me how glad she was to find an old dyke like me to talk to!"

"Uh-oh," said Paris, rolling a pencil between her palms at full speed. "Trouble in River City. Was she real upset when you fessed up to being straighter than a stripe on an American flag?"

"What makes you think I'd tell her that?"

"Didn't you tell me you were when I came out to you?"

Venita squared a stack of papers. "Did I? I was so young and foolish back then."

She emphatically put her pencil down. "It was only last September, Venita."

"Bubba's death, his life, took a lot of getting over."

"You Morton River folks are a kick. Do I get a turn at playing matchmaker now?"

Venita pressed her lips together, but couldn't hide the smile in her eyes.

She and Peg had sometimes conjectured about Venita, but not about themselves. It was all pleasure to be with Peg even though they were never alone.

Those delightful hands touched her chastely, touched her frequently, but she couldn't decide if she and Peg were moving slowly, were moving at all.

Some nights she put herself to sleep imagining a regular middle-class life with all the trimmings in Peg's home. There were mornings when she swore she'd stay away from Peg altogether — she was temptation, complacency, a trap. Then she'd find herself at the mall, turning to the Peg in her head to show her some frilly outfit just to get a rise out of her. Or she'd wake up in a sweat, rubbing against the mattress, on top of her in her dream. She knew they had to talk; she didn't know what to say. She did know that the stress of conflict was as dangerous as the conflict. She might do anything to stop the pulling and tearing inside, like run. Like stay.

It wasn't just the woman, it was the town. She'd gotten involved in it so quickly and deeply she was scared. Somehow that little piece of hermit's land felt like a part of her she was trying to protect. Her survival depended on it. Sure, she could go back to the relative wilds of Montana or the Dakotas, but she was starting to be convinced that she had some kind of responsibility to plunk herself down long enough somewhere, anywhere, to make a difference.

Friday night dinners had become a safe ritual. She could enjoy being with Peg without thinking why or what next. The first week in May Peg was already at the Queen of Hearts when Paris got there from school, flushed from the quick walk and the pulsing scents of spring. John threw her a kiss from the kitchen window. There were huge pitchers of blossoms all over the restaurant, yet there was no escaping the smell of Friday night fish. Elly came for their orders, shoulders drooping.

"Aren't you supposed to be home with your sweetie on Friday nights?" she asked.

Elly's face was drawn, her smile faint. "Giulia called in sick and I'm getting a cold."

"I didn't know she was capable of getting sick." Now that she'd lost her fascination with Giulia as a competent, nurturing, gorgeous, sleek . . . She blinked to put Giulia back into perspective. The woman was an emotionless android.

"She's capable of about anything these days. For the last month or so, ever since the kid took off, she's so unreliable I'd can her if I didn't hope like heck she'd come back to her senses." She looked at Peg. "Any news from New York?"

"As a matter of fact —"

Someone called to Elly just then. "I'll be back." She pushed off into the hubbub.

Avoiding Paris's eyes, Peg offered a photograph. "Annie faxed this up to me today. She wanted to know if it was our girl."

It was a smudged-looking grainy clipping from a New York gay paper. Several very young women and men, heads shaved or in sideways baseball caps, with backpacks, long black capes, skeleton costumes, and other imaginative garb were lying down in the street. People in dark business suits stepped around them. The signs the demonstrators carried read *ACT UP AGAINST DEATH* and *HOMOPHOBIA KILLS!* Frozen in the act of tracing a body with chalk against the pavement was a husky dyke whose wild curls burst from under a Fedora. She was looking

240

up, smiling with an intense excitement from a thinner, exhausted-looking face. Her eyes seemed full of the enormity of what she was doing.

Her vision of Maddy the activist had been real. "That's our girl, all right. I'm relieved, but sadder than a mama bird whose chicks just learned to fly."

"I agree," Peg said, eyes on Paris's face, one hand touching her sleeve. "I also thought you'd be happy."

"I'm glad she's okay, Peg, but, look what these kids deal with today. She's only sixteen and drawing corpses on sidewalks, knowing the boy she outlines might die real soon."

Peg stroked her hand. "Losing my innocence meant learning to smoke cigarettes. Death wasn't exactly an everyday concept unless you knew someone in Vietnam."

"I'll bet being gay in front of the whole wide world wasn't either."

"I even had trouble being gay in front of me."

"You were into women's lib, not gay lib?"

Peg nodded. "Gay lib didn't get going really strong until nineteen-seventy, seventy-one. By then I was too separatist to work with the men."

"You? A separatist?"

Peg traced a line in the condensation on the side of her glass, her fingers careful, tensely sensitive. "I finally decided the only thing I was separating was my two worlds. Gay lib wasn't ever very big up here anyway."

"And feminism was safer?"

Peg crumpled up the straw wrapper. "I didn't feel real connected to men in false eyelashes, darlin'."

"Or women in three-piece suits?"

Peg looked at her for a long time. Finally she

answered, "I was going to say that my suits are socially acceptable, but maybe there is a correlation."

She bit her lower lip to keep from bursting out with a political analysis of drag queens and bulldykes, to keep from proclaiming about being in the front row of the barricades together, about her aversion to passing. If she didn't jump down Peg's throat on every issue maybe they wouldn't be at loggerheads quite so often. She downed her water. "What do we do now? Find a white steed and rescue her?"

"Maybe a yellow steed with its meter off. Turkey's students located her. Maddy's calling herself Mad Hatter. They *rapped* with her, Turkey said, and found out she's staying with three college kids on the Lower East Side. Annie's volunteered to bring her home if she wants to come."

She looked at the picture a while longer, worried. "Is she surviving down there? Do we have any right to interfere?"

Elly brought Paris's Greek salad, Peg's fish and chips. "The kid looks half-starved," said Elly, leaning over Peg's shoulder. "But, jeez, can she live in Morton River after setting the world on fire?"

"Give her the choice," Peg advised. "When I got involved in the women's movement I spent a lot of time in New York."

"I remember," exclaimed Elly, a little of her liveliness returning. "Between Annie taking up with that Yalie and you marching around the city, I never saw either of you."

"You," Peg countered, "were too busy chasing Dusty to notice. I was always glad to get back to

242

the comforts of Brockett Lake, but I knew I'd lost my Valley friends."

"You've never told me about your political side," Paris said, glad to hear Peg confirm it. "You're like a soldier who doesn't want to talk about a war."

Elly laughed and tried to muss up Peg's hair. "Peg gave up the women's movement when she stopped carousing. Don't let her get away with secrets. Especially the carousing parts."

Peg smoothed her hair. "Those days seem tame next to what the kids are doing now."

"But Maddy doesn't feel like she has a home to return to, with Giulia kicking her at one end and the rest of the world at the other." Maybe a fear of being caught in the vandalism would keep Maddy away when she really wanted to come home. She hadn't heard a soul accuse the girl. Who would guess one unruly tomboy could do so much damage? She suspected she could reassure her on that score. "Could you ask your friend to have Maddy call me, Peg? Her mom wants her back bad." Would Sophia let her tell Maddy about her dad? "I have some news that might bring her home."

"Done," said Peg.

Her voice felt rusty all of a sudden, her insides like clanking machine parts grinding against each other. It was only polite to offer. She even wanted to offer, but there it was: the terror that once they started again she'd never be able to let go of Peg. "You can call from my phone," she said. Nothing like a stutter to give away feelings, she thought. Especially to herself. She forced her fingers to stop shredding a napkin.

Peg rose stiffly, eyes downcast. "April showers are a pain in the butt for me, even the first couple of weeks in May," she said with a little laugh. "I've had a bad day and I don't think I want to climb your stairs any more than you do."

"I understand," she said, but a doubt that had been growing under a toadstool way in the back of her brain tripled itself. Maybe Peg hadn't liked being with her as much as she'd liked being with Peg. Maybe it wasn't ambivalence keeping them apart. Peg left the Diner whistling and Paris walked home, incredulous at her disappointment.

The willow trees in backyards and up side streets were unfurling leaves now and their new green seemed to light her way through the dusk. The river was swollen with the same spring rain that inflamed Peg's pelvis and she heard its roiling roar all the time, all over town. It sounded like hot passionate blood hurtling through rivers of the body, like thousands of women breathing in their lovers' ears, like oceans exhaling all their energies on storm-washed beaches. There was a smell of churned-up silt in the air, of earthy promise. She felt like one great big walking need, soggy with longing, burnt-out from dangling desires. Why couldn't anything be light and easy in Morton River Valley? Why was everyone so intense?

Her injured knee, like a souvenir of the Valley, was a barometer of crisis. It skyrocketed in pain as she reached the Pizza House. Giulia sat at the top of her steps. Had she gotten bad news about Maddy?

Inside, Giulia settled on her couch again, bent

over her crossed arms, shivering in a light sweater. Paris, scared, turned on the heat. It had to be Maddy. Why else would the woman be there? If Giulia had ever given the slightest hint of wanting her friendship, beyond that strange winter night when she'd first come to talk about Maddy, she would have gone to her and held her. She looked pathetic, the noble neck bowed, the broad shoulders hunched, the heavy nose thick with crying.

Instead, she switched on every light in or near the living room and brought Giulia a cup of instant coffee.

"You've been to the Diner?" Giulia asked, head down as if to inhale the heat from her mug.

"Yes."

"Am I fired?"

"No one mentioned it."

"I wish they'd fire me. I'll always be a waitress. I'll always live on the Hillside. But I'm tired of fighting to keep Peter. He wants his own kind."

So this wasn't about her sister, she thought. Why in the world had she expected Giulia to show concern about someone besides herself? "Did he break up with you?"

Giulia didn't answer.

"Okay, too personal. I withdraw the question."

"No. There isn't an answer. I don't want him either. Maddy was right for once in her life. Peter's a scarecrow I stuffed full of dreams and pretended was all there because he can do the things a woman can't." She sipped the coffee which, Paris noted, was too scalding hot for human consumption. "One setback and I folded. He's been seeing — another woman. A blonde from Upton. Her father's a big contractor down there. Peter never wanted me, he wanted my ambition."

Paris moved next to Giulia, rested her hand on the shoulder that felt as sturdy as she'd always imagined it would. The scent of spring blossoms was still in her nostrils. It had been a long time since she'd awakened a woman, brought her into the world of lesbian pleasure. "I'm sorry things didn't work out for you."

"Why did he have to say all those hateful things, Paris?" she asked, swinging horrified eyes on her. "He said people talked when he took me to business functions, that I was a nobody waitress who wasn't good enough for him. He said I'd get fat like Mama. He said I was a cheap Italian tease. He said we couldn't have kids because my sister's gay and he wouldn't risk passing it on." Her voice rose in fury and she shook off Paris's hand. "He said it was my fault the Hermitage ran into trouble, my fault for bringing you home, that you're feeding information to the Land Trust people. Is that true? Did you ruin my chance to marry Peter?"

Evasively she answered, "Strange as it may seem, Giulia, as far as I know I've never even met a member of the Trust."

Giulia's eyes looked drained of energy. Only her anger seemed to be keeping her going. "I told him that, but no, he said —"

"If he said I heard more than he'd want me to, if he said I have a big mouth, then he's right. I care about the world surviving men like Peter and scared women like you as much as you care about clawing out of a piece of the pie for yourself."

"That junk heap where his father lived isn't worth saving! What's wrong with you that you put a bunch of scraggly trees before people?"

"That junk heap's got some beautiful growth, some of the only wildlife left in this area, wildflowers galore. As for people — what about all the people who go there to get away from the cities? What about all the things your father taught Maddy there, all the times your family picnicked in those woods? If you're so worried about people, remember that land gives and gives and gives to people. And don't tell me about jobs. That may be the developers' rationale for destruction, but I know your motives were far from humanitarian."

Giulia didn't argue, just looked at her with those empty eyes, dark circles like painted crescents beneath them. "He said I'm no saint for keeping my virginity, just a frigid dyke like my sister."

"Not a very pleasant man. Maybe you're getting out while the getting's good."

"He was everything I'd always dreamed of."

"Then you need to upgrade your dreams, Giulia."

She was silent. Her whole face appeared worn and old, her body diminished, but her eyes, when the anger faded from them, looked stricken with a child's hurt.

After a while Giulia lifted her face and looked at her. "You don't think much of men, do you?"

The woman was pushing. Paris realized that suddenly the heat in the apartment was staggering. They still sat close together. She decided to beat her to it, her heart leaping into its usual pandemonium. "I'm gay, Giulia."

More silence. This was harder than the explosion she'd expected from her. "So he was right about you," she said. "Maybe he's right about me. The night I was up here — he asked if we'd gone to bed, if I was a virgin with women. He *hated* that I wouldn't sleep with him."

"Men do."

"What else do I have to offer? I wanted to be sure I got something back for it. Maybe if I'd —"

She couldn't believe they were talking about this in 1990. She didn't know anyone cared about these things anymore. But this was the town where the fifties furniture came to live. "Then you wouldn't even have that."

"You're not masculine like my sister."

Paris tried to stay calm. "She's not masculine at all."

"Her clothes, her walk."

"She's Maddy. Maddy likes to wear jeans, she walks her own distinctive walk. She doesn't use any man to get what she wants. People call that queer. I call it smart."

Giulia's index finger traced the raised design on her mug over and over. "There's so much I don't understand. I felt safe when I had Peter. Now that I know I was so wrong about him, I'm not sure about anything." Giulia moved closer and laid her head on Paris's shoulder. "Anything."

What was the woman up to, Paris wondered. She'd thought Giulia was so self-possessed, knew how to live life. Like Peter, she'd been attracted to her ambition — no, not ambition, will. Now that her iron will was down for the count there was nothing to Giulia but a soft sad needy woman. She put her arm around her and patted her other shoulder. "You'll find your own answers," she assured her.

Giulia held her face up. "Kiss me, Paris. I need to be kissed."

Her body went stiff, her insides cold, even in the blasting heat. The woman was so lovely. All it would take to begin would be a caress. She could feel all that sensuality coming to life in her arms as she looked into those dark, dark eyes. They were unreadable now. They were bottomless, like a staircase without end. The fall would be petrifying.

She caught herself, broke their contact and crossed the room to the thermostat, which she lowered, then moved to the window. Two cars went by, headlights on. One stopped down the street at the liquor store. A skinny man with a wispy beard went inside. She thanked her lucky stars Giulia hadn't pulled this two months ago — it might have worked and she would have found herself knee-deep in cow-chips, as her Dad would have said.

"No," she replied faster than she could think. "You need to be loved. But you haven't let any of us close enough to love you and I only kiss women I love." Was she saying she loved Peg?

Giulia stood. "I didn't mean that," she spat. "You must have some . . . some . . . lesbian spell you cast. Peter warned me about it."

She laughed. Giulia seemed too pathetic to deserve anger. "Hey, you came to me and you're welcome to leave anytime. But you're welcome to come back and talk too."

"I'll bet," Giulia replied, sarcastic, stuffing her arms into her sweater.

"Don't, Giulia," she said. What a shame, that exquisite woman so bitter. "Don't shut down. Your mom needs you."

"Why is it always me? Why do I have to take care of everybody else? Who's ever going to take care of me? My father runs away, my sister runs away, now my fiance runs away. My mother's a big child who won't take care of herself or she'd run away too." Poised in the doorway, she cried, wild-looking, wiping tears on her sleeves. Some of her dignity had returned with her anger.

The room had cooled quickly. She groped for the words that would reach Giulia. "You're only taking care of yourself, Giulia. You've been trying to hold things together all your life so you wouldn't get hurt when other people failed you."

"Yeah? And what about you?" She spoke with a sharp vindictive tone in the accent of the Hillside, forgetting her college diction. "You're a runaway like the rest of them. You may not like the way I do it, but at least I get in there and work my ass off trying. At least I take the responsibilities I'm given to heart."

Ooof. She sat back down on the couch, deflated. A runaway? She'd only been trying to stay true to herself by moving on, staying clean and unencumbered until — until what? After Giulia slammed the door behind her and she was utterly and dreadfully alone, she strained beyond the clatter of shoes on the iron stairs to hear exactly what the woman had told her.

The responsibilities we're given. It had never occurred to her that people don't get to choose their own responsibilities. Great. Here she'd thought herself brave and strong for doing battle with a staircase. Giulia seemed to think there were more important battles in life.

CHAPTER 17

May was ending with all the excitement of
impending summer. She found Yankee birds
extremely loud, tittering and chortling below her
bedroom window till the last of twilight seeped into
night and the first light of dawn turned to day.

The Jacobs were having a Memorial Day
barbecue. As usual, Peg invited her. As usual, she
started to decline.

"Dad's going to be there," Peg said, no pressure
in her voice. "They've changed medications so his

mood's better and he isn't as fuzzy about what's going on around him."

She'd had a few weeks to stew over Giulia's accusations. Did she have a responsibility to follow through with old Mr. Jacob? She loved Peg's relationship with him, loved Peg for valuing her family ties. She didn't want to pretend to be Peg's permanent partner, yet he might die and this might be as close as Peg got.

For the first time in her life she had insomnia, which she admitted was better than those demented staircase nightmares. She'd wake up in the night with her dumb-ass knee aching so deeply she wanted to massage the bone. Morton River was wearing her out. The term was ending and she was flirting with the idea of canceling the rest of her contract with the Center — that'd save someone's job.

She and Venita had dinner at the Diner at least once a week. It gave her a chance to sort through some of her worries. One night she'd described a nightmare that still brought sweat to her forehead and hands. Venita, finally well and back to full strength, asked where she'd come by her fear of stairs.

"It was the interminable staircases of Europe," she'd replied, laughing. "Half my memories are of being a little kid walking up wide, endless museum steps, or stairs to ruins, or winding staircases inside old buildings. I was always between the *mater* and the *pater,* pulling back, bored, tired, scared."

"Of what? Did they go off on their own?"

"It wasn't that they physically left me. I just always felt extra. They loved me, but I remember my sister telling me how much they'd looked forward to her and Don leaving home so they could tramp around like they had in their early married days. Then, just as they got what they'd waited so long for, they had to wait another eighteen years."

She picked at a huge Greek salad, saving the black olives, savoring the salty feta cheese.

Over the cry of a baby in the next booth Venita said, "Surely they didn't make you feel guilty."

"No. I don't remember them saying a word to anyone about it, but I could feel it. I could feel what passed between them when they looked over my head as we walked, ate in restaurants, climbed steps. If I'm not careful, I still find myself believing I'm too little or don't know how to talk well enough, or I'm plain not enough. Inside, I'm still at the top of an enormous flight of stairs, a teeny girl the wind could blow away."

"Or blow down the stairs."

"And I'm petrified."

Elly refilled their cups. Venita was wearing that slightly silly I-know-a-secret-smile she was seldom without these days. Paris closed her eyes. She heard Venita stir her tea, clinking a spoon against the heavy cup as it went around. She wanted absolute quiet. There was something right on the edge of her consciousness. "On my steps with Peg and Jennifer? I *stopped* myself from falling off," she said in slow astonishment. "It never occurred to me that I could do that. Maybe I banged up my knee, but is that really all I've been fearing all these years?"

Venita surreptitiously adjusted a dental plate in her mouth, then bit into one of Dusty's over-large burgers. After a while Venita asked, "Any word on Maddy Scala?"

"Peg's friend Turkey said her student connections lost her before they could give Maddy my message and number. Did you ever get the feeling everything in your life is on hold? What do you hear from Thor?"

"I saw him a few days ago. He's postponing approaching the investors until he hears from you."

"When I talked to him I admitted that I'm not much good at this kind of thing and haven't come up with a way to accomplish my end of the deal. But, listen to this, he said he'd been looking further into 'this Rafferty's concept' and he's going up to New Avon with a couple of the selectmen next week. Did we get him to bite or what?"

"He always comes through, Paris. He's like most men, he has to pretend he didn't hear it from a woman."

"I'll warn Trixie. I'm sure she has a tactic for chauvinism."

What she hadn't told Venita, she thought later as she parked the Jeep at the Pizza House, was that Thor planned to move soon if he liked what he heard in New Avon. He wouldn't wait for help. She wallowed in guilt over that one. What if he failed because she couldn't get it together? All those birds and animals were depending on her. Then she laughed at herself for pulling a Giulia. They didn't need her; she needed to protect the wildlife because she was the wildlife.

So when Peg had asked her for Memorial Day

she'd said yes. "You need to know," she'd warned Peg, "that I'll be talking to your brothers about the Hermitage."

"It's starting to feel like it wouldn't be a real holiday without you threatening to lock horns with my brothers."

On the eve of Memorial Day she tossed and turned. She had to confront those men. She had to protect the woods to keep herself alive. She felt impossibly tired, though. It'd be so comfortable to move in with Peg, to bask in Mr. Jacob's approval, to take the easy way out with the brothers, trading away the hermit's land for the right to live on Jacob land.

Not me. I'm a sixties kid, universe. You want me, you're going to have to stop me dead — She sat up in the dark, clutching her sheet and blanket around her, shivering. Staying with Peg could be the death of her, at least of her spirit. Or would she be just as dead alone in a first floor rental with a bucket of rock salt for the slippery spots?

Why was she thinking death thoughts? It wasn't that she expected to keel over from some sudden malady, but she knew, deep in her knee maybe, that the aging process she'd thus far been able to ignore had tackled her. She was no longer young enough to simply bounce back from an injury. She had her dad's insomnia, her mom's arthritis and dwindling energy reserves.

Was this what life was really about? You fought to hold true to your dream, whatever it might be, you held on through all sorts of trials, struggled over barricades that seemed impossible to scale — and then you got tired? Cried uncle to the universe and traded in zeal for a good night's sleep? Was she supposed to learn that wisdom was simply surrender?

She fell asleep, exhausted by internal struggle, just as a jay shrieked and dawn disappeared into cloudless blue skies.

When she finally woke she had twenty minutes to shower, dress, gulp coffee and slip Maddy's photos of the hermit's ravaged land — minus Maddy on the CAT — into her purse. Before she'd gone to bed she'd pretended Venita, who was spending the day with Gussie Brennan and Nan Heimer, was with her. Venita stood at her closet, arms folded, foot tapping, looking stern, still in the Russian fur cap she'd sported since her cold. She advised navy blue slacks and a white blouse with a ruffle at the neck. Paris ignored her and chose a loose outfit smacking of liberalism, a white Mexican blouse embroidered with peasants and donkeys. It was hot so she let her unshaven legs show in culottes and sandals. Mr. Jacob, Peg had told her, liked exotic women; she also dressed for the brothers, to make them nervous.

No lipstick, though Venita had recommended it. It seemed like her friend was always with Nan and Gussie these days. That silly little smile. Did Venita have a secret? What had Venita whispered months ago? "Why not fall in love?"

She sped to Brockett Lake but was still the last arrival. Mr. Jacob sat under a grand old blooming cherry tree in his wheelchair, bruised fallen petals littering the ground, Peg at his side while everyone else was active. Kids played and shouted, women set picnic tables and scurried in and out of the house, men distributed cold drinks and prepared the barbecue.

The smell of glowing charcoal pervaded the whole county. Robins hopped across the far fringes of lawn, pulling at worms. One of the smaller kids raced to her with a bag of marshmallows and she popped one into her mouth, forming an "o" around the powdered surface, making faces at the child. Ned gave her a curt hello, and she passed a woman in a white pantsuit — Mr. Jacob's nurse? — but otherwise the field was clear all the way to Peg. She hugged her a little too long for the public eye, hands sliding under Peg's white vest, along her crimson rayon shirt, then hugged the old man.

Peg, in tailored white slacks, gave her a showy bunch of lavender tulips. "From Dad's old garden."

"Are they still producing?" Mr. Jacob asked. "Your mother had them put in."

"I'll take you over later, Dad. You'll see."

"This is a gorgeous setting," she told Mr. Jacob. She could see Peg's jaw line in his, and her gray eyes.

"God planned it, not me," he said in his growly voice.

She laughed. "Not many men would admit that," she said.

"There was a time I wouldn't have," he said. "Like my sons. But at this late date let somebody else do the work and take the credit." His eyes sought hers. "What do you do for a living, Paris Collins? Margaret's told me but I can't keep you all

258

straight. There're too many children and grandchildren all doing different things."

"I teach adults."

"The poor people?"

"Mostly."

"There's no money in that."

"No. Absolutely not."

"Then I hope it makes you happy."

"Watching people learn is a joy. It keeps me young."

"You're young enough."

Peg laughed now. "Your kids are getting on in years, Dad, when their friends admit it."

He closed his eyes. "I can see you crawling in diapers, with practically no hair."

Peg wouldn't meet her eyes, and loosely wrung her hands.

"All those little toes and fingers, perfectly formed. I didn't spend much time with you children. I earned your keep, but I knew what miracles you were. Now you're living in my house, the boys have my stores. Where does the time go?"

She and Peg each took one of his cold, well-manicured hands. They sat in silence under the big shade tree, watching the activity.

Ned strode toward them in red golfing pants and a pink knit shirt. "The kids are starting a soccer game, Dad. I'll wheel you over." Shouts and the butt of a ball against a head became the dominant sounds.

Mr. Jacob waved him off. "I'm much too peaceful to move, Edward. I can see well enough from here."

"Of course you can't," argued Ned. "You can't see across your room with those eyes."

"Edward, I'm on a holiday today. Even the nurse is leaving me alone. Go boss your grandchildren around." Ned scowled but left.

"As for you," Mr. Jacob said. Paris cringed inside as he squeezed her hand, dreading her lies. "I don't see enough of you. How can I know Margaret's happy if she's always alone?"

"Dad," said Peg.

"Shh!" he grouched. "I can see the woman has a mouth of her own. I know you women don't do it quite like the rest of us, but there's no reason in the world why you're not living out here. Peg says you have some rickety old apartment by the old warehouses in Morton River."

"You could call this our courting period, Mr. Jacob."

"If you're as aged as you claim then you don't need a twenty-year-old's courting period. You know your mind. At a certain point, ladies, we stop looking and take what's offered. It's usually the best we'll do and every bit good enough."

She couldn't meet Peg's eyes, nor could she argue with her father. Hadn't Giulia come close to saying the same thing? What was wrong with Peg and her? Venita had suggested that the crazy sixties had turned their whole generation so topsy-turvy they couldn't see clearly.

The nurse was crossing the lawn toward them.

"That woman has to do things to me no man should ever have to endure," said Mr. Jacob. "Don't run away, though. Who knows how much more time I have to get to know you?"

How can I break my contract and leave?

"Would you like to sneak over and see the progress I've made on the old homestead?" Peg asked.

"Sure," she said. She did want to see it and if she had to be alone with Peg, what better time than when she had immediate family obligations?

Once in the shady pines between the old farm house and Brockett's Peg took her hand. "I love that outfit. It suits you and your undisciplined beauty."

"Thank you," she replied, watching the ground, pleased and embarrassed at Peg's insistent admiration.

"Don't let Dad get to you, darlin'. He doesn't have much opportunity to run my life because I'm not in the business."

"Does he know about Hermitage Park?"

"Yes. I told him. I wanted his advice for myself and I wanted him to know what my brothers were doing with his money too. He hasn't been able to supervise them like he used to and Brockett tells him only what he thinks Dad wants to hear. But he's a tough old codger and when he's on the ball he's still very sharp. He didn't tell me what he thought. I imagine he'll let us know one way or another." Peg whistled a jazzy version of "Summertime" as they walked the rest of the way.

She admired the headway Peg had made scraping and painting the house around the new thermopane windows. It was a blue-gray. "I'll trim it in charcoal. What do you think?" Peg opened the door for her.

"Tasteful. Unobtrusive. The colors fit here, you."

"That's what I'd hoped. And look!" She led Paris past new built-in bookcases to the bedroom, gesturing inside.

"You didn't have a bedroom before! That was quick!"

Peg's hands sunk into her white pockets. She looked as embarrassed as she had when her father described her as a baby. She looked at the ceiling. "I was inspired."

"Oh."

"In case."

"I see." Nerve-deep memories of Peg's touches washing over her crotch, she stepped across the threshold. She cleared her throat. "So you're the king-size futon type."

"It's good for my pelvis. Don't you like —"

"Yes! Yes. I love them. If I ever own a bed it'll be a futon." The room smelled of cedar. Peg shifted from one foot to the other, Reeboks gleaming white. She and Peg were as jittery as two crickets in a closet. Peg had chosen a light dresser and bureau to go with the wood of the futon and installed a rattan lounge chair. "Very comfortable-looking furniture," she said to say something, anything at all.

"Let me see you in it."

"The bed?"

"No! The chair."

She arranged herself, wanting Peg to like the picture she made, scared she'd like it too much. Peg, her face a high color from the carmine shirt, spread a heavy old quilt over her legs. It was cool and a little lumpy.

"Family heirloom?" she asked.

"My grandmother made it. Just a little lap quilt from wool scraps."

"I wouldn't think a Jacob would be messing with scraps."

"She was the odd one. Daughter of a Morton River immigrant. No one approved. She never tried to fit in. Dad says that's why Granddad married her, to toughen the stock."

"So that's where you get it."

"What?"

"The backbone to be gay."

She flashed that handsome smile. "Maybe it's not my pelvis at all. Maybe it's my Rafferty back that always hurts."

"Rafferty?"

Peg made a face and played with the quilt. "We don't talk about that connection much, but it's there."

"You don't, by any chance, have any say-so in the operation of the old factory building."

"We own the land, not the building, if that's what you mean. The land's used as a tax write-off, but not much of one. Brockett doesn't want the whole magilla torn down because he thinks he can't sell it or make a profit putting anything else up."

Damn, solutions were so simple if you just opened your eyes to them. "What if there were a way for him to increase its value as a write-off?" She wasn't certain it was even possible. "Or contribute to the community at no cost to the Jacobs?" She told her scheme to Peg.

Peg looked thoughtful. "I'll pave the way for Thor, but any development would have to be with minus publicity. As I mentioned, we don't talk about that connection."

Paris found herself thrilled by Peg's willingness. This was the open door she'd been hunting, for her project as well as into Peg. "Personally, I like it. A streak of other-side-of-the-tracks Irish in the woman." An orchestra-sized string section played "Someone To Watch Over Me" in the background. She couldn't resist. She pulled Peg down next to her and slipped her hands under her vest once more. She loved the solid feel of Peg's firmly-fleshed ribcage. "This chair's big enough for two."

"So's the house, Paris," Peg said, nonchalantly brushing the hair off Paris's neck. There was a quaver in Peg's voice.

The excited feeling thinned out with qualms. She had a feeling of foreboding that came at the top of staircases, of not being enough — substantial enough, she realized, to keep from free-falling through life. "Are we hurting your middle?"

"Not yet." She moved to get up, but Peg had her arms around her now, pulled her back and held tight. "I'll let you know." She lay against Peg, expecting to feel trapped, but Peg loosened her grip. "You can't," Peg said, "live at the top of those stairs another winter."

"I'm not sure there'll be another winter," she said, sorrowful.

Peg's arms tensed briefly around her. "What do you mean? I thought, I mean, your two-year plan? I thought we had at least another year?"

"We? Since when does the eligible bachelor want to be we?"

Peg's breath warmed her scalp. "Since you, Paris.

I'm worried too. I don't want to get hurt again either, but you're just right, everything I've always wanted."

"Ornery ol' me? Environmentalist ol' me? Brazen dyke me?"

"I've always been with women who charged ahead of me and led where I wanted to go," Peg said softly. "I lost my spirit for it somewhere around the second breakup, Paris. We'd done it all together: marching, fundraising, staffing the women's center, answering the hotline. My ex is still doing it, and I needed to get away from her, away from her circles. The last thing I tried was a Take Back the Night March in New Haven. I saw her right away, speaking at the rally. I skulked back down College Street and went to the bar."

"What about Upton?"

She took her mouth away. "Would you believe the other ex is just as active down there?"

"So you hang out with closeted professionals now."

"Yes." Her sigh was heart-breaking. "Sometimes I'm afraid the old pulps were right, Paris. Lesbians can't stay together and no human being can sustain that much pain over and over. I can shut down my emotions or I can stay away from the fire. I didn't even want to consider the other option." Her lips were against Paris's hair again. "Until you."

"How come two big strong women of major moral fiber like you and me can't just walk away from each other? I didn't want this either. Except that I did." Damn, why was it so important for this to work? It was easier not to climb stairs at all than to get all the way to the top and fall.

But Peg was kissing her neck by now and she was twisting to get at Peg and then Peg had a hand between her legs and she was unzipping the culottes but Peg didn't wait, just slid her fingers up and Paris was gushing, just gushing and Peg's fingers felt so good. So did her mouth, her warm tongue, the sheer womanly bulk of Peg against her. She felt Peg go inside her then, but the angle was wrong.

"That hurts a little," she whispered.

Peg came out, but left her hand on her wetness. "I want you all the time," Peg told her, rubbing her mouth against Paris's shoulder. "You're like a tune that's stuck in my head, pretty, but not always welcome."

"I know, Peg. Sometimes I just want you to go away too, but you don't. I'm getting this nagging feeling that I'm supposed to be paying attention to something."

"I wonder sometimes if I should just let the whole tune play until it's a song, or a symphony." Peg's finger was circling her clitoris now.

"Ahhh," she said, without meaning to. "You caught it."

"The song?"

On an exhale she managed to say, "At least a rhythm."

"How would you rate it?" Peg teased, circling and circling.

"I can definitely dance to it."

"Do you hear the words?" Peg whispered right up against her ear.

"I don't hear a thing, Peg, honey. Not a darned —"

Peg held her as she came so powerfully she

found herself clinging to Peg as she had to the stairs after her fall. It hadn't been this good the first night. She'd been right to stay away from her. There was no stopping what happened when they were together.

"I feel just like melted butter," she said in a weak, embarrassed little voice.

"Yes, you do," Peg said, the loving smile back in her eyes. Peg kissed her, open-mouthed. She didn't have the strength to get Peg on her back and it was a good thing.

"Yo, Peg!" came a cry from the wooded path.

"It's Jennifer! We stayed away too long."

"But Peg, how are you going to transport a pool of butter and make it presentable?"

She'd just mopped up in the bathroom and Peg, whistling, was washing her hand at the kitchen sink when Jennifer bounded in. "God, you two are *in* trouble for sneaking off. Brockett's red in the face and Ned's radically white around the lips."

"We didn't sneak off anywhere," Peg said coolly, drying her hand on a dish towel. "And you're supposed to knock on the door to my home. This isn't Girl Scout camp."

"*Sor*-ry. Aren't you grateful I saved your neck?"

Peg patted her shoulder. "Eternally. Dad's coming to see the house before he leaves. You found Paris horrified at the mess it was in and ordering me around to straighten it up."

"Yes, ma'am!"

Peg swept Paris into a one-sided hug and kissed her. Jennifer watched, then laughed and applauded. "So you finally did it! I'm jazzed."

They ran through the woods, then walked

casually across the grass. Jennifer jabbered the story like a big joke to the family. Paris fixed a small plate of food for Mr. Jacob before the sisters-in-law could harass him.

"That's just right. They're always giving me more than I can swallow. Old people don't do enough to need banquets."

She made certain she was by the elder Jacob's side when with a mean eagerness she said to Brockett, "I guess they finally got a court order for that hermit's land." She took out Maddy's photographs of the destruction of the forest and the first CAT and spread them across Mr. Jacob's lap. He stared, squinted at them. Glared at Brockett.

The elder son's head snapped up and he looked as if he'd swallowed something nasty. Then he smiled in a sugary way. "We Jacobs have always had a rule not to discuss business at holiday gatherings."

She was all obsequiousness. "I'm so sorry. You'd said you weren't involved with the industrial park, so I had no idea I was bringing up business, just current events!"

Brockett, incredibly, didn't have an answer to that.

"What's this all about, son?" asked Mr. Jacob. "We're not in on that land deal where the vandalism happened, are we? Everyone was talking about it at the apartments."

"It's something we've looked into, Dad."

"I hope you kept on looking, then, because people around here seem to think that old parcel of land is their personal paradise. It'd be pretty bad for business if they found out we were buying it out from under them." He launched into a story of some of his card-playing cronies at the apartments and their loyalty to Jacob's Department Stores.

She was astonished. All the dialogues she'd had with Brockett in her head were unnecessary. Since she still hadn't come up with anything that sounded threatening enough to scare him away from the development, she'd decided while she lay awake the night before to get nasty about the whole thing in hopes it'd leave a bad taste in his mouth. And now the old man had not only found a good reason for the Jacobs to withdraw from the project, but practically ordered his sons out. She dared to find Peg's eyes as her father told his tale. Peg twinkled at her in that certain way — okay, okay, Peg — certain *butch* way women do so well.

With that done she set about enjoying the food, Peg, Jennifer and Mr. Jacob. They even let him rope them into a card game which she won.

"Only because you young people have tired me out!"

"Then we'd better," Peg said, "get you over to see what I've done with the house before you conk out on us."

Wheeling him through the woods was too difficult, so it was decided that they'd drive and Mr. Jacob would leave from Peg's. When they got to the house the phone was ringing. Peg ran ahead and Paris went beside Mr. Jacob and his walker.

"What kind of colors are those?" he grumbled to Paris about the outside paint job. "How much did those fancy windows cost her?" He was, as Peg had warned him, all complaints, but she fielded them until Peg returned. "I wouldn't recognize the house, Margaret."

"I'll take that as a compliment," Peg said, teasing him. "Since you gave up on it." Peg turned to her, pointing to the phone, eyes anxious.

"Who?" she asked.

"Turkey. Our little friend from New York City is getting a ride home in a taxi cab. They should arrive in about an hour and a half at your pizza palace."

They took Mr. Jacob home before he even saw the plumbing.

CHAPTER 18

The cab made good time. Annie and Maddy were waiting for them outside. Maddy, festooned with political buttons, thinner, but just as hardy looking, leapt from the cab's hood and presented herself to Paris for a hug, then strutted over to Peg and shook her hand.

"This is Annie Heaphy," Maddy told Paris, in her element as mistress of ceremonies. "Don't let the cab fool you, she's really a philosopher."

Annie smiled with a bashful duck of her head and took one hand out of her pocket to punch Peg lightly in the arm. "How's it going, Peglet? When you letting your hair get gray?"

"With this new generation carrying on, very soon. Since when do you wear glasses?"

Annie looked surprised and pulled off the little round wire-framed pair. "They're just for driving," she explained.

She tried dressing Annie as a radical from Peg's era, in a confrontational T-shirt with a lavender bandana around her head. Then she tried a longish skirt, frilly blouse and matching career-woman jacket as befitted a philosophy teacher. Neither fit. "Do you teach?" she asked.

Annie was wearing jeans and a bright rugby shirt. "Sometimes I get a new woman cabbie to train," she answered. "But if you mean philosophy, no. That's just a hobby of mine."

"An excuse," Peg teased, "to hole up in your apartment and be antisocial." Peg's hands were in her pockets too, but whereas Annie looked as if she were burying her hands, Peg looked like she was setting the style for dyke stance. Butch stance, Paris thought, believing in the phenomenon more each time they were together. Butch pockets must be to hands what negligees were to bodies, concealing and revealing all at once.

Annie grinned under a shaggy mop of blonde hair, the edges of her eyes all crinkly. "Maybe," she replied. "Maybe."

Paris carefully led them upstairs and wondered, while she heated water for coffee, if Peg was making a convert of her to this femme/butch thing. It seemed so natural once she'd started thinking in

272

those terms, but it was disconcerting, not knowing exactly what being femme entailed.

"Don't you have any herbal tea?" asked Maddy.

She stifled a laugh. "Is that what you learned with the big city dykes? Yes, I keep some around for you crunchy granola types."

"Count me among them, then," said Annie.

"What brings you home, Maddy?" Peg asked.

Maddy seemed a little bit intimidated by Peg, though she stole admiring glances at her, as if to memorize her style. She answered without the old bravado, but with a confidence she hadn't expressed before she ran away. "I can't get anything but shit work in New York. Under-the-table stuff that pays less than minimum. Besides, there's political work to do outside the big cities and I know I can do it now." She blew on her mug. "You know, when I told people in New York about Dusty and Elly and how they turned some of Morton River's homophobia around just by being strong decent out women, they were impressed. They said I ought to stay in town and make sure all that education wasn't lost."

"So you're going to become the resident agitator?"

"Yes. Starting with Mama. Geeky old Giulia can go jump in the river. I'm going to be who I am where I live or I'll take off again."

"I hope you're not planning any New York antics," Peg said. Paris flinched inside. How could they be together? Peg had retired her political buttons. She probably sat around with pals like Annie Heaphy telling tales of the feminist wars. She'd either dampen Paris's spirit or throw her out.

Annie shook her head. "Haven't changed a bit,

have you, you low-profile Peg? This woman must've racked up a hundred pro-choice marches, but she won't set foot in a gay pride parade. Don't worry. Maddy knows outing's not the only tactic in the book."

"Yeah," agreed Maddy, her mouth full of cookie. "I know what it's like to be scared to death. And I know, Dusty and Elly or not, the Valley's still not the coolest town to be queer. People'll see what happens when I come out in school. If I live through it, maybe they'll decide they can."

The adults were silent. Maddy was making the same decisions Paris had, only a lot earlier, and with a status-quo-challenging "butch" exterior. That was risky. She wondered what Peg was thinking — about her job, her family? And Annie, who just kept grinning into her Red Zinger and could walk away.

"Peg, my woman," said Annie, "I'd love to see Elly again while I'm here."

Paris asked, "Were you and Elly —"

"Not really," Annie answered, "but we all hung out together for a long time, drinking and messing around, trying to figure out what life was about. We were pretty tight."

"When you and Elly were speaking," Peg said with a laugh. "Why don't you plan to bring Turkey up for a reunion sometime?" She looked at Paris. "I'll go over to the Diner with Annie. Shall I drop you and Maddy off?" In her hurry she'd left the Jeep at Brockett Lake.

"Hold it, women," Maddy said, their peer in queerness if not in age. "I need support. Won't one of you be my backup?"

Peg twisted up her face.

274

"Hey, I'll go in with you," said Annie.

Paris hesitated briefly. Would Peg volunteer to be the adult gay who returned the lost sheep to her fold? She decided it wasn't her place to test Peg.

"The Scalas know me," she said. "And Giulia already knows I'm gay."

"She does?" asked Maddy, eyebrows high with amazement.

"Peter left your sister while you were away. She's not the same person."

"Wow. What happened? He didn't guess it was me who —"

"It had to do with Giulia, and being from different classes." She'd get enough bitter details from her sister. She didn't want to reinforce Maddy's part in the breakup.

"We're not good enough for that stupid creep? We're *too* good for him. I bet it's because she wouldn't do it with him. You know what? I'm so glad he's gone I'm not even going to rub it in when I see her."

But Giulia was at work when they arrived at Maddy's house. Maddy walked in yelling, "Hi, Mama! I'm back!"

Sophia came unglued. She cried and hugged and scolded Maddy for ten minutes before Maddy could talk. Paris felt embarrassed to watch such lavishing of emotion.

"Sit down, Mama," Maddy said, pushing her into a chair. "I want to tell you something. Giulia wanted me to keep it from you, but that's not right. Why I left is because I'm gay."

"Gay?"

"A *lesbica.*"

"*Mia bambina?*"

"And I like it. I don't want to change. I love women," she exclaimed, throwing her arms wide. She moved more freely and Paris suddenly realized why. She'd gotten rid of her bra and no longer dug at its cruel straps. "Men are a stupid waste of time. Look at Peter. Look at Papa."

Sophia's eyes finally sought Paris out in the doorway. She said nothing.

"And you ran away to do this?" asked Sophia.

"No. I ran away because I knew it." She told her love story and she told of Giulia's betrayal.

Sophia just sat there, looking sad and confused. "No grandchildren? Giulia says she never marries now. And you want to be one of those women in men's clothes."

"We don't all wear men's clothes, Mama. Look at Paris!"

"Paris?"

"I'm gay too, Sophia."

The poor woman looked stunned now. Maddy went to her and knelt at her chair, putting her arms around her. "See?" she said. "Paris is a good person. It's okay to be gay. I didn't know that when I left, but I've been with lots of gay people and they're just like everyone else. You'll see, Mama. I'll be happy, even happier than Giulia. Than you."

Sophia sat up then, drew Maddy in front of her, holding both her hands. "I am happy. You're home. You can change."

"No, Mama. It's not something you change your mind about. You either are or you aren't."

"I want you to go see your father."

Maddy rocked back on her heels, almost losing

her balance. She stared at her mother, then looked at Paris who waited to see the joy on her face. There it was, first in the eyes, then in that wraparound grin. "Daddy? Where is he?"

"Knee-brass-ka," said Sophia, smiling, looking proud, as if she'd tracked him down herself.

"Nebraska? Is he coming home?"

"He makes better money there. He saves. In a few years we go back to Italy."

"We? I can't live in Italy. It's even harder to be queer there."

"Good. You marry an Italian boy."

"No, Ma, that's not how it works. But I want to see Dad. Let me get a map. I can hitch —"

"There is money. You can fly an airplane."

"I'm dreaming, right?"

"He sends money."

"For me? He wants to see me? You mean he asked for me?"

Sophia nodded, beaming.

Maddy stood, her face earnest. "No. I can't just skip out there in two seconds. I have to write and tell him who I am first. That I'm gay."

"He doesn't want to know," Sophia said. "Just go to him!"

"He'll care. And I care. I want to make sure he's not expecting your innocent little *bambina*." She picked up her pack. "Wait. Did he learn to read English?"

Sophia shrugged. "I don't know."

"I'll call. I'll call right now. Give me his number."

They argued, but Sophia gave in and pulled a postcard from her pocket. She looked toward, though not at, Paris. "I get him to send his number," she explained. Maddy went to the kitchen. In a moment they heard her yelling into the phone as if to make her father hear her halfway across the country.

Sophia wouldn't meet her eyes.

"It's true," she said to Sophia.

"I don't want to know either."

"That's fine with me, but Maddy's not going to let you ignore it." She was so proud of Maddy she felt privileged to be there backing her up.

"There is nothing like this in my *familia*." Just what Giulia said.

"Of course there has been. It's the difference between now and then, Sophia. We're not hiding anymore. We want to see the light of day too."

"It's a mortal sin."

"The same force that made you what you are, made me."

"I love you like a daughter. Now —" Sophia did look at her then, with narrow suspicious eyes. She knew what was coming and steeled herself against feeling insulted, against letting her rage show, against taking her disgust with breeder society out on this one uneducated woman. "You *did* this to my Maddalena? *You?*"

"No one did anything to her," she replied softly. "And no, Maddy announced it to me not much differently that she did to you. She hadn't done anything with anyone at that point. She just knew."

"I tell you, Paris, I don't understand nothing. Is this the same world I wake up in this morning?"

"Having been thrown a few curves myself lately, I can sympathize with you."

"Curves?" Sophia asked.

"No." Maybe this wasn't the time, but she

insisted. "I'm not explaining another expression to you, Sophia. School will bring you to 1990 faster than anything I can teach. Wouldn't it be great if you could read and write as well as you can speak? You could help Mr. Scala run a business here in America and stay near the girls."

"I don't know," she replied, wringing her hands. "He wants to go back home very bad." The look in Sophia's eyes, though, was thoughtful.

Quiet came from the kitchen like a sudden flood. Maddy returned, head hanging. When she looked up it was at Paris, her large dark eyes so hurt she didn't have to say what had happened. She turned to her mother. "He says to send Giulia, Mama. He says he doesn't want any gay kids."

She could see Maddy shrug away the tragic slump of her shoulders. "I don't care. I'll finish school and on time. Then I'll go to college. I'll be a lawyer or a politician. Both. I'll be somebody famous who changes everything for gay people. I'll be president of ACT UP."

Maddy, stiff-shouldered, marched across the room to Paris. The child might be standing taller, but she wondered if she'd ever see Maddy's special brand of unfettered joy in her eyes after this. "Don't you let me forget it, okay, Paris? I'm going to make it so no father ever says that to a gay kid again because they'll know better. I'm going to stay right here and fight it out."

And the words of Maddy's last sentence, of course, were what she heard as she walked down to the Diner in the balmy dark. Even a sixteen-year-old was digging in, making a commitment to roots and a goal.

She stopped on the bridge. The stars flared splendidly against the night sky in this idle, tense town. The Hillside glowed with lights like home fires burning. Spring was a faint sweetness in the air. The last several rainless days had calmed the river. It hummed against the banks lovingly, the time it spent in this town ceaseless yet hurried, like the span of a whole human life. Would it stop and settle if it could? It had no expectations, that vast, mute, desireless body. What if she had none?

She felt dizzy. This was a new thought for her, giving up her expectations, free-falling on purpose.

What *had* she expected? That she would someday flow into a geography of perfection where everything would be in place for her to claim? Did she think her travels entitled her to some sort of finders/keepers code, some no-pain, lots-of-gain paradise? Giulia seemed born knowing what Maddy had just so early and painfully discovered. Maybe she, like them, needed to accept that sort of responsibility for creating the life she wanted right where she was.

The Diner was a neon palace in the distance. She crossed its river moat, her sense of adventure strong, pumping excitement through her body, "Rhapsody In Blue" cresendoing, blending with the river's rising song. Even her knee felt more elastic as she strode ahead.

She didn't know any more answers than the river did, but she suspected Peg would be there with Annie, and Elly, arm through Dusty's, and the stragglers who attached and detached from that family, Giulia a reluctant member despite herself. Maybe Venita was there in her jaunty wide-brimmed straw hat, with news from Thor that the Jacobs had dumped Hermitage Park. Maybe Peg really would take the lead with her brothers and plant a seed about Rafferty's.

Okay, she thought, as she climbed the short steps to the Queen of Hearts, only a slight twinge in her knee, maybe she didn't need to leave town to avoid falling down those stairs again. She could hear the little passenger train pulling out of the Valley, calling *whoo-whoo* to whomever needed to hear its goodbye. She remembered the fantasy she'd brought to Morton River — and she remembered Peg's thermopane windows, built-in bookcases, the futon.

The Diner was soothing cool. In the staff booth at the far end Annie and Peg were laughing. Dusty had her arm around Elly. Giulia, straight-backed, the proudest waitress on earth, gave Paris a brittle, resentful smile. They'd probably told her Maddy was back.

Peg, always the formal gentledyke, got up from her seat and presented her with one white rose. Peg looked startled, but then enormously pleased as she let Paris kiss her hello on the lips. Dusty whistled.

"Have you ever," she asked Peg, smoothing her culottes beneath her and planting herself in the booth, "considered installing a lavender hot tub in your house, just for the sake of decadence?"

A few of the publications of
THE NAIAD PRESS, INC.
P.O. Box 10543 • Tallahassee, Florida 32302
Phone (904) 539-5965
Mail orders welcome. Please include 15% postage.

MORTON RIVER VALLEY by Lee Lynch. 304 pp. Lee Lynch at her best! ISBN 0-56280-016-7 $9.95

LOVE, ZENA BETH by Diane Salvatore. 224 pp. The most talked about lesbian novel of the nineties! ISBN 0-56280-015-9   18.95

THE LAVENDER HOUSE MURDER by Nikki Baker. 224 pp. A Virginia Kelly Mystery. Second in a series. ISBN 0-56280-012-4   9.95

PASSION BAY by Jennifer Fulton. 224 pp. Passionate romance, virgin beaches, tropical skies. ISBN 152680-028-0   9.95

STICKS AND STONES by Jackie Calhoun. 208 pp. Contemporary lesbian lives and loves. ISBN 1-56280-020-5   9.95

DELIA IRONFOOT by Jeane Harris. 192 pp. Adventure for Delia and Beth in the Utah mountains. ISBN 1-56280-014-0   9.95

UNDER THE SOUTHERN CROSS by Claire McNab. 192 pp. Romantic nights Down Under. ISBN 1-56280-011-6   9.95

RIVERFINGER WOMEN by Elana Nachman/Dykewomon. 208 pp. Classic Lesbian/feminist novel. ISBN 1-56280-013-2   8.95

A CERTAIN DISCONTENT by Cleve Boutell. 240 pp. A unique coterie of women. ISBN 1-56280-009-4   9.95

GRASSY FLATS by Penny Hayes. 256 pp. Lesbian romance in the '30s. ISBN 1-56280-010-8   9.95

A SINGULAR SPY by Amanda K. Williams. 192 pp. 3rd spy novel featuring Lesbian agent Madison McGuire. ISBN 1-56280-008-6   8.95

THE END OF APRIL by Penny Sumner. 240 pp. A Victoria Cross Mystery. First in a series. ISBN 1-56280-007-8   8.95

A FLIGHT OF ANGELS by Sarah Aldridge. 240 pp. Romance set at the National Gallery of Art ISBN 1-56280-001-9   9.95

HOUSTON TOWN by Deborah Powell. 208 pp. A Hollis Carpenter mystery. Second in a series. ISBN 1-56280-006-X   8.95

KISS AND TELL by Robbi Sommers. 192 pp. Scorching stories by the author of *Pleasures*. ISBN 1-56280-005-1   8.95

STILL WATERS by Pat Welch. 208 pp. Second in the Helen Black mystery series. ISBN 0-941483-97-5   8.95

MURDER IS GERMANE by Karen Saum. 224 pp. The 2nd
Brigid Donovan mystery.   ISBN 0-941483-98-3   8.95

TO LOVE AGAIN by Evelyn Kennedy. 208 pp. Wildly
romantic love story.   ISBN 0-941483-85-1   9.95

IN THE GAME by Nikki Baker. 192 pp. A Virginia Kelly
mystery. First in a series.   ISBN 01-56280-004-3   8.95

AVALON by Mary Jane Jones. 256 pp. A Lesbian Arthurian
romance.   ISBN 0-941483-96-7   9.95

STRANDED by Camarin Grae. 320 pp. Entertaining, riveting
adventure.   ISBN 0-941483-99-1   9.95

THE DAUGHTERS OF ARTEMIS by Lauren Wright Douglas.
240 pp. Third Caitlin Reece mystery.   ISBN 0-941483-95-9   8.95

CLEARWATER by Catherine Ennis. 176 pp. Romantic secrets
of a small Louisiana town.   ISBN 0-941483-65-7   8.95

THE HALLELUJAH MURDERS by Dorothy Tell. 176 pp.
Second Poppy Dillworth mystery.   ISBN 0-941483-88-6   8.95

ZETA BASE by Judith Alguire. 208 pp. Lesbian triangle
on a future Earth.   ISBN 0-941483-94-0   9.95

SECOND CHANCE by Jackie Calhoun. 256 pp. Contemporary
Lesbian lives and loves.   ISBN 0-941483-93-2   9.95

MURDER BY TRADITION by Katherine V. Forrest. 288 pp.
A Kate Delafield Mystery. 4th in a series.   ISBN 0-941483-89-4   18.95

BENEDICTION by Diane Salvatore. 272 pp. Striking,
contemporary romantic novel.   ISBN 0-941483-90-8   9.95

CALLING RAIN by Karen Marie Christa Minns. 240 pp.
Spellbinding, erotic love story   ISBN 0-941483-87-8   9.95

BLACK IRIS by Jeane Harris. 192 pp. Caroline's hidden past . . .
                                       ISBN 0-941483-68-1   8.95

TOUCHWOOD by Karin Kallmaker. 240 pp. Loving, May/
December romance.   ISBN 0-941483-76-2   8.95

BAYOU CITY SECRETS by Deborah Powell. 224 pp. A Hollis
Carpenter mystery. First in a series. ISBN 0-941483-91-6   8.95

COP OUT by Claire McNab. 208 pp. 4th Det. Insp. Carol Ashton
mystery.   ISBN 0-941483-84-3   9.95

LODESTAR by Phyllis Horn. 224 pp. Romantic, fast-moving
adventure.   ISBN 0-941483-83-5   8.95

THE BEVERLY MALIBU by Katherine V. Forrest. 288 pp. A
Kate Delafield Mystery. 3rd in a series. (HC)   ISBN 0-941483-47-9   16.95
                       Paperback   ISBN 0-941483-48-7   9.95

THAT OLD STUDEBAKER by Lee Lynch. 272 pp. Andy's affair
with Regina and her attachment to her beloved car.
                                  ISBN 0-941483-82-7   9.95

PASSION'S LEGACY by Lori Paige. 224 pp. Sarah is swept into
the arms of Augusta Pym in this delightful historical romance.
                                  ISBN 0-941483-81-9   8.95

THE PROVIDENCE FILE by Amanda Kyle Williams. 256 pp.
Second espionage thriller featuring lesbian agent Madison McGuire
                                  ISBN 0-941483-92-4   8.95

I LEFT MY HEART by Jaye Maiman. 320 pp. A Robin Miller
Mystery. First in a series.   ISBN 0-941483-72-X   9.95

THE PRICE OF SALT by Patricia Highsmith (writing as Claire
Morgan). 288 pp. Classic lesbian novel, first issued in 1952 . . .
acknowledged by its author under her own, very famous, name.
                                  ISBN 1-56280-003-5   8.95

SIDE BY SIDE by Isabel Miller. 256 pp. From beloved author of
Patience and Sarah.   ISBN 0-941483-77-0   8.95

SOUTHBOUND by Sheila Ortiz Taylor. 240 pp. Hilarious sequel
to *Faultline.*   ISBN 0-941483-78-9   8.95

STAYING POWER: LONG TERM LESBIAN COUPLES
by Susan E. Johnson. 352 pp. Joys of coupledom.
                                  ISBN 0-941-483-75-4   12.95

SLICK by Camarin Grae. 304 pp. Exotic, erotic adventure.
                                  ISBN 0-941483-74-6   9.95

NINTH LIFE by Lauren Wright Douglas. 256 pp. A Caitlin
Reece mystery. 2nd in a series.   ISBN 0-941483-50-9   8.95

PLAYERS by Robbi Sommers. 192 pp. Sizzling, erotic novel.
                                  ISBN 0-941483-73-8   8.95

MURDER AT RED ROOK RANCH by Dorothy Tell. 224 pp.
First Poppy Dillworth adventure. ISBN 0-941483-80-0   8.95

LESBIAN SURVIVAL MANUAL by Rhonda Dicksion.
112 pp. Cartoons!   ISBN 0-941483-71-1   8.95

A ROOM FULL OF WOMEN by Elisabeth Nonas. 256 pp.
Contemporary Lesbian lives.   ISBN 0-941483-69-X   8.95

MURDER IS RELATIVE by Karen Saum. 256 pp. The first
Brigid Donovan mystery.   ISBN 0-941483-70-3   8.95

PRIORITIES by Lynda Lyons 288 pp. Science fiction with
a twist.   ISBN 0-941483-66-5   8.95

THEME FOR DIVERSE INSTRUMENTS by Jane Rule. 208
pp. Powerful romantic lesbian stories.   ISBN 0-941483-63-0   8.95

LESBIAN QUERIES by Hertz & Ertman. 112 pp. The questions
you were too embarrassed to ask. ISBN 0-941483-67-3   8.95

CLUB 12 by Amanda Kyle Williams. 288 pp. Espionage thriller
featuring a lesbian agent! ISBN 0-941483-64-9 8.95

DEATH DOWN UNDER by Claire McNab. 240 pp. 3rd Det.
Insp. Carol Ashton mystery. ISBN 0-941483-39-8 9.95

MONTANA FEATHERS by Penny Hayes. 256 pp. Vivian and
Elizabeth find love in frontier Montana. ISBN 0-941483-61-4 8.95

CHESAPEAKE PROJECT by Phyllis Horn. 304 pp. Jessie &
Meredith in perilous adventure. ISBN 0-941483-58-4 8.95

LIFESTYLES by Jackie Calhoun. 224 pp. Contemporary Lesbian
lives and loves. ISBN 0-941483-57-6 8.95

VIRAGO by Karen Marie Christa Minns. 208 pp. Darsen has
chosen Ginny. ISBN 0-941483-56-8 8.95

WILDERNESS TREK by Dorothy Tell. 192 pp. Six women on
vacation learning "new" skills. ISBN 0-941483-60-6 8.95

MURDER BY THE BOOK by Pat Welch. 256 pp. A Helen
Black Mystery. First in a series. ISBN 0-941483-59-2 8.95

BERRIGAN by Vicki P. McConnell. 176 pp. Youthful Lesbian —
romantic, idealistic Berrigan. ISBN 0-941483-55-X 8.95

LESBIANS IN GERMANY by Lillian Faderman & B. Eriksson.
128 pp. Fiction, poetry, essays. ISBN 0-941483-62-2 8.95

THERE'S SOMETHING I'VE BEEN MEANING TO TELL
YOU Ed. by Loralee MacPike. 288 pp. Gay men and lesbians
coming out to their children. ISBN 0-941483-44-4 9.95
ISBN 0-941483-54-1 16.95

LIFTING BELLY by Gertrude Stein. Ed. by Rebecca Mark. 104
pp. Erotic poetry. ISBN 0-941483-51-7 8.95
ISBN 0-941483-53-3 14.95

ROSE PENSKI by Roz Perry. 192 pp. Adult lovers in a long-term
relationship. ISBN 0-941483-37-1 8.95

AFTER THE FIRE by Jane Rule. 256 pp. Warm, human novel
by this incomparable author. ISBN 0-941483-45-2 8.95

SUE SLATE, PRIVATE EYE by Lee Lynch. 176 pp. The gay
folk of Peacock Alley are all cats. ISBN 0-941483-52-5 8.95

CHRIS by Randy Salem. 224 pp. Golden oldie. Handsome Chris
and her adventures. ISBN 0-941483-42-8 8.95

THREE WOMEN by March Hastings. 232 pp. Golden oldie. A
triangle among wealthy sophisticates. ISBN 0-941483-43-6 8.95

RICE AND BEANS by Valeria Taylor. 232 pp. Love and
romance on poverty row. ISBN 0-941483-41-X 8.95

PLEASURES by Robbi Sommers. 204 pp. Unprecedented
eroticism. ISBN 0-941483-49-5 8.95

EDGEWISE by Camarin Grae. 372 pp. Spellbinding
adventure.   ISBN 0-941483-19-3   9.95

FATAL REUNION by Claire McNab. 224 pp. 2nd Det. Inspec.
Carol Ashton mystery.   ISBN 0-941483-40-1   8.95

KEEP TO ME STRANGER by Sarah Aldridge. 372 pp. Romance
set in a department store dynasty.   ISBN 0-941483-38-X   9.95

HEARTSCAPE by Sue Gambill. 204 pp. American lesbian in
Portugal.   ISBN 0-941483-33-9   8.95

IN THE BLOOD by Lauren Wright Douglas. 252 pp. Lesbian
science fiction adventure fantasy   ISBN 0-941483-22-3   8.95

THE BEE'S KISS by Shirley Verel. 216 pp. Delicate, delicious
romance.   ISBN 0-941483-36-3   8.95

RAGING MOTHER MOUNTAIN by Pat Emmerson. 264 pp.
Furosa Firechild's adventures in Wonderland.   ISBN 0-941483-35-5   8.95

IN EVERY PORT by Karin Kallmaker. 228 pp. Jessica's sexy,
adventuresome travels.   ISBN 0-941483-37-7   8.95

OF LOVE AND GLORY by Evelyn Kennedy. 192 pp. Exciting
WWII romance.   ISBN 0-941483-32-0   8.95

CLICKING STONES by Nancy Tyler Glenn. 288 pp. Love
transcending time.   ISBN 0-941483-31-2   9.95

SURVIVING SISTERS by Gail Pass. 252 pp. Powerful love
story.   ISBN 0-941483-16-9   8.95

SOUTH OF THE LINE by Catherine Ennis. 216 pp. Civil War
adventure.   ISBN 0-941483-29-0   8.95

WOMAN PLUS WOMAN by Dolores Klaich. 300 pp. Supurb
Lesbian overview.   ISBN 0-941483-28-2   9.95

SLOW DANCING AT MISS POLLY'S by Sheila Ortiz Taylor.
96 pp. Lesbian Poetry   ISBN 0-941483-30-4   7.95

DOUBLE DAUGHTER by Vicki P. McConnell. 216 pp. A Nyla
Wade Mystery, third in the series.   ISBN 0-941483-26-6   8.95

HEAVY GILT by Delores Klaich. 192 pp. Lesbian detective/
disappearing homophobes/upper class gay society.

                                        ISBN 0-941483-25-8   8.95

THE FINER GRAIN by Denise Ohio. 216 pp. Brilliant young
college lesbian novel.   ISBN 0-941483-11-8   8.95

THE AMAZON TRAIL by Lee Lynch. 216 pp. Life, travel & lore
of famous lesbian author.   ISBN 0-941483-27-4   8.95

HIGH CONTRAST by Jessie Lattimore. 264 pp. Women of the
Crystal Palace.   ISBN 0-941483-17-7   8.95

OCTOBER OBSESSION by Meredith More. Josie's rich, secret
Lesbian life.   ISBN 0-941483-18-5   8.95

LESBIAN CROSSROADS by Ruth Baetz. 276 pp. Contemporary
Lesbian lives.   ISBN 0-941483-21-5   9.95

BEFORE STONEWALL: THE MAKING OF A GAY AND
LESBIAN COMMUNITY by Andrea Weiss & Greta Schiller.
96 pp., 25 illus.   ISBN 0-941483-20-7   7.95

WE WALK THE BACK OF THE TIGER by Patricia A. Murphy.
192 pp. Romantic Lesbian novel/beginning women's movement.
                                  ISBN 0-941483-13-4   8.95

SUNDAY'S CHILD by Joyce Bright. 216 pp. Lesbian athletics, at
last the novel about sports.   ISBN 0-941483-12-6   8.95

OSTEN'S BAY by Zenobia N. Vole. 204 pp. Sizzling adventure
romance set on Bonaire.   ISBN 0-941483-15-0   8.95

LESSONS IN MURDER by Claire McNab. 216 pp. 1st Det. Inspec.
Carol Ashton mystery — erotic tension!.   ISBN 0-941483-14-2   8.95

YELLOWTHROAT by Penny Hayes. 240 pp. Margarita, bandit,
kidnaps Julia.   ISBN 0-941483-10-X   8.95

SAPPHISTRY: THE BOOK OF LESBIAN SEXUALITY by
Pat Califia. 3d edition, revised. 208 pp.   ISBN 0-941483-24-X   8.95

CHERISHED LOVE by Evelyn Kennedy. 192 pp. Erotic
Lesbian love story.   ISBN 0-941483-08-8   9.95

LAST SEPTEMBER by Helen R. Hull. 208 pp. Six stories & a
glorious novella.   ISBN 0-941483-09-6   8.95

THE SECRET IN THE BIRD by Camarin Grae. 312 pp. Striking,
psychological suspense novel.   ISBN 0-941483-05-3   8.95

TO THE LIGHTNING by Catherine Ennis. 208 pp. Romantic
Lesbian 'Robinson Crusoe' adventure.   ISBN 0-941483-06-1   8.95

THE OTHER SIDE OF VENUS by Shirley Verel. 224 pp.
Luminous, romantic love story.   ISBN 0-941483-07-X   8.95

DREAMS AND SWORDS by Katherine V. Forrest. 192 pp.
Romantic, erotic, imaginative stories.   ISBN 0-941483-03-7   8.95

MEMORY BOARD by Jane Rule. 336 pp. Memorable novel
about an aging Lesbian couple.   ISBN 0-941483-02-9   9.95

THE ALWAYS ANONYMOUS BEAST by Lauren Wright
Douglas. 224 pp. A Caitlin Reece mystery. First in a series.
                                  ISBN 0-941483-04-5   8.95

SEARCHING FOR SPRING by Patricia A. Murphy. 224 pp.
Novel about the recovery of love.   ISBN 0-941483-00-2   8.95

DUSTY'S QUEEN OF HEARTS DINER by Lee Lynch. 240 pp.
Romantic blue-collar novel.   ISBN 0-941483-01-0   8.95

PARENTS MATTER by Ann Muller. 240 pp. Parents'
relationships with Lesbian daughters and gay sons.
                                  ISBN 0-930044-91-6   9.95

THE PEARLS by Shelley Smith. 176 pp. Passion and fun in
the Caribbean sun.   ISBN 0-930044-93-2   7.95

MAGDALENA by Sarah Aldridge. 352 pp. Epic Lesbian novel
set on three continents.   ISBN 0-930044-99-1   8.95

THE BLACK AND WHITE OF IT by Ann Allen Shockley.
144 pp. Short stories.   ISBN 0-930044-96-7   7.95

SAY JESUS AND COME TO ME by Ann Allen Shockley. 288
pp. Contemporary romance.   ISBN 0-930044-98-3   8.95

LOVING HER by Ann Allen Shockley. 192 pp. Romantic love
story.   ISBN 0-930044-97-5   7.95

MURDER AT THE NIGHTWOOD BAR by Katherine V.
Forrest. 240 pp. A Kate Delafield mystery. Second in a series.
                                      ISBN 0-930044-92-4   9.95

ZOE'S BOOK by Gail Pass. 224 pp. Passionate, obsessive love
story.   ISBN 0-930044-95-9   7.95

WINGED DANCER by Camarin Grae. 228 pp. Erotic Lesbian
adventure story.   ISBN 0-930044-88-6   8.95

PAZ by Camarin Grae. 336 pp. Romantic Lesbian adventurer
with the power to change the world.   ISBN 0-930044-89-4   8.95

SOUL SNATCHER by Camarin Grae. 224 pp. A puzzle, an
adventure, a mystery — Lesbian romance.   ISBN 0-930044-90-8   8.95

THE LOVE OF GOOD WOMEN by Isabel Miller. 224 pp.
Long-awaited new novel by the author of the beloved *Patience
and Sarah.*   ISBN 0-930044-81-9   8.95

THE HOUSE AT PELHAM FALLS by Brenda Weathers. 240
pp. Suspenseful Lesbian ghost story. ISBN 0-930044-79-7   7.95

HOME IN YOUR HANDS by Lee Lynch. 240 pp. More stories
from the author of *Old Dyke Tales.* ISBN 0-930044-80-0   7.95

EACH HAND A MAP by Anita Skeen. 112 pp. Real-life poems
that touch us all.   ISBN 0-930044-82-7   6.95

SURPLUS by Sylvia Stevenson. 342 pp. A classic early Lesbian
novel.   ISBN 0-930044-78-9   7.95

PEMBROKE PARK by Michelle Martin. 256 pp. Derring-do
and daring romance in Regency England.   ISBN 0-930044-77-0   7.95

THE LONG TRAIL by Penny Hayes. 248 pp. Vivid adventures
of two women in love in the old west.   ISBN 0-930044-76-2   8.95

HORIZON OF THE HEART by Shelley Smith. 192 pp. Hot
romance in summertime New England.   ISBN 0-930044-75-4   7.95

AN EMERGENCE OF GREEN by Katherine V. Forrest. 288
pp. Powerful novel of sexual discovery.   ISBN 0-930044-69-X   9.95

THE LESBIAN PERIODICALS INDEX edited by Claire
Potter. 432 pp. Author & subject index.   ISBN 0-930044-74-6   29.95

DESERT OF THE HEART by Jane Rule. 224 pp. A classic;
basis for the movie *Desert Hearts*. ISBN 0-930044-73-8 8.95

SPRING FORWARD/FALL BACK by Sheila Ortiz Taylor.
288 pp. Literary novel of timeless love. ISBN 0-930044-70-3 7.95

FOR KEEPS by Elisabeth Nonas. 144 pp. Contemporary novel
about losing and finding love. ISBN 0-930044-71-1 7.95

TORCHLIGHT TO VALHALLA by Gale Wilhelm. 128 pp.
Classic novel by a great Lesbian writer. ISBN 0-930044-68-1 7.95

LESBIAN NUNS: BREAKING SILENCE edited by Rosemary
Curb and Nancy Manahan. 432 pp. Unprecedented autobiographies
of religious life. ISBN 0-930044-62-2 9.95

THE SWASHBUCKLER by Lee Lynch. 288 pp. Colorful novel
set in Greenwich Village in the sixties. ISBN 0-930044-66-5 8.95

MISFORTUNE'S FRIEND by Sarah Aldridge. 320 pp. Historical Lesbian novel set on two continents. ISBN 0-930044-67-3 7.95

A STUDIO OF ONE'S OWN by Ann Stokes. Edited by
Dolores Klaich. 128 pp. Autobiography. ISBN 0-930044-64-9 7.95

SEX VARIANT WOMEN IN LITERATURE by Jeannette
Howard Foster. 448 pp. Literary history. ISBN 0-930044-65-7 8.95

A HOT-EYED MODERATE by Jane Rule. 252 pp. Hard-hitting
essays on gay life; writing; art. ISBN 0-930044-57-6 7.95

INLAND PASSAGE AND OTHER STORIES by Jane Rule.
288 pp. Wide-ranging new collection. ISBN 0-930044-56-8 7.95

WE TOO ARE DRIFTING by Gale Wilhelm. 128 pp. Timeless
Lesbian novel, a masterpiece. ISBN 0-930044-61-4 6.95

AMATEUR CITY by Katherine V. Forrest. 224 pp. A Kate
Delafield mystery. First in a series. ISBN 0-930044-55-X 8.95

THE SOPHIE HOROWITZ STORY by Sarah Schulman. 176
pp. Engaging novel of madcap intrigue. ISBN 0-930044-54-1 7.95

THE YOUNG IN ONE ANOTHER'S ARMS by Jane Rule. 224 pp. Classic
Jane Rule. ISBN 0-930044-53-3 9.95

THE BURNTON WIDOWS by Vickie P. McConnell. 272 pp. A
Nyla Wade mystery, second in the series. ISBN 0-930044-52-5 7.95

OLD DYKE TALES by Lee Lynch. 224 pp. Extraordinary
stories of our diverse Lesbian lives. ISBN 0-930044-51-7 8.95

DAUGHTERS OF A CORAL DAWN by Katherine V. Forrest.
240 pp. Novel set in a Lesbian new world. ISBN 0-930044-50-9 8.95

AGAINST THE SEASON by Jane Rule. 224 pp. Luminous,
complex novel of interrelationships. ISBN 0-930044-48-7 8.95

LOVERS IN THE PRESENT AFTERNOON by Kathleen
Fleming. 288 pp. A novel about recovery and growth.
ISBN 0-930044-46-0 8.95

TOOTHPICK HOUSE by Lee Lynch. 264 pp. Love between
two Lesbians of different classes.   ISBN 0-930044-45-2   7.95

MADAME AURORA by Sarah Aldridge. 256 pp. Historical
novel featuring a charismatic "seer."   ISBN 0-930044-44-4   7.95

CURIOUS WINE by Katherine V. Forrest. 176 pp. Passionate
Lesbian love story, a best-seller.   ISBN 0-930044-43-6   8.95

BLACK LESBIAN IN WHITE AMERICA by Anita Cornwell.
141 pp. Stories, essays, autobiography.   ISBN 0-930044-41-X   7.95

CONTRACT WITH THE WORLD by Jane Rule. 340 pp.
Powerful, panoramic novel of gay life.   ISBN 0-930044-28-2   9.95

MRS. PORTER'S LETTER by Vicki P. McConnell. 224 pp.
The first Nyla Wade mystery.   ISBN 0-930044-29-0   7.95

TO THE CLEVELAND STATION by Carol Anne Douglas.
192 pp. Interracial Lesbian love story.   ISBN 0-930044-27-4   6.95

THE NESTING PLACE by Sarah Aldridge. 224 pp. A
three-woman triangle — love conquers all!   ISBN 0-930044-26-6   7.95

THIS IS NOT FOR YOU by Jane Rule. 284 pp. A letter to a
beloved is also an intricate novel.   ISBN 0-930044-25-8   8.95

FAULTLINE by Sheila Ortiz Taylor. 140 pp. Warm, funny,
literate story of a startling family.   ISBN 0-930044-24-X   6.95

ANNA'S COUNTRY by Elizabeth Lang. 208 pp. A woman
finds her Lesbian identity.   ISBN 0-930044-19-3   8.95

PRISM by Valerie Taylor. 158 pp. A love affair between two
women in their sixties.   ISBN 0-930044-18-5   6.95

THE MARQUISE AND THE NOVICE by Victoria Ramstetter.
108 pp. A Lesbian Gothic novel.   ISBN 0-930044-16-9   6.95

OUTLANDER by Jane Rule. 207 pp. Short stories and essays
by one of our finest writers.   ISBN 0-930044-17-7   8.95

ALL TRUE LOVERS by Sarah Aldridge. 292 pp. Romantic
novel set in the 1930s and 1940s.   ISBN 0-930044-10-X   8.95

A WOMAN APPEARED TO ME by Renee Vivien. 65 pp. A
classic; translated by Jeannette H. Foster.   ISBN 0-930044-06-1   5.00

CYTHEREA'S BREATH by Sarah Aldridge. 240 pp. Romantic
novel about women's entrance into medicine.
                                                      ISBN 0-930044-02-9   6.95

TOTTIE by Sarah Aldridge. 181 pp. Lesbian romance in the
turmoil of the sixties.   ISBN 0-930044-01-0   6.95

These are just a few of the many Naiad Press titles — we are the oldest and
largest lesbian/feminist publishing company in the world. Please request a
complete catalog. We offer personal service; we encourage and welcome direct
mail orders from individuals who have limited access to bookstores carrying
our publications.